COLD DAYS AT CASTLE DRAX

CHARLOTTE E. ENGLISH

Cold Days at Castle Drax (Chronicles of Vexx, 1)

by Charlotte E. English

Published by SpellBounde Press
Copyright © 2024 by Charlotte E. English

Cover design by MiblArt

Ebook: 978-9-49282-473-8

Paperback: 978-9-49282-474-5

Hardback: 978-9-49282-475-2

1

The Vexxed Question

In a land far from anywhere you know, in a town by an emerald sea, atop a cliff overlooking prismatic green waves, there's a castle looming. A dark and stormy castle, thoroughly forbidding, which is unfortunate: for among the crumbling parapets and grime-ridden spires, a hand-lettered sign reads: FOR SALE (Enquiries: Percy and Bell, Estate Agents).

'You have set it far too high up,' said Miss Luna Vexx to her father, the Count. 'No one will see it. Ask Fane to bring it down.'

'Nonsense,' answered Count Vexx, waving this off. 'Fane has enough to do.' This was true, the old manservant being a prominent part of a much-reduced household staff, in these straitened times.

'Then I shall fetch it down myself,' decided the damsel, and rose from her threadbare seat before the pleasingly blazing hearth. The flames were as cold as the sea, and at least as green, which rather compromised its comforts;

but the effect, Lulu considered, was delightful. The light flickered off the black marble floor most attractively.

'It is fine where it is,' the Count drawled, slumped and idle in the familiar embrace of a chair he'd favoured for a century at least (and it showed). 'It's jaunty. Like a flag.'

Lulu frowned down at her feet. They were bare; she'd forgotten shoes, again. It only now occurred to her to notice the penetrating cold. 'You do *want* to sell Castle Drax, I suppose?'

'Of course!'

'Well! You never will, if nobody knows it is for sale.'

Count Vexx waved this off, too. 'They know.'

It is possible no one intended for the place to be so lugubrious. The town above which it loomed, Andirac, offered several advantages to its residents: bracing sea air, sulphuric hot springs, and a deep quarry of black lava stone, now much depleted. A long-ago Count Vexx, finding the local stone economical, had plundered it liberally; Castle Drax was the striking result.

Furnishing every inch of the interior in marble as black as the depths of Hell, though, there could be no excuse for that.

Lulu acquired for herself a sock (not black), and then another to match it (near enough). She trotted up the three winding flights of stairs to what had once been Aunt Maud's painting-tower, and stretched her long, strong arms out of the window (three of its diamond-shaped panes absent, and letting in the wind). Retrieving the FOR SALE sign was the work of a moment, and she soon had it installed by the front door. The Count rarely left the house; it'd take him at least a week to notice.

It took everyone else a week to notice, too, or rather more. Lulu soon forgot about the prospective sale of the castle, busily occupied (as always) with her favourite springtime pursuits. She'd be down in the kitchens with Magwell, the cook, baking up batches of gooseberry pies (which her father declined to eat). She'd be out in the walled garden pruning the peach trees, neatly espaliered, or gathering fat peonies to put in glass vases (the Count tended to throw them away again, if he chanced to notice them at all). She'd even be up in Aunt Maud's painting tower, with a canvas before her, and a box of water-colours; the Count threw her paintings away, too, when-ever she was so bold as to display them, though in this, at least, he had the right of it. Lulu had neither talent nor taste, though was never so poor-spirited as to let it stop her.

Her days proceeded so much as usual, that when a tinny ringing sound shattered the sepulchral silence at Castle Drax she could not immediately identify what it was.

The morning had barely started. Lulu was down in the cloakroom, removing the curl clamps from her bobbed blonde hair. The mirror warped her reflection somewhat, age-spotted as it was, but every other mirror in the house being long since shattered, it sufficed. The ringing began when she was only halfway finished; she froze with her arms raised over her head, staring at her own wide green eyes in the mirror.

Fane's heavy footsteps added to the tumult. He was crossing the hall, towards the—

'Gracious! The telephone!'

Lulu abandoned her hair, ran out into the hall with half her head bristling with metal, like a semi-styled porcupine. 'I'll get it, Fane!' she called, and trotted past him.

'Very good, Miss,' said the slow-moving Fane, placid as always, and paced away again.

Lulu caught up the heavy black receiver and clamped it to her ear. 'Hello!'

A voice buzzed and rattled in answer. 'Hello, is that Castle Drax?'

'Ha! See! It still works!'

'I beg your pardon?'

Lulu performed a little dance of victory. 'I am sorry. Only I'm so delighted to receive a telephone call! I had begun to think that the device was irreparably broken.'

'To whom am I speaking?' Her interlocuter was male, and sounded severe. Well, she could hardly expect him to understand her point of view; he probably lived in a house where everything worked.

'Sorry,' Lulu said again. 'This is Luna Vexx.'

'Miss Vexx. This is Percival Percy, of Percy and Bell's. We have received a request to view your delightful home—' he could not suppress a slight, embarrassed cough after the word "delightful" —'And I would like to conduct this interested person around this afternoon.'

Lulu suppressed an impulse to say "sorry" again, she had said it twice already—what came out instead was scarcely any better—'What?' she blurted.

'Oh dear, is there something wrong with the connection? Can you hear me? Operator—'

'I hear you,' Lulu hastened to interrupt. 'At least, I believe I do. You said somebody wants to buy the castle.'

'Oh, no,' said Mr. Percy at once. 'Somebody wants to *see* the castle.'

'Aha.'

'If they are sufficiently pleased with the place, then, I imagine, an offer of purchase will naturally follow.'

'Aha.'

'Yes.'

'Well.' Lulu cast a brief, desperate glance around the great, empty hall in all its dilapidated glory. The distant ceiling thick with dust-ridden cobwebs; chilly black marble walls and floor, all of it shimmering with warped old magic, and grime; an acid-green witchfire crackling in the hearth, spitting frost in a halo over the floor.

Fane, hovering in the far doorway, his black jacket threadbare and his craggy skin reminiscent, in hue and texture, of mould.

'What time shall we expect you?' said Lulu, brightly.

'At two o'clock,' said Mr. Percy, and her doom was sealed.

'Six hours!' said Lulu, five minutes later, to the obliging (if unresponsive) Mr. Fane. 'We ought to be able to do a lot with the place in that kind of time, no?' They'd had over a week to "do a lot with the place," of course, and now she wished they had; only she'd never thought anyone would actually visit. Putting up a sign was all very well, but when the property in question was Castle Drax—

'Get rid of a few of those spider's webs, for starters,' she suggested, pointing. 'Will you, Fane? You're by far the tallest of us, and there's a ladder in the cellar, I believe. Only do take care not to stray into Father's summoning circle, he will keep leaving it lying around—' She wandered off before she had quite finished this speech, in quest of a bucket, and a mop. It surely couldn't take more than half an hour to spruce up the dark marble floor; it could even look quite elegant, if she put her back into it.

Lulu put her back into it, and everything else, too. By two o'clock, half of the floor gleamed glossily black, Fane had dislodged a small colony of spiders from the vaulted ceiling, and Lulu was only just getting around to taking the rest of the curl clamps out of her hair.

Mr. Percy was prompt, as always, to a fault. As the six or seven ancient clocks across Castle Drax weightily tolled the hour, the doorbell clanged. Fane had been waiting; he heaved the heavy iron door open (it groaned), and there stood Percy, with a stranger.

Mr. Percy's appearance varied as little as his manner. Lulu had met him twice before, and found him curiously colourless: pale of face and hair and eyes, clothes, even, with a crumpled ivory jacket and a white cravat. 'Miss Vexx,' he said tonelessly, as Lulu sallied forth to meet him. 'You're looking very well.'

Lulu dimpled at him. 'Mr. Percy. May I compliment you on your excellent time-keeping?'

'This is Lady Rondel,' he announced. Lulu dimpled at her ladyship, too, and hoped (far too late) that she had not missed any of her curl clamps. The back of her head did feel oddly weighty...

'Charmed to meet you, Miss Vexx,' said Lady Rondel, and swept past her and Mr. Percy both. She planted herself in the centre of the hall like a gnarled old tree, and loomed. Gracious, she was almost as tall as Fane, and very nearly as elderly. Wealthy, judging from her lavishly embroidered gown and sumptuously condescending manner.

'Excellent bones,' she declared, subjecting the great hall and everything in it to narrow-eyed scrutiny.

'Thank you,' said Lulu.

'Sadly out-dated,' continued her ladyship. 'One expects as much with these grand old places, of course. Now, with new fittings I really think we could achieve something very tolerable. There's a charming ivory-coloured marble quarried down at Pedieu, with the merest *suggestion* of gold about it. All of this must go—' Lady Rondel, equipped with a sharp-pointed walking stick, rapped this article smartly against the cold-black marble hearth— 'New fireplaces throughout—*green* flames, I never saw so tasteless a conceit—white and gold, I rather think, with the new marble—'

She swept out of the hall, Mr. Percy (and Lulu) trailing after. 'I suppose there is little to be done about the cold,' she opined as she went, opening every door she passed, and dismissing the chambers beyond with a series of contemptuous sniffs. 'Hopeless to heat, castles, but something might be managed—'

'—Various options your ladyship might like to consider—' Mr. Percy concurred, and so it went: Lady Rondel, tireless in spite of her antiquity, escorting herself over every inch of Castle Drax, and transforming it, in her own mind at least, into the epitome of modern glamour.

Lulu, unattended to, felt her spirits sink lower by the minute, though she could not have said quite why. Impressed or not, Lady Rondel clearly meant to buy the place, which had, after all, been the goal—or at least, the necessity. Even Mr. Percy and Mrs. Bell had cautioned the Vexx family to expect a long wait, before an eligible purchaser might be found—'Owing to the, er, disarray,' Mrs. Bell had said, with some tact. What luck, then! A buyer, and after only a week. Lulu had not even considered the question of where the Vexxes were to go, afterwards.

The tour concluded in Count Vexx's library, where (perhaps unfortunately) the Count himself happened to be at that moment in residence. 'Aha!' carolled Lady Rondel, advancing upon the Count like a general upon the enemy. 'Count Vexx, I declare! Delightful. The past owner and the next ought to get acquainted with one another, no?'

'No,' said Count Vexx. The library was ill-lit, as always, only a single lamp poised upon an ebony table at the Count's elbow. The dim emerald glow cast lurid shadows over his pallid face, as he sat still and sombre in his black wing-backed chair. Even the gilded, leather-bound tomes crowding upon the shelves seemed to loom with disapproval.

'And Lady Vexx?' persisted Lady Rondel. 'I should very much like to—she *is* in residence, I suppose?'

'No,' said Count Vexx again.

'Yes,' corrected Lulu. 'After a fashion. She went down to the cellar.'

'Oh? You confuse me, my dear. When exactly was that?'

'About 1912, wasn't it?'

'About that,' agreed her father.

'A jest. Very droll, I declare.' Her ladyship's face pinched with disapproval. 'Well, perhaps you are right to spurn my acquaintance,' she said with a forced little laugh, already turning away. 'It is unlikely we should ever meet again, after all—Percy, these bookcases! Have you ever seen the like?'

'Rarely, my lady,' said Mr. Percy with cool disdain.

'They must all go, and at once. Blonde wood, I think—high varnish—handsome collection of ivory-bound volumes, titles stamped in gold—very charming—'

Count Vexx came alive, his marble countenance flooding suddenly with vigour. He leapt from his chair, and made his bow to Lady Rondel. He had the silver-grey hair of a wolf's pelt, and a smile to match it, when he chose: he was wearing the latter now.

Lulu's heart sank a little further.

'I see your ladyship possesses a most discerning eye,' smiled the Count, his teeth glinting white and sharp. 'I really must apologise for the state of the old place. The times, you know, the lamentable times... I trust you are not too daunted?'

'My dear fellow, I? Daunted?' Lady Rondel gave another of her little laughs. 'No, no. I shall soon have this place in order. Why, you will not even recognise it yourselves!'

'Ah, but the cellars,' answered the Count, shaking his handsome head. 'They will all have to be rebuilt, naturally. So often flooded—no keeping the water out, I'm afraid, it is quite the problem. You have seen the cellars?'

'I have not! Percy, the cellars, and at once.'

'Papa—' Lulu remonstrated.

Her noble parent held up an admonishing hand. 'No, Lulu. It would not be right to conceal anything from our eminent purchaser, now would it? She must know exactly what she will be getting for her money. Warts and all.' He smiled his wolf's smile.

'I commend you for your honesty, Count Vexx,' said Lady Rondel, already halfway out the door. 'I believe we shall deal extremely well together, in spite of—' She was gone, without saying what, exactly, she was to spite. Mr. Percy went with her, leaving Lulu and her reprehensible parent alone.

The Count raised one of his expressive brows at his disapproving offspring. 'Well, Lulu?'

Lulu threw up her hands; there was no arguing with her father when he got into this sort of mood. 'I shall go and see if there is anything to be done,' she said, severely.

Count Vexx laughed, and accompanied her along a passage or two, gloom-shrouded and achingly cold (the passage, that is. Well, and also the Count). Lulu wrapped her shawl more tightly around herself, without much effect; Count Vexx stuck his hands into his jacket pockets, and whistled a thin, jaunty tune.

Lady Rondel's resonant tones emanated from somewhere below, echoing hollowly. '—Truly deplorable—shocking neglect—all have to be rebuilt, to the last brick—'

'—Significant impact on the purchase price—' agreed Mr. Percy. '—Offer to be much reduced—cost of renovations—'

'What's this?' said Lady Rondel. 'A pentagram? Daubed in blood, I declare! Dear me, how *dreadfully* vulgar—' A thin shriek followed, and then silence.

Count Vexx grinned, and dusted off his long white hands. 'I'll be in the library,' he informed Lulu. 'Do send Magwell up with some wine, will you? And cakes. Those little marzipan ones.'

'Papa.'

'Yes, dear.'

'We do *want* to sell Castle Drax, recall?'

'Of course we do!' He beamed upon his daughter, and wandered off, whistling.

Lulu rested her shoulders against the frigid blackstone wall, permitting herself a long sigh. She was quite tired, what with one thing and another. Her arms and back ached.

Half an hour drifted past before Lulu heard the footsteps. Someone was coming up the cellar stairs, very slowly, and with a heavy tread. Iron hinges squealed, spraying rust: the oaken door opened.

Lulu shook herself awake. 'Hello!' she said brightly. 'Welcome to Castle Drax.'

The newcomer was short and stout, with well-muscled arms and leathery, bone-white skin. He wore his white hair cropped short, and had an ivory jacket on rather like Mr. Percy's. He sniffed his broad nose, idly swinging a sharp-pointed walking stick in one large hand. 'I am Stormdust,' he informed her. 'What is your desire?'

Lulu thought of the floor in the hall, only half polished. Her lower back twinged. 'Well,' she ventured. 'Are you perhaps any good at cleaning?'

2

Simply Storming

The talents of Stormdust, newest inhabitant of Castle Drax, were myriad, eclectic, and, in the main, useless. His size and bulk might have lent themselves well to the more pugnacious arts, were it not for the absolute lack in him of anything resembling a fighting spirit. He had gently shepherded the pestersome mice of Castle Drax out of the great front door, rather than slaughter the creatures, even if they had got into Magwell's flour store.

Fresh from Count Vexx's summoning circle in the cellar, Stormdust would not be parted either from his ivory jacket or his sharp-pointed walking stick. He whistled much more melodically than the Count, possessed a smooth baritone singing voice which he often exercised, displayed a surprising talent for watercolour painting (much more so than Miss Lulu Vexx, to her mild regret), and could recite reams of presumably ancient poetry in a snarling language nobody understood but himself—not even Fane.

He had neither the skill nor the inclination for any of the various cleaning arts, to Lulu's greater regret. His one useful quality was a decided interest in motor cars and an accompanying facility for the piloting of them. Thus did Castle Drax acquire a chauffeur for its sole vehicle, should the family ever be minded to actually go anywhere—and if the car should consent ever again to function. It was at least restored to its former, gleaming-green glory, once Stormdust had had a go at it (the one thing he consented to clean, soaping its bodywork lovingly as he sang a succession of old ballads, and polishing its headlamps with the softest chamois leather).

After the escapade with Lady Rondel, Lulu set herself a daily task of housekeeping. There would be more prospective purchasers turning up at the castle in time, and the place ought to look a little brighter for its eventual new owners. Well, cleaner, anyway; there was no brightening an edifice built from black lava stone, and kitted out inside with polished midnight marble, to boot.

She half expected someone to enquire after Lady Rondel, her ladyship last seen sweeping through the heavy iron doors of Castle Drax, and never (yet) seen to emerge. No one did, however (yet), and a week or two drifted past in a happy haze of scrubbing, polishing, and landscape painting.

Count Vexx, as was his wont, remained inflexibly opposed to cleaning, or any other pursuit, save reading. His favoured emerald flames roared in the library's hearth, spitting frost over the Count's shoes as he sat with a succession of slim volumes, large folios, and weighty tomes; he hardly noticed. He was impervious to cold and entreaty, both.

Spring was wearing on, and the world beyond the castle flourishing in green and gold, before the next visitor manifested. The telephone shrilled, for the first time in a fortnight; Luna was halfway up the massive marble staircase, with her bobbed hair wrapped up in cloth and wielding a feathery duster in both hands. 'Coming!' she shouted, forgetting for a moment that neither the telephone nor the caller could hear her. She had just polished the glinting black stairs, and was then engaged in dusting the elaborate banisters; the former hindered her as she attempted to run for the telephone, and she slipped.

Stormdust's heavy tread sounded. 'Castle Drax, goodest of mornings,' he rumbled in his forbidding baritone.

A voice answered, faintly, tinnily. Lulu picked herself up off the frigid marble steps, straining to hear.

Garble, garble; then Stormdust said, 'Eleven o'clock. It shall be the best of days for your presence in it, madam,' and set down the receiver.

He would have thundered away again without remark, save that Lulu got herself down into the hall again, and intercepted him. 'Well, Stormdust? Who was it?'

'A Mrs. Bell,' he answered, and began a song, something lugubrious.

'And? She is coming here at eleven?'

Stormdust declined to break off his ballad, only nodded, and went away, leaving Lulu wondering.

Mrs. Bell was a partner in the firm of Percy and Bell, Estate Agents. They had in their management the selling of Castle Drax, a monumental task. If Mrs. Bell was coming, then she was likely bringing a prospective buyer with her: delightful! Only this time, Lulu would contrive to keep her father out of the business, if she could. Perhaps she would stock the library with wine, and cakes—the little ones, with marzipan in them—and then quietly lock the door. That should hold him.

The hall, at least, glimmered, sumptuous and elegantly dark (she hoped; alternatively heavy and miserably depressing; it all depended on one's taste). The rest of the castle retained all its shabbier, grimier characteristics, there being few to tackle these, only Lulu. Ah well.

Lulu hastened to the cloakroom, to take the cloth wrappings from her hair, and primp it: she looked passable, so the spotted mirror informed her. This time, she would butter up the visitors with hospitality; accordingly, she ran down to the kitchens to consult with Magwell, about the cakes (and the wine).

'Well, isn't this lovely,' proclaimed Mrs. Bell at eleven, entering the castle with a false smile on, and a young gentleman at her heels.

Lulu hoped she was referring to the state of the vast and echoing hall, freshly polished, the proud product of so much labour. More likely she was speaking of Fane, looming though he was, hard of feature, and the approximate colour of mould, yet he was carrying in his capable hands a silver tray, and on it were glasses of the Count's best vintage, really a rather good one. Magwell had made chocolate truffles for the occasion.

Luly eyed Mrs. Bell with a little unease. The lady didn't appear distressed, at least, or even wary. She had a comfortable bulk about her, worn with the greatest pride, her chin high. Her hair had not been permitted to grey, and was swept up in a chic chestnut chignon; her dress, mauve jacquard trimmed in ebony, must surely have been made by Madame Neve. She absorbed three truffles with great relish, and took up one of the Count's heavy silver goblets, brimming with wine.

Lulu expected a certain question, any moment now, prepared herself to meet it. But Mrs. Bell smiled, gulped her wine, and said: 'My client, Mr. Florrin.'

Lulu had scarcely glanced at their new buyer (possibly). He came forward with a bright, open face, and shook her hand much too heartily. 'Miss Vexx, goodness. You are a local legend!' he said, much too enthusiastically.

Lulu discovered him to be a head shorter than herself, his hair slicked back with too much brilliantine, and his face shining with the fresh glow of unimpeded youth. In short, he was only a boy.

'Mr. Florrin,' she said, recovering herself enough to smile, though she couldn't match the bruising alacrity of his handshake. 'You would like to buy a castle, would you?'

'Who wouldn't!' He adjusted the dark waves of his hair, a gesture Lulu interpreted as nervous, and beamed at Mrs. Bell. 'I suppose I might..?' He gestured at the tray of truffles, and wine.

'It would be rude not to,' said Mrs. Bell gravely, with the faintest wink for Lulu. 'I shan't tell.'

Young Mr. Florrin seized a goblet with what appeared to be his customary enthusiasm, and a truffle, too. 'Well,' he said with his mouth full, 'Let's get on!'

Either Mr. Florrin ('It's Boris!' he insisted after five minutes) experienced unmitigated delight from every feature of the capacious and gloomy Castle Drax, or he was accustomed to manifesting a mendacious facsimile of it. He followed Mrs. Bell and Lulu down every draughty passage, through a succession of creaking old doors with the hinges half rusted away, into disused antechambers, and the craggy old ballroom, with its peeling wallpaper and cracked flooring. He bounded up and down shadowed staircases to all the attic garrets and turret-top rooms; he even managed the water-logged and mildewed cellars with apparent aplomb (Lulu was careful to avoid the bit with her father's summoning-circle in it).

Mrs. Bell did her best to talk the place up, not that she needed to bother herself overmuch: Mr. Florrin declared himself entranced. 'I am delighted!' he said, more than once. 'Positively enchanted! I don't know how you could bear to part with the place!'

Lulu laughed politely, incredulously, and hoped her father hadn't managed to get himself out of the library. There hadn't been a peep out of him, which might be a good or a bad thing, depending.

They saw all of the castle, really very almost all of it, and arrived at last back in the hall. Fane had caused the great hearth to be lit, and a cheerful, electric-green fire cast unearthly shadows over the gleaming marble surround. Lulu, shivering, trusted that this at least would impress itself suitably upon the young master, especially after he dashed straight over to it and held out his hands to the fire, to warm them. As well he might, after a lengthy, near hour-long trek over Castle Drax; he could hardly help but be half-perished with cold.

'Ha!' he said. 'A cold flame! Fascinating,' and fell, apparently, to deciphering how such a marvel worked.

Lulu could not help the look of pure incredulity she directed at Mrs. Bell. There was a question in it, or several, all of which the estate agent plainly read; she coughed. 'Boris.'

'Yes.' The young man ceased his scrutiny of the fireplace, snapping upright like a willow sapling in a high wind. 'I'll take it,' he beamed. 'All of it. It's perfect.'

'Perfect?' echoed Lulu faintly, curiously appalled.

'Down to its last brick! I won't need to change a thing.' Mr. Florrin smiled upon the world as though it had personally gone out of its way to please him. 'No! I tell a lie. There *is* one thing—I suppose you *do* have a library?'

'Well, yes,' Lulu admitted.

'You see? Perfect!' He waited, smilingly, to be taken there, and Lulu couldn't think of a single excuse not to do so.

'Oh yes, the library,' put in Mrs. Bell. 'It seemed shut up, but I suppose it isn't, is it?'

Lulu entertained wild visions of dissembling: '*Oh, entirely shut up, quite infested with rats, the books all eaten, we never go in there now,*' she would say, or, '*I'm afraid it burned down yesterday, it's a marvel the castle survived.*' No, that wouldn't do.

At least they had already tackled the cellars.

'Well then,' she sighed, with a strange feeling of impending doom. 'Come this way.'

The lock turned, and the door opened, with traitorous ease; not even a pretence at sticking fast. Lulu peeked inside, hoping, by some inexplicable miracle, to find the room empty.

It was rather dark. Shadow-drowned, one might even say sepulchral; nothing much to be wondered at in that. Count Vexx stood leaning one hand against the mantelpiece, staring into the leaping flames illuminating the dark maw of the hearth. He looked up, smiled, and green fire seemed to leap in his eyes. Just a reflection, no doubt. 'Come in,' he invited.

Mr. Florrin didn't hesitate. Lulu winced as the door closed behind him, with a bang and a cloud of dust.

She and Mrs. Bell eyed one another.

Lulu's composure crumbled a bit around the edges. 'About Mr. Percy—'

'Yes, much obliged to you for that,' interrupted Mrs. Bell.

Lulu's silence spoke a couple of volumes.

'I shall just mention, however,' continued that lady, 'I shan't be thanking you if anything were to happen to Boris.'

Lulu sighed. 'Does he really want to buy a castle?'

'Oh, passionately. Last week he was wild to take up horse-racing, and become a jockey. Next week it will be motor cars, I expect, or something else altogether.'

'Motor cars,' said Lulu. 'I see.'

The library door wafted open again; voices emerged. '...Chasuble's treatise on economics—' came Mr. Florrin's excitable tones. 'Positively ripping stuff, though it did have one or two weaknesses—'

'Ah yes, well, if you're a Chasuble enthusiast then you must read—if you would just fetch that volume down from the third shelf above your head there—that's the one—' Count Vexx, this, almost as boyish as Boris.

'I think he'll be fine,' Lulu observed to Mrs. Bell, meaning Boris (or her father, or both).

'He's very likeable, Boris,' Mrs. Bell replied. 'It's one of his faults.'

'The Count isn't, in the least. Usually.'

Mrs. Bell snapped her fingers with lazy authority; Fane appeared, with admirable promptitude and a drinks tray, freshly refilled.

'I hope you are going to tell me what became of darling Percy,' she said, selecting a goblet. 'And in detail.'

'Father took him down into the cellars,' said Lulu, with meaning.

'Too unfortunate,' murmured Mrs. Bell.

'Quite. Though Stormdust is a perfect delight. And so well-dressed.'

Count Vexx came out into the passage, glossily handsome, and supremely pleased. Boris was with him, a bounce in his step, despite the weight of the seven or eight tomes in his arms. 'Ah, Fane,' said the Count, swiping a goblet off the tray. 'Just the person. Be a good fellow and take Boris out to the garage, will you? He'd like to play with the motor car.'

'And a few books, I see,' put in Lulu.

'Oh, yes. He's to enroll at Devervale in the autumn. Economics. Clever chap.' He clapped Mr. Florrin on the shoulder with brutal heartiness, and disappeared back into his library.

The door closed.

'Devervale?' Lulu queried, of Boris and Mrs. Bell both.

'Oh, yes. The Count's going to arrange it. I never heard he was such a capital fellow!' This, of course, was young Mr. Florrin; Mrs. Bell merely looked bemused, or amused, or likely both.

'I never heard that he was, either,' said Lulu. 'I suppose you won't be needing a castle when you're at university?'

'I suppose not. Marvellous place, though. Simply storming.' He went off with Fane and a goblet of wine, chattering about opera seats, and horsepower.

'I'll show myself out,' said Mrs. Bell, and did so, without further remark.

Lulu permitted herself just one, little sigh, and went back to her watercolours.

3

The Counting

There can be no doubt that the sinister and silent Castle Drax has seen its fair share of terrible events. A succession of unwanted visitors, tiresome guests and an occasional family member have disappeared into the cellars, never to be seen again (so far); a Lady Vexx, a century past, was stabbed to death with a steak knife in the middle of a particularly disharmonious society dinner; and a past Count Vexx, out on his morning constitutional, slipped on a slick of unfortunately positioned mud and fell into the dark waves of the emerald sea, which promptly swallowed him.

There are still greater calamities afoot, however. While the weather had continued fair through much of the spring—a strengthening sunshine only occasionally enlivened by a sprightly and invigorating shower—there came a lowering week, a week of impending doom presaged by the massing of black clouds over that same malachite-green sea.

In short, it began to rain, and in earnest.

Monday wasn't so bad; by the end of it, only half the contents of the kitchen cupboards had been pressed into alternative service, positioned at disparate intervals around the castle's draughty corridors and vault-ceilinged rooms, wherever the leaks were the most severe.

By Wednesday, Magwell had scarcely a pan left to cook in, or a dish to serve anything onto. Every lacquered vase, porcelain tea cup or disused chamber pot in the castle had been requisitioned, and sat quietly spilling the relentless rainwater onto the mouldering floors of the first, second and third best parlours, the guest bedrooms, the long gallery, and the attic garrets (long devoid of guests and inhabitants alike).

By Friday, the determined efforts of Miss Luna Vexx, Magwell the cook, Fane the butler and Stormdust the chauffeur to preserve Castle Drax from a relentless washing-away had ebbed. For five days together, a dark sky boiling with storms had entrenched itself over the village of Andirac. The ocean had lost its prismatic quality in a frothing rage, sending up walls of water near as high as the turrets; a gale of furious currents had whistled and howled and screamed down all the twisted chimneys of the castle, plunging the customarily frigid temperatures down into the regions of the arctic; and, of course, a malevolent rain, intent on destruction, had driven itself in a mad frenzy against the rattling windows until the corridors were awash with rivulets of rainwater slowly washing the dust away. And since, by Friday evening, there was no sign of it letting up, not the slightest sliver of a silver lining to lighten the glowering sky, really there was no point anymore.

'I dare say it will clear up tomorrow,' declared Miss Luna, a bright hope ringing in her clear, low voice and wreathing itself in a smile about the elegant bones of her face. Her blonde hair in its stylish bob was wringing wet, like everything else in the castle; remarkable, really, how she could muster anything like cheer under the circumstances, but some people are marvellous like that.

She was addressing her father, the current Count Vexx, who sat in a miserable huddle in his library (as usual), glowering as darkly as the storm outside, and radiating displeasure.

'By what possible logic can you suppose any such thing?' answered that gentleman, pausing in his anxious scrutiny of his collection of books to shoot a look of wondering exasperation at the light of his life (his daughter). And well he might worry: though his several hundred excellent volumes were arranged with great care over the tall, deep, ebony shelves of his book-room, and were dusted regularly (with his own hands, no less), nothing could keep the roof from leaking, or the rain from seeping in, and trickling in gleaming streams down the walls. As any book lover will know, little is as fatal to a library as water.

Lulu knew this all too well, and regarded the storm's intrusion into her father's sanctuary with feelings as anxious as his own. But since it was out of her power—or his, apparently—to do much about it, it was not in her nature to fall into a sulk.

Several articles of ancient bed-linen, full of holes and thick with dust, had already been spread over the black-glittering floor, and wedged against the walls, in the vague and fading hope that they might somehow preserve every book in the room by absorbing all the rainwater themselves. They were wringing-wet, of course, and there was nothing dry to replace them with.

It was in this state of mutual dissatisfaction and mounting despair that something extraordinary happened.

The doorbell rang.

A previous Count Vexx had actually liked people, indeed possessed a spirit of expansive bonhomie that had seen many a society dinner held at Castle Drax, and it was probably the last time the great, echoing ballroom had seen use. This same Count Vexx had overseen the installation of a stupendous system of bells, the better and more dramatically to announce the arrival of visitors.

The doorbell, then, resounded around the castle with sufficient clamour to make itself heard, despite a terrific clap of thunder happening to occur at that same moment. The bell sounded in a descending, increasingly lugubrious scale, pleasurably discordant, and left Luna's ears ringing. She despised it almost as much as her father did, but there was no changing it; that would cost money.

It didn't help that this inexplicable visitor, choosing a darkening night in the midst of a terrible storm to impose themselves upon the castle, was so eager to be admitted that they sounded the doorbell again—and *again*.

'To blazes with them!' roared the Count, clapping his hands over his ears. 'Lulu, this infernal intruder is to be hurled into the cellars without delay, and the door *slammed*.'

This was no insignificant threat, considering what had become of most of the other unlucky souls whose stars had guided them down those ringing stone stairs, slick with mould, and into the dark bowels of the castle.

Lulu patted her father's hand in a vain attempt to pacify him, and got up. 'I'll see to it at once,' she promised. 'We shall have this importunate person tidily eviscerated by dinner time, I've no doubt.'

This mollified the count, though—if he had known his daughter at all, and he ought to—Lulu had no intention of eviscerating anybody. He subsided into his black wing-back chair and subsequently into his sulk, the natural state of a man besieged by difficulties and powerless to much alter them, and Lulu hurried away.

Fane had answered the door, and stood unflinching in the savage squall of rain that came through it; whoever had caused the doorbell to so thoroughly discompose the count stood wreathed in shadow.

'And are you expected, sir?' Fane was saying, with commendable patience under the circumstances.

Lulu might have laughed. Expected? A guest? At dinner time? The stranger proffered a polite negative, without apology, and Lulu arrived in time to hear him saying: 'I've come to see the house.'

Lulu strayed into the watery patch spreading slowly over the fathomlessly black tiles, and tried to ignore the cold dampness seeping into her stockings. 'In this weather?' she couldn't help saying.

Their visitor made a daunting figure, she immediately discovered: almost as tall as Fane, and preternaturally still; quite unmoved by the weather. His clothes were extraordinarily well tailored, a dark, sleek, crisp suit, and seemed equally impervious to the elements. 'May I come in?' he said, without answering Lulu's question.

Lulu looked past him for Mrs. Bell, her estate agent, but saw no one. She could hardly turn him away in the midst of a storm, even if a searing flash of lightning did at that moment illuminate a sharp, angled face cast in an unnatural pallor. 'Of course you must come in,' she said. 'Thank you, Fane. Please tell Magwell to wait dinner.'

It might have been sociable, at such a moment, for the enigmatic visitor to make some apology for his uninvited intrusion, but he did not. He came in, his polished black shoes making almost no sound as he moved, and did not even trouble to smile at his hostess, or to shake her hand, or to introduce himself. His green eyes turned up at once, to survey the distant ceiling; 'Marvellous,' he said, in a cool baritone.

Lulu glanced up, briefly. It was marvellous, of course: a shadowy, echoing, vaulted, splendid ceiling, liberally painted with a roiling, thunderous firmament just like the one still wreaking destruction outside. 'That? Oh yes, quite,' she agreed. 'Are you interested in the castle?'

'Extremely,' he said, still studying the painted empyrean in all its faded glory. 'The work of Stittlegarth, surely?'

'Yes! Or so it has been said—never entirely confirmed, though the style—'

'—is unmistakeable,' he finished. 'There can be no question.'

Lulu studied him with greater interest than before. He wasn't at all handsome, really, with his cheekbones jutting like cut glass and his skin as pale as the grave. In fact, he was the sort of man she might infinitely prefer not to be left alone with, if she could help it, an effect in no way improved by the smile he finally bestowed upon her: it didn't reach his eyes.

She might wish her father had not chosen to lock himself in the library, and refuse to come out; or that she had not dismissed Fane.

Still, he was a scholar of Molly Stittlegarth: there was nothing savage in *that*.

'Well, I'll show you the rest of the house,' Lulu decided. She did not know how else to get rid of him, and he probably wasn't going to murder her, even if he looked like he might like to. 'Though really,' she added, a belated and admittedly feeble attempt, 'The house is really only open for viewing by appointment with Mrs. Bell, of Percy and Bell.'

'I will remember that next time,' he promised, with the ghost of another smile.

Lulu made one last effort. 'Miss Luna Vexx,' she informed him, and held out her hand to shake.

He took it, and shook it, and said: 'Enchanted, Miss Vexx.'

'And you are?' she said, in tones turning as arctic as the air of the grand hall.

'I am an admirer of castles.'

'And Molly Stittlegarth, I gather, but that doesn't—'

'You do have more of her work?' he interrupted, eyes brightening.

'Well... yes, actually we do have another mural that's said to be hers. In the ballroom. And there's a bit of a fresco on the west wall of the Long Drawing-Room, sadly unfinished, she unaccountably went missing before she could finish it—' Lulu, betrayed into something like enthusiasm, led her strange guest off to the ballroom, first, where they admired a mural depicting a midnight forest of wizened trees lit by deathly pale wisps; thence to the Long Drawing-Room, to absorb the generally tragic effect of a half-painted figure shrouded in a rippling silver cloak. Along the way, the admirer of castles identified several statues of Grimspound's work, carved from the local black lava rock, and depicting the Five Attitudes of Death; an expanse of emerald-and-garnet stained glass, undoubtedly designed by Mordale; a rare example of lace worked rib vaulting suspended over the library passage; and a succession of airy, unusually narrow pointed-arch windows in every part of the castle, sheathed in obsidian, and etched in a silver tracery not seen outside of the legendary Winter Palace, at Tausent (so he said).

Lulu saw all this, and saw besides acres of peeling wallpaper, hundreds of cracked floor tiles, a suffocating quantity of dust and cobwebs (frequently occurring together), and myriad streams of clear rainwater industriously forming fresh channels down the ancient black walls.

'Really, it needs a lot of work,' she said more than once, appalled anew at the general state of dilapidated decay; it had been a long time since she had really looked at most of it.

'Oh, I should think it would cost millions to restore everything,' her companion agreed comfortably, seeming unperturbed. Lulu's hopes rose; perhaps he was an eccentric millionaire, with no qualms about paying a fortune for a house the size of a small hamlet, and then hurling another one at it in repairs.

But he didn't make any kind of an offer, only withdrew a leather-bound notebook from some hidden pocket, and began sketching the outlines of a massive ebony armoire that lurked like a giant spider in a corner of the Ruby Bedchamber (last occupied by the count's maternal grandmother, who expired there, at an improbably advanced age).

'An interesting piece,' he said by way of an aside. 'Dagny's Dark Period. Quite valuable. Whoever chose this one had excellent taste.' His grin hinted at secrets held out of Lulu's reach, which he patently enjoyed; Lulu didn't, so much.

'Did you come here to view the house or to study it?' she said, folding her arms, and subjecting him to one of her mother's best and most devastating stares.

'There's a lot here you could work with,' he answered, without answering. 'Do you have any more Dagny?'

'A jet-inlaid sideboard in the dining room, a matched pair of console tables in the Little Hall, and a set of four parlour chairs with marbled upholstery, though one of them's got a leg missing.'

'You know your Dagny.'

'I know my castle,' Lulu retorted.

He bowed to her, with exquisite grace, and said, to her mingled mystification and surprise: 'A worthy Vexx indeed. I'll show myself out, shall I?'

'By way of the dining room, the Little Hall, and all the parlours, I suppose, though pray, for your own good, stay out of the cellar.' Lulu honoured him with a brief curtsey, only because he had been so extremely well-mannered as to bow, and left him finishing his sketch of the ebony armoire. She ought not to, perhaps, but she was perishing with cold and hunger, and besides that, quite tired of him.

She did take the precaution of asking Fane to keep an eye on him, and further stationed Stormdust at the top of the cellar stairs.

Having partaken of a solitary dinner of venison steaks and cheesecakes in the Oval Salon, chosen for its proximity to the library (with her father in it) and the dark descent below (with Stormdust on guard before it), she opened a novel, and sat with three blankets around her shoulders and spread over her lap, attempting to focus on the adventures of the lachrymose Evangelina. She did not meet with any great success, her mind blossoming with questions about their strangest visitor yet. What could he mean by his peculiar behaviour? What had he been suggesting, when he'd said "there's a lot here you could work with?" He surely wasn't suggesting that she *sell* the contents of the castle—the Dagny furniture and the Grimspound statues? Was she to peel the Stittlegarth murals of the ceilings and the walls? And to call her a worthy Vexx, as though he had the smallest right (whoever he was) to judge!

Lulu's sunny temper had been, for a little while, significantly shadowed, which was not at all her way; she did not linger long in her depressed mood. She had jollied herself out of it before long, reflecting that it had, after all, been nice to talk to someone knowledgeable, and interested. She turned a more tolerant ear, then, to the stranger's baritone voice when it came drifting past her salon, and was gratified to hear Stormdust answer: all was well.

But then came a creaking, shrieking sound of protesting hinges, and the heavy swing and thud of a massive door opening: the cellar! She heard no footsteps, but then, this fellow had a strangely soft tread—she was out of her chair in an instant, her novel hurled aside, and running fleetly out into the passage.

She saw Stormdust, a stout, solid figure past which no one would easily go, if he were to set himself against it. But he no longer guarded the stairway, and she saw no sign of the dark man with his sketchbook.

'Stormdust! You cannot have permitted our guest to go down there!'

Stormdust gave a little half-bow in acknowledgement of her words, but said: 'The Count ordered it, Miss Luna.'

'My father? But he cannot have. He has locked himself in the library all this while, and has not yet come out. I would have heard him.'

'The other one, Miss Luna,' said Stormdust, and took himself off, crooning something deep and dreamy.

Lulu let him go, choosing instead to hare down the stone steps after their guest. They had already lost one prospective buyer to the dark depths of the cellar; she could not square it with her conscience to lose another (even if he had been so foolish as to directly disobey her clear instructions). She could picture him all too well, marking the pages of his silly sketchbook with the stark outlines of her father's summoning circle; five dark points daubed in something deep and red—straying too close in his absorbed interest, a flash of sickly light, and—

She did not get more than halfway down the steep stairway, however, before she bumped into somebody else coming up.

'Oh, thank goodness,' she was halfway through saying, before she realised: it wasn't him.

A woman was huffing and puffing her way up the stairs, a very large woman perfectly strange to Lulu. Paint in diverse colours marked the loose, threadbare shirt and long coat she wore; her arms were full of brushes, canvas, palettes, and other materials of the artist's trade; and the light of a strange zeal lit her fierce gaze as she glanced at Lulu.

'Well?' she snapped. 'Where is it?'

Lulu could only look her surprise and incomprehension.

'The Long Drawing-Room,' said the woman, struggling up another step. 'Not that it was among my finer works; I'd have finished the thing if it *was*, now wouldn't I?'

'The fresco?' suggested Lulu, beginning, vaguely, to understand.

'Quickly. I've only got until midnight.'

Lulu lead the way, wondering. That the enigmatic man with his sketchbook had vanished into Count Vexx's summoning circle seemed indubitable; that the late, great Molly Stittlegarth had somehow come out of it as a consequence seemed equally so.

And there were Stormdust's words to consider...

She would interrogate Stormdust, later, without much benefit; whether he was intentionally keeping secrets or simply failed to comprehend her question, he would only repeat that "the Count had ordered it all".

When Lulu next entered the Long Drawing-Room, she found a completed fresco of a shimmering, impossible beauty, the shrouded figure's silvered cloak whipping in an unseen wind—and no sign of Molly Stittlegarth.

Lulu took a soft cloth to the ebony armoire in the Ruby Bedchamber, and to the marble-upholstered chairs, the matched console tables, and the jet-inlaid sideboard. When they were gleamingly clean, she took herself off to the library, to consult her father's collections on Stittlegarth, Grimspound, and Dagny's Dark Period.

It took another week to stop raining, by which time Lulu had made herself an expert in all three. There was too much mopping-up of rainwater, scraping-up of mud and mould, and cataloguing of fresh damage for her to much consider these various mysteries after that. But she had the settled feeling that they had not seen the last of the Dagny-appreciating man and his sketchbook; and in this, she was likely to be proved correct.

4

A Fine Night for It

A cool blue twilight settled over Castle Drax, deepening the shadows (never entirely absent) about its gleaming black contours, and deepening the chill (never entirely absent, either) that haunted its agéd halls.

The castle was haunted by Stormdust, too, at the present time, though not unpleasantly. He was singing as he wound the looming ebony grandfather clock in the great hall. His mellow baritone echoed off acres of polished black marble and stone; Lulu could hear him all the way up in her painting tower, if distantly.

Twelve o'clock, twelve o'clock, a howl in the night,
One o'clock, one o'clock, you'll perish of fright
If you dare to step into
the Eventide...

Lulu hummed along as she daubed silvery paint onto her canvas. It was a fine night for painting, the skies clear, strewn with dawning stars. A bright moon, fat and full, floated through the darkening firmament, bathing the overgrown grounds in a dulcet white light.

'*They're gonna get yoouuu,*' sang Stormdust, eerily. '*Don't let them get yooouuuu...*'

She'd grown distracted, and painted something odd into her tranquil twilit landscape. A dark patch of shadow beneath an age-bowed yew tree had sprouted eyes from somewhere, the kind that glowed with an unearthly light.

She looked out over the tangled thicket that might, once, have been attractive pleasure grounds, searching the shadows: no malevolent stare. She had painted in the eyes in a moment of abstraction, doubtless a consequence of Stormdust's eerie serenade.

Lulu prepared her brush with black paint, but hesitated on the point of obscuring the eyes. They gave an otherwise typical landscape a note of interest, drew the viewer's own eyes to the curious feature. Raised a haunting question, perhaps? It might prove to be the best thing she had ever painted.

She left the eyes where they were, and went back to sweeping swathes of pale moonlight across her canvas, limned in white.

Stormdust completed his clock maintenance, an event heralded by nine resonant strikes from below. Two voices floated up along with them: her father, Count Vexx, had joined the evensong from his customary station in the library, singing harmony in a light tenor.

Lulu smiled, and added a third part to the medley, and by the time the song finished she had also added a trail of dark footprints to her painting, marking a path out into the darkness beyond the reach of the moonlight.

'Hmm,' said she, and put her paints away. She took up the canvas carefully and carried it downstairs to the kitchen, the only room in the castle with the faintest breath of warmth about it (from the cooking).

'Magwell,' said Lulu, breezing in. 'Guard this with your life. It may be my masterpiece.'

Magwell had concluded her culinary efforts for the day. The kitchen gleamed with cleanliness, pristine; the enormous oaken table in the centre, marked and scored and stained with the remnants of decades—centuries—of chopping and kneading and rolling, bore myriad covered ceramic bowls, filled with delectable substances ready prepared for the morrow.

Magwell herself sat in a pine rocking chair near the blackstone hearth, knitting something unfeasibly lengthy. She was unfeasibly large herself, mightily strong, though with a softness to her air and manner that had beguiled Lulu as a child, and ever after. 'And what have you made this time, lovie?' said she, without looking up.

'A monster, I think.' Lulu held up her painting, mostly for her own perusal, and frowned at it. 'Definitely a monster.'

'How lovely. Put it on the mantel there. I'm sure it will be all dried out by morning.'

Lulu balanced it carefully over the dying coals in the hearth, pausing to savour a waft of warmth herself before she left it there. She had often trotted down the stairs to the kitchens to help Magwell kneading dough or mixing pastry, and it had only been partially motivated by a strong desire to absorb some warmth into her chilly bones.

'What's that you're making?' Lulu enquired, as Stormdust began another song. His voice floated down the stairs, crooning.

'A suit for Vera. She gets awfully cold, poor dear.'

Vera, hearing her name, glanced up from her spot upon the warm stones of the hearth, her crimson beak set in a smug smile. Magwell's hens were not normally permitted in the kitchen, but Vera evidently considered herself a fixture.

Lulu frowned at the knitted thing, worked in fetching ochre yarn. It seemed formed for a snake, or some such elongated creature, if a snake were likely to possess five—no, seven—legs.

'How lovely,' Lulu answered, meaning it without reservation, and pinched a nugget of cinder toffee from the nearest bowl. It crunched satisfyingly between her teeth as she wandered back upstairs.

Stormdust had finished winding and singing and the castle had fallen back into its usual silent torpor. Then, dropping into the stillness like a rock into lakewater, a horrific, bestial scream split the air, emanating from somewhere beyond the walls.

Lulu thought at once of the glowing eyes in her painting. 'Ah,' said she, and went to fetch her coat.

Count Vexx was faster. Lulu had donned only her coat and one wellington boot when her father brushed past her, wielding a wickedly sharp sword—black, of course—almost as tall as he was.

She ought not to have bothered with the boots, perhaps, but it was too late now; she stomped hastily into the second one and hurried through the porch and out of the back door. Count Vexx's imposing figure was some way ahead of her, moving at speed; already he had nearly reached the dark line of yew trees that flanked the garden, clearing ferns and brambles out of his path with impatient chops of his sword. Lulu followed in his wake as best she could, urged on to greater haste by a second roar, shatteringly loud.

Snarling followed, and cursing.

Lulu ducked under the low-hanging fronds of a knotted yew, and cursed herself for wasting time on boots instead of fetching a lantern. Count Vexx had melded entirely with the deepening shadows under the boughs, and she could see little of him—or of the monster, either.

Something moved. Eyes flashed bright silver in the gloom.

The creature gathered its breath, began another screaming bellow—which broke off in a yelp.

'FANE!' bellowed Count Vexx. 'Blazing Hells, man! What in the Nine Circles has got into you?'

A whimper answered him. The glinting silver orbs turned on Lulu, and fixed there.

Lulu reached out a hand, half blindly; her fingers encountered a thick ruff of fur. 'Now, Fane,' she murmured. 'Everything will be well, I promise.'

Fane had been a resident of Castle Drax since long before Lulu was born. He was an odd, looming sort of fellow, with skin the colour of freshly sprouted mould and a visage best described as horrifying. But he had played hide-and-go-seek a hundred times with Lulu in bygone times, picked her up after countless falling-downs and scraped knees, and had functioned as a species of butler for a great many years, and with considerable aplomb.

Lulu struggled to remember the last time he had gone monster, though.

Count Vexx rested the gleaming point of his sword against the dark earth, and leaned on it. 'You've nicked me,' he grumbled. 'I am bleeding.'

Lulu wound all of her fingers into Fane's rough fur, and tugged gently. 'Leave be, Father. Poor Fane is upset.'

'Of course he is,' snapped the Count. 'We're all upset. We're selling Castle Drax.'

Was that the cause of Fane's distress? Lulu scarcely needed to shape the question before she knew the answer: of course it was true. Where would Fane go, once the ancestral Vexx residence had passed into someone else's possession? Where would Magwell and Stormdust go?

Where would *she* go, or her father either?

These were not questions either of them had addressed, when laying plans for the castle's sale. They couldn't. The mere thought of it had fractured Lulu's heart every time she brought it to mind, and her father's, too (a state of distress he displayed chiefly through heightened irascibility, and a near total refusal to leave the library).

She had put off the whole bushel of problems for future resolution; after they had managed the difficult business of finding a buyer for the castle, say.

But that wouldn't do. The state of uncertainty was sending Fane crackers, and everyone else, too.

'Father. You do *want* to sell Castle Drax, don't you?'

'About as much as I would like to flay you alive, or eat Fane for dinner.'

Lulu took a moment to consider this remark. 'Just to be quite clear, that is a no, isn't it?'

'Oh, Lulu.'

'Sorry.'

He sighed, gustily and irritably. 'I will never want to sell it. But the castle seems to grow larger and colder and greedier every year, and our sources of income have not, I needn't remind you, grown to match it.'

The costs of repairs and heating and food and everything else had climbed and climbed; the income from rents and crops and investments had fallen and fallen. Times were hard, for everyone.

'Perhaps,' she ventured, 'We should not have permitted Lady Rondel to go down into the cellar?' Her ladyship had been the only likely purchaser they had yet encountered, even if she had been full of plans to alter, irrevocably, every brick and stone and chair in the castle.

'Lulu. I would rather die than see *this castle* in the hands of a person with so little taste, sense or feeling.'

'She did have rather strong opinions,' Lulu agreed. Fane whined, and lay down at her feet. A stray beam of moonlight filtering through the needled canopy illuminated a vast, dark shape, with the customary number of eyes but far too many legs. 'We have to sell it,' she said. 'None of us can think of any feasible alternative, can we? But I promise, Fane, we will find a new place for us all.'

It wasn't enough, as assurances went, but it was all she had. Fane remained out in the woods at the end of the garden, a monster, and Count Vexx stayed there with him.

Lulu lingered until the chill sank too far into her bones, and then returned inside, heavy at heart.

Some time afterwards, voices rose once again in mournful serenade—three. The Count and Fane, out in the yew-trees still, and joined by Stormdust. Well, and it was a fine night for it, after all.

Lulu woke to a quiet castle. There was no sign of Count Vexx as she shuffled, shivering, down to the kitchens to collect her bread and butter for breakfast, or of Fane either. Stormdust she encountered in the dank, black passage between the kitchen and the cellar door; he was whistling softly, and carrying a bundle of oil-smeared rags under one arm.

'Morning, Miss Lulu,' he greeted her, smiling toothily all over his broad face. 'Though the mournest of mornings it is, I must say.'

'What?' Lulu stopped dead, her heart thudding with dread. 'Why do you say that?'

'Why, did you not hear the song yestereve?'

'Your beautiful serenade? Why yes, and I was glad of it, for it meant that poor dear Fane must have got back into his legs and arms. He could not have sung so, otherwise, more of a howl—' Lulu, petrified of unnameable things, babbled on, as though the news Stormdust had to share could be warded off by it.

'It was!' Stormdust agreed, beaming. 'The beautiest of serenades. It is a farewell, Miss Lulu, as you must know. We sing them, sometimes, when we are sad.'

By "we", she supposed he meant himself and Fane and Magwell—those who had come through her father's summoning-circle in the cellar, at one time or another, and stayed.

It now struck her that Stormdust had been walking and whistling rather close to the cellar stairs; had he been coming back from the deep places below? 'Tell me at once,' she pleaded. 'It's Fane, isn't it? He has gone back. And—no, surely my father has not gone with him?'

'Neither, yet.' Stormdust whistled a few bars of some melody Lulu didn't recognise, while her nerves screamed with impatience. 'But it must be so that they will, once the castle is sold. No doubt we shall all go. Perhaps you might like to come with us, Miss Lulu.'

Lulu's heart sank into her socks. Of course; she ought to have known. The wretched question of what was to become of the Vexxes, without Castle Drax; how could it have any other resolution? What other possible place could they hope to find for themselves, out beyond the familiar black walls and penetrating chill of their own beloved home? Fane would go below, Magwell and Stormdust with him—and her father. The world above never had made any sense to him. Would he fare any better in another one?

Stormdust may well be at ease; he was a new Vexx, only recently arrived at the castle. But Fane's faithful heart was breaking over it, and her father's, too.

And her own.

'Stormdust,' she said. 'Don't let them do it, not yet. Stop them, somehow, if they try to go. I will make this right. I'll save the castle somehow. Do you believe me?'

Stormdust's toothy smile returned, along with a scattering of merry notes. 'Why, of course I do!' He patted her arm, gentle taps of his great, brawny hand which fell on Lulu like hammer blows, and went on his way.

Lulu was left to all the dangerous satisfaction of having staved off immediate disaster, but only temporarily, and by way of a reckless promise she did not know how to keep.

She trailed back upstairs, fetching a bucket and a mop and an armful of cloths and dusters on her way, and set to cleaning the summer breakfast-room. She always got her best ideas when she was up to her elbows in honest work.

The results of her cogitations were not of the most encouraging sort. No extraordinary stroke of genius blessed her, as she wiped layers of dust off the mantelpiece, and scrubbed an odd, brownish stain off the flagstones under the long window. No harebrained but marvellous solution to all their problems darted into her mind, as though gifted from some obliging deity. There would be no such scheme; the castle, she knew, could only be saved by ordinary mortal efforts, or in the plainest of terms: work.

None of the Vexxes had anything like a marketable skill between them, of course, save possibly Stormdust's way with the motorcar. But they had other assets—one or two, at least. They had space. And there was a wide world out there, full of misfits and lost souls. Surely something like a solution lurked in all of that.

By the end of the day, the FOR SALE sign hung still by the front door—Lulu's confidence in her own brilliance was not quite such as to permit her to take it down, yet—but it had been joined by a second sign, painstakingly lettered in Lulu's own hand. ROOMS TO LET. ENQUIRE WITHIN.

5

A Spot of Chicanery

Sunny weather dawned on Castle Drax with the onset of summer, the ragged remnants of spring taking the rains away with it, as it went. After so many drowning-wet days, and so much water damage, this alteration in the firmament came as a great pleasure, at least for a day or two. The vast, black monstrosity of a castle dried out at last—the outsides, at least. The insides didn't especially, but at least they didn't get any wetter.

Lulu Vexx, tired of wielding mop and cloth against a never-ending tide of rainwater, welcomed the signs of balmy weather burgeoning. Mingling with the pervasive smells of mould and wet cloth came a whiff, here and there, of verdure freshly grown; should the windows be unlatched and thrown open, there might be warm air coming in, bringing wafts of flowers with it.

One bright morning, several days after the storms had passed, Lulu went about the castle with the reviled mop in hand, and a bucket, and a quantity of (mostly) dry cloths; a little heavy at heart to still be at it, but her spirits rising, for whenever she passed a heavy casement window she hurled it open, and a summery breeze came dancing in.

There had been no strangers about since the midst of that one great, shattering storm, and Lulu had forgotten to expect any. It had been weeks since Mrs. Bell had last telephoned, with word of an interested buyer wanting to be toured around the place; nor had any other dark and mysterious gentlemen seen fit to pop in, and air opinions about the furniture. The ROOMS TO LET sign at the door had yet to bear any fruit whatsoever. Blissfully, the lugubrious doorbell had not shattered the peace (or what passed for it) about the castle in some time, though Lulu would have given much for a lodger—just one, to start with.

How it could come about, then, that anybody could be wandering around the gardens (or what passed for them), quite unattended, and without the smallest warning of their arrival, Lulu could not venture to guess; but so it happened.

She caught a glimpse of this invading presence from the window of the Long Drawing-Room, having thrown it open to the breezes, and smiled sunnily down upon the jungly verdure below. How delightful to see things growing again! Even if they were at it with a bit too much enthusiasm—a great deal of rain, followed by sunshine, being an encouraging combination to plant life, they went wild for it. There had once been an elegant shrubbery down there, probably, but it had vanished under rambling ivy and an assortment of shrubs quite unidentifiable. If she were to take a strong pair of shears to it, perhaps something might be achieved—

Then came a flicker of movement—more than that, a furious rustling and waving of shrubbery, as though some very large animal might be about to surge out of it. Lulu's heart quickened in surprise and brief alarm, before she discerned the nature of the creature creating the ruckus: a person, female-looking, and not at all dressed for such an adventure.

'I say!' Lulu called down, waving. 'What are you doing in the shrubbery?'

Her words went unheard, or ignored, the lady continuing to do battle with the garden in a state of grim silence.

Lulu watched for a moment, with rather an encouraging spirit; wrangling with the gardens was no pursuit for a faint-hearted maiden. This lady had gumption.

She had better discover what exactly this courageous person thought she was doing hacking a path to a side-door with her bare hands. After all, they were not entirely devoid of valuables inside the forbidding walls, even if they were still a little soggy; there were the Dagny furnishings, Dark Period. Quite nice, if not especially portable.

There was some distance to be covered on her way down from the Long Drawing-Room, out of the side-door, and into the shrubbery. By the time Lulu had achieved it—discarding, as she went, the old rags wrapping up her hair, and neatening her blonde waves as best she could—the intruder had almost reached the castle. So intent was she upon her task that Lulu was obliged to shout to get her attention, such was the cacophony created by rustling leaves, snapping branches and swearing matrons. She looked up; her eyes met Lulu's, dark and angry; and she said, crisply, and with superb vowels: 'Well, that's torn it.'

She was a stout woman, probably quite strong, with grey threads in her auburn hair and a permanent line etched between her brows. Her grey suit and cream silk blouse had probably been neat and presentable, an hour ago.

'I expect you have torn a few things,' Lulu agreed. 'Your stockings for certain, and possibly a muscle or two.'

She expected apology, possibly chagrin, but the interloping lady whipped a notebook out of nowhere Lulu could fathom, and took up a pencil, too. 'Luna Vexx?' she barked, the words fired like missiles.

'Yes?' said Lulu, bewildered.

'I'm from the—well, I'm from an important newspaper and I'd like to ask you a few questions about Castle Drax.'

Lulu looked past the reporter, to the trail of devastation she had left in her relentless passage through the undergrowth. 'You're a journalist?'

'Yes, and it's very important that I speak with you—'

'You couldn't have come to the front door?' Lulu ventured a smile. 'I assure you, we don't bite.'

This prompted a flurry of scribbling. '—Maintains the rumours of savagery are lies—' said the reporter under her breath. 'Miss Vexx, is it true that Castle Drax is currently up for sale?'

'It—yes, it is, but if we must interview one another, perhaps in an alternate locale?' Lulu suggested. 'I am sure we could rustle up some refreshment for you—'

'—Blatant attempt to suborn this reporter with blandishments—' More scribbling.

Lulu's smile turned fixed. 'Just tea, and possibly a scone, if our cook has made any. Nothing extravagant, I assure you.'

'—Possible attempt to avert publicity by poisoning—'

The fixed smile faded altogether. Lulu, uncharacteristically, glowered. 'Which paper are you from?'

'The De Montford Observer.'

'Are you, though?' There ought not to have been a slight hesitation when the lady spoke, not if she was a prominent reporter for so major a paper as the De Montford.

'Yes?' came the answer.

Lulu, inflexible, waited.

And the reporter sighed. 'The Ladies' Journal of Architecture, Archaeology and Flower-Craft.'

'Nobody sent you, did they?' said Lulu. 'You're looking for a sensational scoop you can take to the De Montford Observer.'

'If I have to write one more story about the Andirac Annual Flower-Arranging Competition—'

'You'll burn the town to the ground,' Lulu suggested helpfully. 'With all the flower-arranging ladies in it.'

'We do have one or two gentlemen competing, most years,' said the reporter, and sighed again. 'Why do I know that.'

'Did you know Castle Drax was built five hundred and ninety-three years ago by the architect known only as La Belle? There's a local quarry of pure black lava rock that's mostly empty on account of it.'

'La Belle? Surely you're making that up.'

'Well, I'm not.' Lulu glanced up at the serene blue sky, a few wisps of cloud drifting through it. 'We'll have tea on the terrace, I think. It's mostly clear of undergrowth. I think we might be able to help each other.'

The reporter's name was Fannie Danvers, and she had been married, once. 'A no-good husband's a terrible curse, Miss Vexx,' she opined over a cup of sugared black tea and a slice of Magwell's dark fruit cake, sticky with treacle. 'Take care you don't get caught yourself, that way.'

'I shan't marry at all,' Lulu said with decision. What could possibly persuade her to do so? She had been born at Castle Drax, had played away her childhood in its chilly corridors and draughty turret-top chambers; had lost herself in its attics, nearly died of a chill caught in one of the guest bedrooms (she'd locked herself in by mistake; it had taken all day for anybody to find her).

She had been the castle's chatelaine, moreover, since Mama had gone down to see what all the fuss was about in the cellar. She could never willingly leave it, nor would she be so unreasonable as to expect anybody else to live in it with her.

Fortunately, solitude suited her.

'La Belle is thought to have built three houses,' Lulu said, pouring more tea. She'd cleared the terrace herself at the end of the winter, baring its dark flagstones and uncovering the ancient stone table. It had turned out fairly pleasant, if stone cold. 'Castle Drax was her most ambitious project, but she is also thought to have conceived of House De Winter, and the ruined palace at Ashfen.'

'I've seen House De Winter,' said Miss Danvers, casting a keen-eyed glance up at the looming black walls of Castle Drax above her. 'It's as fanciful as this place. Alabaster and diamonds.'

'It's plausible that the same mind created both, hm?' Lulu suggested. 'Now, nobody has ever done a full exposé on Castle Drax, to my knowledge. Neither its architectural features, nor its—intriguing history.'

'And which am I to produce?'

Lulu smiled. 'Both. One for the Ladies' Journal—we've got an original set of plans from the castle's construction in the library, with La Belle's notes on it, all done in her own hand. You can borrow it, and I'll tell you everything I know about the place.'

'I'd need a personal angle, and La Belle won't suffice. Not if we don't know anything about her.'

'How about me? I was born and bred here.'

'Nobody's heard of you, Miss Vexx. Your father certainly—'

'They have heard a great deal of nonsense about my father,' Lulu said firmly. 'If your questions earlier were any measure to judge by.'

Miss Danvers, surprisingly, grinned. 'But is it nonsense?'

'Officially, the most profound rubbish I ever heard.'

'Unofficially?'

'That brings us to your second article, Miss Danvers. I cannot give you tales of my father, but the previous Count was a shocking character. I'm sure we can come up with something that would interest the De Montford Observer.'

Miss Danvers had a keen, uncompromising gaze, and missed very little. She would make a fine journalist for a national paper. 'You found me trespassing on your private grounds and now you are offering me two exclusive stories? Why?'

'Because we have one or two problems at Castle Drax just now, and if they are to be resolved in a fashion that suits me then we shall be needing plenty of publicity.'

'You won't squirrel up a buyer that way,' Miss Danvers warned. 'The more unique the property, the more punishing the costs of maintaining it. And while scandals sell newspapers, they don't sell castles.'

Lulu nodded, unruffled. 'I know. Don't worry about that.'

Miss Danvers polished off a third slice of cake, and gulped her tea with the air of a woman being taken to her probable execution. 'Very well. Take me to your library.'

'Don't mind the fireplace,' Lulu warned, rising. 'It probably won't hurt you.'

Turfing her father out of his precious library proved no easy task. Lulu had never had cause to do it before; she had been more in the habit of keeping him in, than of ushering him out. In the end, she was obliged to bribe him.

'Did I mention that the motorcar is working? Stormdust has done something magical to it, I hardly know what.'

'Miraculous,' answered Count Vexx savagely. 'Next you'll be proposing a jaunt around the countryside.'

Ensconced in his black wingback chair as usual, with a tome of monstrous size open on his lap and the glow from the fireplace casting flickering green shadows over his chiselled, haughty features, the Count made for a forbidding figure. Lulu had prudently left Miss Danvers in the kitchens talking to Magwell. 'Not precisely,' she answered. 'But a jaunt to Harper's? Stormdust will drive you.'

He looked up. 'What, is that still there?'

'It's been there for two centuries at least, Father. Of course it's still there.'

Count Vexx developed a look of acute and feral hunger; Lulu hoped it was the thousand books of Harper's Emporium he was hungering for. 'Tell Stormdust to bring the car around,' he ordered, and sprang out of his chair, his heavy tome sliding down to land on the floor with a thud, and a cloud of dust. 'And don't wait dinner for me.'

He would be gone for at least a week, Lulu judged, which would give her time to sort a few other things out in his absence. Perfect.

'They've got a copy of Cortauld's Booke of the Nine Circles, I hear,' Lulu added, by way of a closing manoeuvre.

The Count, already on his way out the door, barely paused. 'Don't think I can't see what you're doing, Lulu.'

'What am I doing, Father?'

'You are being devious, in pursuit of ends presently unknown to me.'

'But I am doing it well, am I not?'

'Very. But if you permit any harm whatsoever to come to my library in my absence, I shall send you after your mother without a moment's regret.'

Lulu adopted an air of sober responsibility. 'I shall die before I permit any harm to come to our library, Father dear.'

Count Vexx grinned, always a savage expression whether he had violence on his mind or not. 'That's the spirit.' With these encouraging words he was gone, out to the motorcar, and Stormdust.

Lulu beamed at nothing in particular, and went off in search of Fannie Danvers.

'The fourth Count Vexx was said to bathe in the blood of maidens every seventh day. It is what kept him looking so youthful, and he did live an unconscionably long time.' Lulu sat in the vacated library, posed before a wall of handsomely-bound volumes, freshly dusted. It was two days later, and Miss Danvers had telephoned for a photographer to come to the castle; the chap was rather twitchy, for some reason, but he knew his business.

Lulu had donned a stylish tweed suit for the occasion—not new, but respectable enough. The blonde waves of her hair were, for once, perfectly arranged, and she had assumed an enigmatic smile for the photograph.

'An implausible tale,' Miss Danvers replied, paused over La Belle's hand-annotated plans for Castle Drax. 'Nobody would believe it.'

'Hold,' interposed the photographer, disappearing under the black drape of his camera. Lulu held her pose and her smile; 'Excellent,' declared the photographer after a long pause, and Lulu resumed her train of thought.

'He lived surrounded by a legion of demons summoned up out of Hell, and half the town of Andirac disappeared into his dungeons at one point or another.'

Miss Danvers threw down her pencil. 'Miss Vexx, may I entreat you to please take this matter seriously? I can't print the half of these wild claims.'

Lulu thought. Something acceptably plausible. 'He was married five times, and all of his wives died or disappeared in highly mysterious circumstances.'

'Oh. Now, that I can use.' Miss Danvers reclaimed her pencil, and gave a magisterial wave. 'Carry on.'

'The first of his wives was the beautiful Anne de Vere, rich, but with the most shocking temper...' Lulu recounted Vexxish histories while the photographer took several more pictures of the Chatelaine of Castle Drax, and its would-be biographer toiled away at her investigations into La Belle. It was rather companionable. Later, they would take luncheon together, and discuss the details of Fannie's articles; there were to be at least three, now, and very likely more.

A satisfactory day's work, all told.

These comfortable ideas came to an abrupt end halfway through Lulu's tale of the fourth Count's third wife, Elisabeth Vantry. 'Devious beyond compare, and quite malevolent, she hatched a shocking plot against the Count himself—'

'Luna. Just what in the Blazes are you doing?'

Lulu's creative visions of the fourth Count Vexx faded away, for here was the current one come back, days before she had expected him, and looking by no means pleased. He stood looming in the doorway—blocking the exit, thereby—with a forbidding demeanour, positively thunderous in fact. Cradled in his arms was the most ancient book Lulu had ever seen, a delicate thing of faded leather bound with tarnished silver clasps.

'Is that the Cortauld?' Lulu beamed up at her glowering parent. 'I'm so glad you were able to get it. Have we sufficient photographs, Mr. Lovett? I believe Magwell will be serving luncheon shortly.'

The photographer shot a nervous glance at the Count, who continued, bristling with displeasure, in the doorway. 'I believe we'll manage, Miss Vexx.' His patent desire for escape saw him working far faster than seemed to be his wont; he had his equipment packed up in a matter of minutes, though the Count remained an obstacle insuperable.

'Shall you join us, Father?' Lulu rose with some relief, and stretched the knots out of her limbs. Posing for pictures had proved a laborious business.

'I shall not. I shall, however, be glad to have the use of my library without further delay.' He condescended to clear the exit as he spoke, and Mr. Lovett was the first to go through it, moving at speed. Miss Danvers, sensibly, followed.

Lulu bestowed a kiss upon her father's cheek. 'Really, you can be awfully inconvenient sometimes.'

'Inconvenient? Me?' The Count swelled with indignation. 'I can be forbidding, foreboding, magnificent, terrible beyond comprehension, and entirely devastating, but never merely "inconvenient".'

Lulu patted his arm. 'Quite true. You go ahead and be terrible beyond sense or reason in your favourite chair. I'll ask Magwell to send a tray in for you.'

Count Vexx ensconced himself, still clutching his book like a babe to his breast. 'Are you going to tell me what this scheme is about?'

'Not yet.' Lulu moved towards the door into the hall, and lunch; she felt half starved. 'You'll see soon enough.'

'Mind what you're about.' He sounded absent, now; he'd opened the Cortauld.

'Please, Father. I know exactly what I'm about.'

Fannie Danvers' articles appeared in the Ladies' Journal a fortnight later—two of them, at least. "The Enigmatic Chatelaine Poised to Take Society by Storm" featured Mr. Lovett's photographs of Lulu, looking pale and stylish and (she hoped) rather mysterious; "Castle Drax: An Architectural Marvel by a Lost Genius" had a great deal to say about La Belle, about the black lava stone, and about the myriad details and curiosities built into Castle Drax, more even than Lulu knew.

Lulu was delighted with them both, the more so because they evaded her father's notice altogether. What use had he for Ladies' Journals, when there was Cortauld's Booke of the Nine Circles?

The third article, the scandalous one, would take some time yet to appear; Miss Danvers would crack The De Montford Observer, without question, but perhaps not immediately.

It was hardly necessary just yet, as it turned out, for not three days after the second article ran, Lulu took a telephone call. 'Castle Drax, Luna speaking,' she said brightly into the receiver.

'Miss Luna Vexx? Chatelaine?'

'Yes! Have you an interest in coming to see us? We are open for the next two days, and again next week. You'll have seen our admission prices in the Ladies' Journal, of course?'

'Do you offer a discount for groups?'

'Certainly! We can also offer a personal tour of the castle, and a spot of luncheon on the terrace.'

'Delightful. There'll be twelve of us. Tomorrow at eleven?'

Lulu chirped her agreement into the receiver, and re-placed it with care. She then performed a victory shim-my down the long length of the great hall, stopping only when she encountered a nonplussed Fane.

'Fane! We shall have visitors tomorrow. Paying ones. Will you wear your best livery? And ask Magwell to make those little marzipan cakes that Father likes. And if Stormdust could see to it that the motorcar is parked in the driveway—buff it up a bit more first, of course—'

Full of joy and plans, Lulu went in search of the key to the cellar door, and the summoning circle that lay beyond it. It wouldn't do to lose any of the ladies to it—not yet, at least. That would be a story for another time.

6

As Beautiful As a Dream

Came the third hour after midnight, a sliver of a white moon struggling bravely against the drowning dark of a night devoid of stars. A cold wind whistled down the chimneys of Castle Drax, and rushed along the passages, singing hollowly; upstairs, in a vast, black-walled bedchamber hung forlornly with patterned silks, Lulu Vexx lay dreaming.

The thick brocade drapes about her four-poster bed had long since fallen into holes, and the embroidered blankets in which she lay nested had fared still worse. Lulu lay untouched by the decay, comfortably aslumber, her fair hair spread over her pillow and a slight smile softening the lines of her face. It was a pleasant sort of dream, probably.

She was still at Castle Drax, in this dreamland of her imaginings, but it was a different sort of place. Still dark and frigid and looming, crouched atop a cliff on the shores of an emerald sea like a great spider deprived of a meal, but inside—oh! Inside it glittered with light and rang with music, every gramophone in the craggy old place pumping jaunty tunes into the night. There was laughter, too, for the castle swarmed with guests; ladies in silken dresses shimmering with beads, their hair gorgeously coiffed and their lips dark with rouge; gentlemen in smart suits and natty ties, glossily lacquered, boisterous with wine.

And the lady of the house, a bright, ravishing dream of a woman with hair just the colour of Lulu's and a smile to light up the world. She was holding court at a polished grand piano, leaning her slim elbows upon it while a gentleman drew melodies from its ivory keys; her ladyship sang along.

There was no sign of the master of the house, if such a person existed at all; to look at the place, you wouldn't think so.

Lulu was singing, too, under her breath, the words half-slurred with sleep and the notes wandering off-key; long ago, she had sat on the stairs with her face pressed to the cold black banisters and dreamed of being old enough, smart enough, beautiful enough, to join in, but none of that appeared in this mirage of the past. Where would be the fun in that? Lulu-in-the-dream was older and infinitely more glamorous, a sheathe of gold satin rippling like water over her hips as she danced in the arms of—of—well, a man, probably, though there was something very much amiss with his face and he had altogether too many arms—

A shattering noise shook the sleeping castle, a raucous, thundering, discordant abomination of a sound: Lulu started awake, stared groggily into the blank darkness of her bedchamber while her mind fought to free itself from her dream—goodness, had there been *champagne*—?

The cacophony sounded again, horrifyingly loud in the crisp stillness of the night; Lulu clapped her hands to her ears and struggled out of her bed. Who in their right mind could be ringing the doorbell at such an hour? It could only be someone who was not in their right mind, some lunatic wandering the hills of Andirac, armed (probably) with an axe and intent upon violence—Lulu, with an aggrieved sigh, thrust her arms into a quilted dressing-gown and hurried for the stairs.

When the lugubrious tones of the doorbell split the air for a third time, Lulu broke into a run.

'*What* is it?' she snapped, having arrived at the massive front door, and, sweatingly, hauled it open. 'If you have come to murder us all in our beds, I must ask you to return at a more sociable hour.'

The stranger on the doorstep carried no axe, nor any weapon of any sort at all; Lulu's mind, still half-fogged with sleep and nightmares, registered this fact with a dim surprise. She was short and thin and beskirted, garbed in the fashions of decades before, with a wide-brimmed hat shading her face from sunlight that would not dawn for several hours yet.

No more could Lulu discern in the wan light of that pathetic slip of a moon, but when the lady spoke her voice sounded flat and cold. 'I am looking for a room.'

Lulu waited for the situation to start making sense; it didn't. 'I beg your pardon?' she said.

'A room,' the stranger repeated, and pointed to one of the several hand-lettered signs hanging around the doorway. FOR SALE, said one; VISITORS ARE KINDLY ASKED TO KEEP OUT OF THE CELLARS AT ALL COSTS read another (the final three words painted in red, and underlined); and ROOMS TO LET—ENQUIRE WITHIN.

'In the middle of the night?' Lulu replied.

'If I had a room to be in at night then I would hardly need to enquire for one, would I?' answered the stranger, tartly. 'You must have something available, surely,' and the brim of her overlarge hat tilted up in a glance, pregnant with meaning, at the enormous, hulking mass of castle looming above them both.

'Well, yes, of course we do, but this is rather peculiar,' Lulu protested. From behind her, sounds echoed across cold stone: footsteps, doors opening, questioning voices. 'You've woken up the whole house.'

'Give me a room, then, and we can all go back to sleep.' There wasn't a trace of apology in the clipped words, and Lulu was within a breath of sending the woman away with a blistering curse or two to show for her efforts, when—she was obliged to pause.

Highly irregular and disorderly as her appearance past the witching hour might be, she *was* a prospective lodger. A paying guest, probably. Hopefully. At last.

Lulu told her the rate, and added, 'That's all right, is it?' It sounded such a lot, when she said it out loud.

'Do you imagine I wake people in the middle of the night in order to cadge a free room?'

'I cannot imagine why you felt it necessary to arrive at such an hour under any circumstances—'

'Yes, yes, it is fine,' interrupted Lulu's new lodger. 'Now please, let me in. I'm frightfully tired.'

Lulu capitulated. Some fading memory of her dream caused her to don a veneer of gracious charm, as her mother would have; she ushered her disagreeable lodger into the dark maw of the castle, pleased to discover the solid bulk of Fane standing at the ready in the hall. He had lit two lamps; the steady golden light cast fearful shadows over the polished black marble. Fane's seemed especially monstrous. 'This is our butler, among other things,' Lulu introduced him.

The new lodger took in the spectacle of Fane, getting on for twice her diminutive height, with skin of a texture and hue best described as fungal, and an ageing black suit hanging about his cadaverous frame. 'Delightful,' said she, shortly. 'Do not trouble yourselves to show me to my room. Just point the way and I'll find it myself.'

Lulu glanced at the mouth of the formidable staircase, as wide across as two motorcars drawn up side-by-side, gleamingly black, and wreathed in a profound darkness. Above them lay a warren of passageways and disused chambers (most of them), alcoves and galleries, cold hearths lit with freezing emerald flames, windy attic garrets half-filled with the detritus of many generations of residence—staircases, dark and slippery and winding, why, they might have been expressly designed to send inattentive creatures tumbling to their deaths, they could hardly do a better job of it if they had— 'Truly, you had better let me show you,' Lulu decided.

Nothing was seen of the new lodger at breakfast the following morning. Hardly surprising, Lulu allowed; she had arrived very late, and might likely have suffered a poor repose thereafter, suddenly transplanted into a strange place, without anything familiar about her (she had hardly seemed to possess any luggage). Lulu busied herself with the interminable task of housekeeping, roping Stormdust in to assist as she scrubbed, dusted and polished anything their new lodger was likely to encounter.

She was sweeping out the grate in the dining-room, humming a working song to beguile away an otherwise stupefying sensation of boredom, when her father wandered by. She heard his footsteps crossing to the sideboard, where the dregs of breakfast lay under bright silver covers; 'What was that infernal racket last night?' he idly enquired, helping himself to comestibles that must be long gone cold.

'An arrival,' Lulu answered, a touch out of breath; the powdery black ash left by the cold green flames seemed to cling to everything, including Lulu. 'We've a new lodger for you to be civil to, Father, if you please.'

'They are not paying for civility, Lulu, they're paying for a room.'

'And I should prefer you not to frighten them straight out of it again.'

'Frighten? Nonsense. They will find me the most charming host in the world,' came Count Vexx's answer, to Lulu's profound scepticism; 'Provided they stay out of my library,' he added, which made rather more sense, all told.

'Father, if you aren't busy perhaps you could help Stormdust with—' He had gone, taking his plate away with him. '—dusting the paintings upstairs,' she finished with a sigh. No matter. He would only make a dreadful mess of it, like the time she had persuaded him to mop the tiled black floor in the—no. No, it was best not to think about it.

Lulu went down to the kitchens, to wash the smothering grime from her skin, and help Magwell with the pastry.

The new lodger was not seen at luncheon, either. Neither was Count Vexx, which was not unusual; he'd be deep in a treatise on rune lore by now, or the history of Andirac, or possibly a technical manual on the art of beekeeping; he wouldn't emerge until dinner, if then.

The lodger's absence, not to mention silence, began to disturb Lulu. Was there anything amiss? Perhaps her ill-temper of the night before was due to sickness, and she lay abed and suffering, in need of help. Perhaps she had taken the castle in dislike, somewhere between the ponderously weighty front door and the neat, but shabby and frigid chamber Lulu had conducted her to, and left again shortly after.

Perhaps she had died in the night, of cold or of fright or both, and her lifeless remains even now lay upstairs in the oaken box bed, her eyes staring sightlessly at the dark ceiling Lulu had but just swept free of dust-ridden cobwebs.

A round of baking with Magwell settled her restless imaginings, a bit; Magwell's reassuring bulk was ever steadying, and the fat venison pies looked so attractive with their decor of spiders, and leaves.

An hour of painting had rather the opposite effect, for though Lulu went up in the later hours of the day, to watch the light dying out of the sky from her turret-top vantage, and paint it, she found herself instead daubing nightmar-ish scenes onto the white paper before her, resplendent with corpses and bones. She set her paintbrushes down with a sigh. Eventide had come, which meant dinner, and she was wearing almost as much watercolour paint as the paper; she went away to wash.

Darkness settled over Castle Drax, bringing the pene-trating cold seeping up out of the marble floors and down out of the chimneys. Fane rang the dinner-gong, mightily: the terrific, booming *crash* of it rattled the walls.

Lulu hurried downstairs, her skin pink and tingling from a ferocious scrubbing, one of her mother's ravishing dinner-gowns glittering greenish in the firelight as she went. She could not have said what had prompted her to put it on; dressing for dinner was by no means the custom, what would be the point, but this one was silver and luscious and they had a new guest, if the woman hadn't died in the night—

'Oh!' said Lulu, and came to a sudden and ill-advised halt three steps from the bottom of the grand staircase.

The new lodger frowned down at the recumbent form of her new hostess, collapsed in a shimmering silver heap upon cold black marble. That was the trouble with cleaning the stairs, Lulu thought bitterly; perhaps less polish, next time. 'Was that intentional?' asked the lodger.

Lulu scowled up at her, too winded, for the moment, to move. 'Why would I fall down the stairs on purpose?'

'Oh.' Something galvanised the new lodger to civility; she extended a hand to Lulu, who employed it in hauling herself upright again.

'Thank you,' she said with as much dignity as she could muster. 'I'm Lulu Vexx, if you hadn't guessed it.'

A nod from behind a length of gauzy veil. 'Minerfa,' offered the new lodger in return. She stood for a moment in silence, then said, 'My room is very cold.'

'Yes,' said Lulu. 'If this is disagreeable to you then I advise you not to attempt lighting the fire.'

'Curious,' said Minerfa.

'Dinner?' suggested Lulu.

Minerfa had come to the end of what passed for her sociable instincts; she attended Lulu into the dining room in silence, the quality of which Lulu could not gauge. Thoughtful? Appalled? Bristling with offence? Or perhaps just frozen to a point near death; truly, the castle was doomed if the relentless cold were to do away with the lodgers.

'If there is anything you need,' Lulu began, wishful of breaking the terrible silence somehow, 'In order to be more comfortable, I hope you will let us know.'

'Except a warmer room,' answered Minerfa.

'Except that, yes,' Lulu admitted. 'There is no getting several centuries of murderous cold out of the stone anymore. It's been tried.'

'Ah? And what happened?'

Lulu remembered it well. It had been at her mother's insistence; she'd borne down every possible objection or obstacle, smilingly, until at last Count Vexx had given way. A fire, a proper one, had been set, and lit; it had burned thrillingly ruddy in the hearth of the great hall, and then all the way up the chimney.

From there, it had spread further still.

'We lost quite a few tapestries and paintings,' Lulu answered. 'And a cousin.'

'Oh.'

Count Vexx presided over an empty dining-table as the ladies stepped into the room. The table was, of course, excessive, an enormous, overlong conceit with the polished, mirror-black shine of a grand piano, its surface decked with a small forest of silver candlesticks and cutlery, black brocade napery, dark crystalline goblets, and a puzzling epergne carved from onyx with a hundred tortured faces engraved into its convoluted design. The Count sat at the head of it with a book laid open upon the tablecloth. He was absorbed.

'I was going to say, how good of you to suspend your studies in order to attend upon us at dinner!' Lulu said, taking the chair to her father's right. 'But I see that you haven't. Is it a frightfully good book?'

'Second Ung Dynasty porcelain,' answered Count Vexx, without looking up. 'Coffee pots, for the most part. They seem to have been obsessed by it.'

'How interesting,' said Lulu, politely but doubtfully.

'Not especially.' Count Vexx turned a page.

'Well, stop reading and say hello to Minerfa, then.'

'I will when I finish this chapter, I've got three more to go before—' He looked up. 'Minerfa?'

'Our new lodger.' Lulu beamed, hoping her father might find it possible to display some of his better manners. And that Minerfa would, too, supposing she possessed any.

'Lodger.' Count Vexx uttered the word with a kind of suppressed loathing.

'Your lordship. What an honour.' Minerfa's words emerged flatly from behind her veil, tinged, faintly, with scorn.

The silence that followed spoke volumes, albeit in a language Lulu had no chance of reading.

'Do you perchance happen to know anything about coffee pots?' Count Vexx enquired, with passable civility.

'I do, yes,' said Minerfa.

Silence.

Lulu made an urging-encouraging motion with her hand, and widened her eyes in her father's direction.

'The most superior of them tend to be silver,' Minerfa opined. 'Ung Porcelain is among the best of its sort, but it is inferior in craftsmanship to the exquisite wrought-silver coffee and chocolate pots made by Karonesian artisans in the third to the fifth century.'

Count Vexx pondered this. 'I should have thought they would be awfully heavy. Solid silver, you say?'

'Heavy, and likely to burn the unwary,' Minerfa agreed. 'But we speak of art and conspicuous display, not practicality. Leave *that* for the Ung Second Dynasty Porcelain.'

Dinner came in, conveyed and expertly served by Fane; Lulu awarded him several beaming smiles by way of thanks, considering that Minerfa and her father were absorbed to the point of inattentiveness. The debate raged all the way through the casserole of tender rabbit meat and spring vegetables, continued unimpeded by Magwell's venison pies, however buttery the pastry, and came to an end halfway through the cherry pavlova Lulu had made with her own hands, and layered thickly with cream.

'A *Dagny*?' Minerfa said, letting her silver spoon fall into the midst of her half-eaten pavlova with a sad *thunk*. 'You have an original Dagny here?'

'Dark Period,' Count Vexx confirmed. 'More than one. Here, I'll show you—'

Minerfa pushed back her veil and her chair both, and rose with alacrity; Lulu caught a glimpse of an angular face with wings of black hair and a complexion like old cheese, as purple as a bruise. Then she was gone, whisked away in the wake of Count Vexx, still talking stridently about murals and statuary as he went.

Lulu smiled to herself, and finished her pavlova, then Minerfa's, too. She'd had doubts about introducing lodgers: how would someone ordinary, someone *normal*, take to life at Castle Drax?

As it turned out, she needn't have worried—about Minerfa, at any rate. Clearly there was nothing ordinary about Minerfa at all.

7

About Time For a Change

Miss Lulu Vexx, daughter of Count Vexx, and present chatelaine of the mighty, weighty and windy Castle Drax, had done her hair. Not in the sense that she had thrust a pin or two into it, or a barrette, and left it at that; no, she had *done* her hair, really gone to town on it. She was the proud, if temporary, owner of a shiny, sleek blonde bob, crimped in elegant waves, and what was more, she had donned a good suit of clothes, too. There were hardly any rips or tears in her cream-coloured silk blouse, and the tweed of her jacket and skirt was free of stains or wrinkles.

Her heels were hell to walk in, especially up and down so many of the castle's dark stone stairs, but it was all in a good cause.

'Now, here we see several notable works by the well-known sculptor, Cavendish Grimspound,' said Lulu, indicating, with a graceful sweep of her arm, a set of five statues carved from the local black lava rock. They marched down the length of a distant hallway, a long and draughty room whose purpose in existing Lulu had never been able to determine. 'They depict the Five Attitudes of Death: here we have Death by Disease, beside it Death by Savagery...' Lulu's voice echoed pleasingly off the bare, black walls, giving her words a compelling resonance. Her audience absorbed every syllable, entranced (Lulu hoped) by the splendour of the artworks before them.

'How did Cavendish Grimspound come to construct such works *here*?' asked one among her visitors, a thin woman with a dark chignon and a far better grade of tweed than Lulu's.

'I suppose it does seem an unlikely spot,' Lulu agreed, smiling. 'But Castle Drax is among the most substantial residences in the country. Several great artists have exhibited their work here, and with pride.'

Lulu hadn't convinced; the thin lady cast a doubtful look around the hall, empty besides the statues, its ceiling so thick with decades' worth of cobwebs and dust as to entirely obscure whatever might lie beneath them.

'And on that note,' Lulu went on, 'our next destination shall be the Long Drawing-Room, which features a delightful fresco by Molly Stittlegarth.'

A collective intake of breath at that; even the doubtful woman in tweed seemed impressed. Molly Stittlegarth, highly eccentric and sought-after in her day, had enjoyed only a short career as a painter of frescos and murals. Consequently, there were few known works attributable to her—and Castle Drax had three of them.

The rest of the tour proceeded well. The Stittlegarths perked up Lulu's guests enormously, and the Dagny pieces furthered the generally positive effect. Lulu led them back down to the dining-room feeling pleased with herself, and optimistic: with enough visitors, not to mention the new lodger, perhaps Castle Drax would not have to be sold, after all. Perhaps.

Magwell, the quietly talented cook who presided over the castle's kitchens, had laid out a splendid spread for the guests. Fane, the butler, had set the long, gleamingly black table, too, and exquisitely at that; three candelabras bore long black candles, casting their emerald-green glow over acres of silverware and napery.

Minerfa, the new lodger, sat at the head of the table, in the seat ordinarily reserved for Count Vexx. She, short and slight, diminished to almost childlike proportions in the imposing chair, its tall, black back towering over her head. She was black-clad and veiled and her presence would not have occasioned any discomfort had it not been for the nature of her repast.

'Gracious me,' said the matronly lady who'd asked a *lot* of questions about the Dagny. 'Is that a calf's head?'

Minerfa did not deign to look up. She speared a staring eyeball on the prongs of her shining silver fork, and slipped it under her veil. An audible crunch sounded. 'I'm afraid you can't have any,' said Minerfa by way of answer. 'But Magwell has prepared plenty of inferior delicacies for your—delectation.'

This remark neatly disposed of the elegant, crustless sandwiches stacked upon silver platters; the delicate pastry-tarts arranged upon tiered stands; and the jugs of fragrant cordial waiting to be poured into clear crystal glasses.

Lulu sighed. 'I can assure you, the food is of an entirely different sort—' she began, but it was no use. Her guests, doubtless envisaging sandwiches dripping with uncooked brain matter and tarts stuffed with the raw remnants of some unfortunate creature's organs, were leaving en masse. Lulu heard muffled exclamations of horror and outrage mixed in with the horde of fleeing footsteps.

Minerfa took up a forkful of something that oozed. 'See,' she said. 'They do not like sandwiches, either.'

Lulu briefly considered taking up one of the heavy candelabra, and braining her new lodger with it. Being a civilised woman, she refrained. 'Perhaps you might prefer to take your meals in your own room?' she suggested instead. 'Or one of the parlours may very easily be prepared for you.'

Minerfa thought about this, over a heaped forkful of glistening calf's brains. 'No,' she decided. 'It would be terribly rude of me to shut myself away from the household like that. Wouldn't it?'

'I am sure nobody would much regard it,' Lulu replied, attempting an encouraging smile.

'No; I've made up my mind,' said Minerfa, and popped a sliver of bone into her mouth, biting down upon it with an audible crack.

Lulu abandoned the conversation, and went below, to consult with Fane. Her paying visitors—supposing there were any more, after today's debacle—would be just as comfortable taking their complementary luncheon in the Long Drawing-Room, surely.

'Miss Vexx, how well you look. What a treat.' The hearty voice, rather booming, belonged to Mrs. Bell, of Percy and Bell, Estate Agents. Mr. Percy had not been seen in some time—detained, no doubt, by some urgent matter—but Mrs. Bell persisted in her attempts to find a buyer for Castle Drax. She had brought a prospective one now, today; the pair of them swept past Fane, the towering and silent butler who'd opened the door, and beamed at their hostess. Matching smiles, both of them over-bright: disturbing.

Lulu adjusted the fall of her jacket. Mrs. Bell was early; Minerfa and her gristly repast had but just vacated the dining-room. The bloody smell of it lingered in the air.

'Charming to see you, Mrs. Bell,' murmured Lulu with dutiful mendacity. The woman was over-dressed and over-brisk, as usual, large and loud, her chestnut hair exuberantly coiffed. The buyer was an iron-grey sort of woman, from the artfully arranged waves of her hair to the steel in her eyes. She was short, and slender, but she had presence. Lulu felt an inexplicable wariness creep over her, despite the woman's smile.

'This is Madame Delavigne,' said Mrs. Bell. 'She has been most eager to see your—'

'Of course, the viewing is merely a formality,' interrupted Madame Delavigne, taking Lulu's hand, and shaking it: her grip was bone-crushing. 'My people are making the arrangements for the purchase and I daresay they shan't require more than a few days to complete them. I trust you shall be ready to leave within—shall we say, a week? Two?'

Lulu, too astonished to do otherwise than stare, said nothing. Her mouth hung open: she closed it, swallowed, and ventured: 'I'm sorry?'

'There is only one little thing I am anxious to verify,' Madame Delavigne swept on. 'I must have the castle and its contents, Miss Vexx. Of course, you are free to take any of your personal items with you—I could hardly object to so reasonable a request—but not a stick of furniture, nor any of the paintings or statuary, or—well, anything!' She laughed gaily, falsely. 'I am so looking forward to becoming the new chatelaine. You may rest assured, Miss Vexx: your ancestral home will be safe in my hands.'

Lulu looked at Mrs. Bell, wonderingly. The estate agent had the grace to appear a little uncomfortable; her smile had faded. 'It is a remarkably generous offer,' said Mrs. Bell. 'Madame is a great admirer of art in all its forms, and a noted collector—'

'When I heard you had a Dagny,' interjected Madame, 'and several Grimspounds, well! Nothing would do for me but to telephone Mrs. Bell immediately. Astonishing, Miss Vexx! Simply astonishing.'

'We also have a Stittlegarth,' Lulu said absently, her thoughts—and her stomach—churning. 'Three of them.'

'Finished?' said Madame Delavigne, urgently. 'Surely not. While several partial murals have been attributed to

Molly Stittlegarth—and those claims are, in my opinion, credible—there are scarcely five completed works in existence. To find three, in the same—'

'They are finished,' Lulu said. 'One of them recently.'

Madame stared. 'Come, do you think me ill-informed? Molly Stittlegarth vanished out of all knowledge years ago, leaving much of her work incomplete. It has been speculated that she grew tired of public acclaim, and emigrated—or that she is dead, which is equally likely in my opinion. But perhaps you have been hiding her at Castle Drax all this time!' A laugh, gay and hearty, concluded this speech.

'Perhaps we have,' said Lulu.

Madame Delavigne stopped laughing. 'I must see the rest of the castle,' said she. 'At once!'

Lulu could hardly refuse. She wanted to—badly—but Madame Delavigne was here by appointment, with Lulu's own estate agent at her elbow, and she had, presumably, the means to purchase even so large and splendid a castle as the Vexx family abode. She was the answer to all Lulu's prayers, on the face of it—and the woman who would break Fane's heart, and Magwell's, and Count Vexx's (if he had one).

Lulu's too. She ought, of course, to have taken the FOR SALE sign down. She had known for some time that nobody wanted to sell up, and move; she didn't, either. But she had not dared to turn her back on what had seemed the only solution to the enormous problem of maintaining a dwelling whose monstrous proportions and magnificent decor were far beyond the Vexx family's diminished means to manage. They had one new lodger, Minerfa, and several small groups of visitors had paid for a tour of the place; but these measures, excellent in themselves, were hardly enough to keep the castle going. Besides, they had an awkward way of cancelling each other out, as Lulu's rather trying morning had proved.

She followed Mrs. Bell and Madame Delavigne in something of a daze, hardly venturing any remark whatsoever as Madame admired and coveted every treasure in the house. One week, perhaps two. A fortnight, and they would put Castle Drax behind them forever. Where were they going to go?

'I suppose we will use the money to buy a nice, normal castle somewhere else,' Lulu said later, down in the kitchens with one of Magwell's loaves of dark rye bread before her, oven-fresh, and a dish of butter. She had got through half of it without much noticing, and was working on the rest.

'That is what most people would do, isn't it? Madame Delavigne's offer is extremely generous. It ought to be plenty.'

She supposed it was rampant ingratitude, to lament so happy a happenstance as an enormous purchase offer on a house that had seemed unsaleable, the week before. They would go from straitened circumstances to something like fabulous wealth, and in a single week. Many would kill for such a chance.

But Lulu's heart felt like a stone in her chest, heavy and dull.

'I daresay we shall,' answered Magwell, placidly enough, and hurled her ball of black rye dough at the table. It hit with the force of a hammer blow; Lulu jumped.

'Perhaps somewhere a little warmer,' Lulu ventured, spreading salted butter onto a new slice of bread. 'With a proper, blue sea nearby, or even just a grey one.' She bit, and chewed. 'We could even have fires in the hearths. You know, warm ones.'

Magwell kept hurling the dough, bang-bang-bang. She didn't answer. Lulu glanced at her broad, familiar face and found it set like stone, lips tight, all the lines in it deeply graven.

She set down the bread. The half-loaf she had consumed felt like a stone in her stomach, too. She was a whole quarry of sadness.

'No, you're right,' she said. 'Of course you're right. We can't leave. It's unthinkable.'

'I said no such thing,' replied Magwell, grimly.

'And why not? It is what you're thinking, isn't it?'

'Because,' said Magwell, without looking up, 'It is you and the Master as has to find a new place. Fane and Stormdust and me, well, it's back where we came from, for us.'

Lulu's heart sank even further, somehow. 'Fane doesn't want to go back there,' she answered. 'I know he doesn't. Do you?'

Magwell glanced at her, something like scorn in her gaze. 'No,' she said. 'But where else are we like to be welcome?'

'You will always be welcome with Father and me, wherever we may be living. I promise.'

'In your modern house, warm from wall to wall, and with *neighbours* all about?' Definitely scorn; it dripped from every word. Magwell went back to throwing her dough; the table shuddered.

Lulu wilted over the table, pressing her cheek to the cold surface. Magwell was right. They couldn't leave Castle Drax; it was the only place they belonged. But what was she going to do? The place was falling down around them.

'Magwell,' said Lulu, closing her eyes. 'I don't know what to do.'

Bang-bang-bang went the dough. 'Well,' said Magwell presently, 'First we'll need to get rid of Madame Delavigne.'

'I will telephone her,' Lulu offered, 'and tell her we are withdrawing the castle from sale.'

'If you think that will do the trick,' replied Magwell.

'It won't. She would sell her soul to get her hands on those Stittlegarths, and so she told me.' The woman wouldn't easily give up. It wasn't as though she could purchase some other Stittlegarth frescos from someplace else; there weren't any. Not like these.

'Besides,' Lulu added, 'If we take down the FOR SALE sign then we also have to dispense with Mrs. Bell. She's expecting her commission from the sale. It'll be vast.'

'It will have to be the cellar, then,' said Magwell, cheering up with the words: her smile was coming back. 'It'll be so nice to have another new face or two about the place. Stormdust was such a lovely addition.'

Lulu felt tempted to give in, and agree; it was by far the simplest solution. But they had dispatched one or two unwitting souls into the cellar already, of late. If more were to disappear from Castle Drax without explanation or warning, they could have far greater problems on their hands than a lack of funds.

'We can't use father's summoning circle as the solution to every problem,' she objected. 'It's for emergencies only.'

'What do you call an emergency, if it isn't this?'

Inarguable. Lulu sat up, and began again upon the bread. Chewing helped her think, sometimes.

Molly Stittlegarth. Her mind snagged on the word, and kept returning to it. Something about the artist's renowned and mysterious name felt like an inkling of promise...

'Oh!' blurted Lulu, thickly, her mouth stopped with bread and butter. She swallowed hastily. 'Magwell! I think I have it.'

'Clever girl,' said Magwell, as she had when Lulu was a child, and had accomplished some complicated sum, or spelled a difficult word correctly. 'I knew you'd get there.'

Lulu barely heard; she was already on her way out of the kitchen, thundering back up the stairs.

Madame Delavigne arrived promptly for her appointment. Very promptly; the denizens of Castle Drax were treated to another rendition of the castle's boomingly lugubrious doorbell at a most unseasonable hour.

This time, Lulu didn't mind it at all. She had lain awake, waiting: confident, with smiling certainty, that Madame would act as she wished, yet with a secret kernel of doubt and disquiet that rendered it useless to close her eyes.

The hour had ticked past three o'clock, Lulu had taken to a restless and chilly pacing up and down the faded carpet of her room, and the world lay night-drowned and silent when at last the summons came.

The bell. Its peals of discordant chorales crashed and boomed over the castle; by the time the melody, if such it might be called, came to an end, Lulu had already hurled off the cosy dressing-gown she wore over her dress and clattered down and down the stairs.

She arrived to find Fane already admitting their visitor—Madame Delavigne, in the flesh.

Lulu arrested her hurtling progress just outside the hall, and slipped her chic heeled evening slippers back onto her feet. She was sheathed in a ripple of liquid black satin, her hair lacquered and shining and her throat clasped with her mother's garnets. She looked the part, and must act it, too: her smile as she entered the hall was all charm.

'Hush, Madame,' crooned Lulu, interrupting the lady's effusions. 'The process is very delicate. We must act with all possible care and decorum.'

'Of course,' answered Madame in a half-whisper, and bowed very low to Lulu. 'Miss Vexx, may I say how very honoured I was to receive your invitation. I couldn't be prouder.'

She had obeyed Lulu's instructions, thus far: she wore a glamorous golden evening gown with a fur wrap, and shoes as stylish as Lulu's. She must be perishing with cold, but her manner spoke of suppressed excitement, overlaid with reverence.

Lulu inclined her head, all graciousness. 'We do not often issue such invitations, nowadays,' she replied. 'Few are worthy of the honour. I'm sure you understand.'

'Perfectly,' Madame Delavigne breathed, her eyes shining in the leaping green light from the hearth. 'You will find me quite prepared, Miss Vexx.'

'Yes? As I indicated in my letter of invitation, there is a price. No such opportunity can be bestowed without cost.'

'I am ready to pay any price.' She meant every word: Lulu could read that on her, clearly enough.

And here, for a moment, the honourable Miss Vexx's resolve wavered a little. She could extract more than one price from the eager woman before her: money, first, possibly even enough to save Castle Drax. It would be paid, and without question.

Something in her balked at the notion. Perhaps it was the shining anticipation in Madame Delavigne's eyes; for all her repulsive qualities, she was a true and sincere appreciator of the finer things in life. Nay, an obsessed devotee, or this would never have worked.

'The artist,' said Lulu, 'is of a difficult temperament, as you may imagine'—Madame nodded emphatically, everyone knew artists were difficult after all—'and she may not warm to your presence immediately. You will have to prove your worthiness to her.'

'I am ready to do so.'

'And I must further emphasise that the site of your studies will be of an unusual nature. It is a place few will ever reach, and fewer still return from it.'

'I understand,' said Madame Delavigne, straightening her shoulders, and lifting her chin. 'You will find no cause to question my dedication, Miss Vexx.'

Lulu nodded. 'The papers, then, please.'

Madame reached into her sequined evening bag, and withdrew the document Lulu had caused Stormdust to deliver, earlier in the day. The contract was simple enough; Lulu was no lawyer, to craft a complex one; but it stated

Madame's intentions clearly enough, and absolved Castle Drax and the Vexx family of any possible responsibility for the undersigned's fate once the aforementioned ritual had been completed, etc, etc. Lulu browsed it quickly, discovered a suitable signature in the proper place, and handed it off to Fane.

'Very well, Madame,' she smiled. 'Come with me.'

The solemnity of the occasion required a slow procession down into the cellar, conducted in heavy, portentous silence. Madame Delavigne asked no questions, expressed no doubts: she was all resolve and delight, and Lulu enjoyed a few moments' hope that she might even be contented with the outcome of the night's undertaking. It was not wholly impossible, surely.

How the artist might feel about it, well. That was a problem for another time.

Lulu had acquired the heavy, half-rusted key to the one cellar door that was, almost always, kept locked. She paused before the great, black-oaken door at the foot of the draughty cellar steps, and negotiated the lock with as much dignity as she could manage. It was ancient and ill-kempt, like the rest of the castle, and it stuck; Lulu experienced a moment's heart-jolting terror that it might not open, that her scheme might be foiled here and now through time and rust alone.

Then the lock clanked, most satisfyingly, and the bolt swung back. The door creaked slowly open, its ancient iron hinges groaning in protest.

'Are you ready?' Lulu said, with solemn grandeur, to her guest.

'I am,' answered Madame Delavigne. 'Oh, Miss Vexx, I have never imagined I might be offered such a privilege—'

'Then, proceed,' Lulu interjected, for she was perishing with cold even if Madame wasn't, and she wanted to go to bed. 'She is waiting for you.'

Madame Delavigne ventured into the darkened room beyond the portal. No lights burned there, save for the smouldering red glow of the summoning-circle itself. It was enough. Madame hesitated only for a moment before stepping into the centre of the five-pointed star daubed, bloodily, over the floor.

'Do give my regards to Miss Stittlegarth,' said Lulu, waving.

The circle pulsed, flared with an unholy ruddy glow—and Madame Delavigne disappeared, probably forever.

Lulu breathed out a long sigh.

She had cause to feel confident that the great Molly Stittlegarth resided somewhere on the other side of her father's summoning-circle—had received tolerable proof of it, recently. In that, she had not deceived Madame Delavigne. Whether the artist would be remotely interested in receiving the dogged devotion of an obsessed disciple of art—as Lulu had perceived Madame Delavigne to be, underneath her brashness of manner—well, that was Madame's problem. It was all in the contract, after all.

Lulu turned back to the door, and the steps, and the bed that lay awaiting her beyond them both. A fine night's work; the problem of dispensing with Mrs. Bell's services remained before her, but at least their importunate buyer was taken care of, to everybody's satisfaction. Delightful. Lulu took a step.

'Darling!' someone said behind her. 'My beautiful Luna, how much you have *grown*.'

Lulu froze with one foot on the road to freedom. She had forgotten, for a while, that the circle in the cellar was not for dispatching; it was for *summoning*. She had fed it Madame Delavigne, and someone had duly been exchanged for her.

Someone Lulu knew, distantly at least.

She turned around. 'Mama?'

The lady in the circle was a vision still, unchanged, apparently, since her long-ago vanishment. Like Lulu in every way, save that she was brighter somehow, more golden, more vivacious: to Lulu's candle-flame, she was an inferno.

She wore a ravishing crimson gown that clung to her curves, with her golden hair dressed high, and decked with jewels. Her clear blue eyes sparkled more brightly than her jewellery: she might never in her life have been so overjoyed as she was in this moment, reunited with her darling girl, at last.

She spread wide her graceful arms, bracelets humming upon her slim wrists; Lulu, frozen, was engulfed in scent and softness. 'My darling!' said Lady Vexx again. 'How much you must have missed me!'

Lulu swallowed a sigh, and permitted her arms to form some semblance of an embrace around her long-absent parent. How exactly was she going to explain *this* to her father?

Perhaps she would lead with the successful dispatch of Madame Delavigne, first. It couldn't hurt to try, anyway.

'Welcome back, Mama,' said Lulu, endeavouring to mean it. 'Why don't I take you up to your room?'

8

Facing the Music

Miss Lulu Vexx, drooping like a fading rose, sat majestically ensconced in a tall, black chair fit for Counts and Kings—specifically, Count Vexx. It possessed all the plush comfort of a slab of granite, and Lulu wondered that her father could stand it.

In fact, he practically lived in it: poised, grim and glowering, before cold, leaping flames of a glowing emerald fire, surrounded on several sides by walls bristling with books. The library was the Count's refuge—or it had been, until recently.

Not that it could fairly be termed the library, anymore. The onyx-carved shelves stood stripped of their erstwhile contents, glinting icily black, and brooding. Three volumes remained: a book of psalms, a collection of ancient recipes half burned away, and a pamphlet of somebody's memoirs chiefly recounting a great many fruitless endeavours to win a cooking competition.

Much of the rest had retreated with his lordship into the west wing, and lay behind barricaded doors. The remainder—novels, biographies, and anything containing fashion plates—had gone with Lady Vexx into the east wing.

The battle had raged for days, in true Vexx fashion. The Count, his grave displeasure expressed in a wooden countenance and tightly-compressed lips, had maintained a frigid silence as he piled books into the arms of the ever-obliging Fane. Her ladyship's had manifested in a vivacious flow of airy chatter, layered with barbs delivered ruthlessly, and with a smile.

Castle Drax was a castle divided, an invisible line drawn through its centre, and impassable, and least by the combatants. Lulu, dispossessed, had withdrawn to the kitchens, preferring the company of Magwell; except today, when some sorrowing impulse had brought her into the sadly divested library, and marooned her there.

Her mother had been gone for many years; so many, the world at large generally presumed her dead. Lulu had, too. Her return ought to have been a triumph, thought Lulu bitterly, though the outcome could not surprise her: theirs had been no happy home, when she was a small child.

The door creaked, and groaned. 'Your mother wants you,' said Minerfa, their lodger, in her peremptory way.

'Oh no,' said Lulu involuntarily. 'What about?'

'Party business.' Minerfa, the colour of a bruise and with a glare to put a basilisk to shame, came farther into the library-as-was and drifted near to the hearth. She liked the emerald flames, and they liked her: they leapt higher, and a halo of frost crept farther over the blackstone floor. 'She has dresses,' Minerfa added, holding her thin-fingered hands towards the fire.

'And why are you the bearer of these tidings? I am sorry, Minerfa, you ought not to be employed as messenger.' She was a paying guest, not staff, but it was typical of Mama to misunderstand the difference.

Minerfa grinned; a pair of long fangs peeped. 'I find her exhilarating. So vicious! So smiling! Quite beautiful, altogether.'

Lulu paused, awaiting the arrival of some impulse to defend her parent: none came. 'I'd better go, then,' she said with a heavy sigh, and hauled herself out of her father's chair. 'I shall have no peace until the dress is selected, shall I.' None after that, either, for party business never stopped: not until the party was partied through, and finished, and that halcyon moment lay days away.

Minerfa turned a gleaming eye on Lulu. 'I should bash her a bit, if I were you. Do her good.'

Lulu mustered her sunshine. 'I am sure that won't be necessary. We are choosing a gown for a dazzling event!

What could be a more delightful pastime for a mother and daughter, after all.'

'Butchery,' suggested Minerfa. 'Or tarot-reading. I have a deck with extra Death cards in.'

'Have you? How ingenious.' Lulu made a note to borrow the deck, another time: perhaps when she visited her father.

For now, she stepped smartly out of the library, sternly ordering her slippered feet not to drag on her way upstairs. She lifted her chin, and straightened her slender shoulders: she was a Vexx, and no Vexx had ever gone cringing into battle.

'There you are, darling,' said her ladyship, beaming. 'How slow you are! I began to think you were never coming.' She stood in a riot of colour, for she'd ordered fresh curtains hung about the windows and her bed, in exciting shades of raspberry. An explosion of colours lay strewn in gowns of silk and lace and velvet, tinted every hue from blood-crimson to jaunty yellow. Beads glittered, sequins sparkled, satin shimmered; Lulu felt a headache begin to throb behind her eyes.

'Sorry, Mama,' she said, shutting and barring the door behind her against the enemy. 'I came as soon as I got your—'

'I think this one,' said Lady Vexx, holding against her own lithe figure a froth of cerulean gauze. She scarcely looked older than Lulu, and had far superior hair: lush, bronze-tinted waves tumbling to her waist, crowned with jewelled combs. Her eyes were like amethysts, some used to say, and it was, Lulu realised, absolutely true.

'It is pretty, but not to my usual—' Lulu began.

'It is perfect,' said Lady Vexx, twirling the dress about so the layers frothed. 'Youthful, playful, charmingly fun! You'll look a perfect dream in it.'

'I don't like it,' said Lulu firmly. 'It would be like wearing a powder-puff. It would be like *being* a powder-puff.'

'My darling Luna, how difficult you've become. You were such a sweet child! This is all your father's doing.'

'I don't think—'

'Very well then, not the blue.' Her ladyship tossed it carelessly on the bed, and snatched up a violet gown with enough beads embroidered into it to sink a small boat. She shook it: it glittered painfully.

Lulu scanned the array of discarded finery. 'I like this one,' she said, selecting a column of liquid satin coloured a chic and sumptuous silver.

'Ah! What a pity. I shall be wearing that one myself. You get your taste from me, darling, along with your looks of course. But the violet, now? I really think it would suit you charmingly.'

Lulu, defeated, accepted the violet dress, and permitted herself to be ushered into a trying-on. It might not fit, there was always a possibility: it would snag on the width of her hips, or gape about the bust.

'There, it's perfect on you. I knew it would be.' Lady Vexx, triumphant, turned her daughter this way and that, like a mannequin on the shop floor of some costly boutique.

The dress swished and clattered with every motion. Dreadful. No, it would not do.

'It's so lovely to see you, of course, Mama,' said Lulu brightly. 'What brought you back, after all this time? We quite thought you were never coming home.'

'Is that what your father thought?' Lady Vexx's lovely face set into hard lines; her glorious eyes flashed.

'If you want to know what father thought, you must ask him,' said Lulu, hoping she would not. The ensuing argument might shatter the walls.

'Well, I shall.' Lady Vexx's anger melted into a little smile: the prospect of discomfiting her husband charmed her. 'Word reached me, darling, that the two of you had taken an awfully silly notion into your heads. You needed me, clearly.'

'What n—oh, you mean selling the castle. It is quite all right, we have since—'

'Sell Castle Drax! Insupportable. I leave you alone for five minutes, and look what happens.'

'Well, this party,' ventured Lulu. 'It can hardly be inexpensive, can it?'

'Sometimes, darling, you must spend a little money if you want to get anything done.'

A little money. What with the sumptuous catering, the extra staff taken on for the event, the cases of champagne, and the finery—not to mention the appalling quantity of beeswax candles brought in for the evening, Lady Vexx's complexion taking exception to stronger light—the costs of Lady Vexx's little soiree could bankrupt a small town.

Lulu was no longer puzzled by the state of the Vexx family's finances. Mama had been the chatelaine for years before she'd strolled into the Count's summoning-circle.

'And what is it we are getting done, exactly?' Lulu pressed. 'We cannot afford this party, Mother.'

'Precisely,' beamed her ladyship, smoothing folds of beaded silk over Lulu's waist. 'If your father cannot afford even a cosy little evening party, clearly matters have become desperate in my absence. We must consider our assets, Luna, and utilise them to their fullest effect.'

'And our assets chiefly consist of a shadowy old castle lit with a thousand black beeswax candles?'

'Silly girl.' Lady Vexx cupped her daughter's face in her slim, cool hands, and surveyed her critically. 'You haven't my nose or my complexion, sweetheart, and I wish you had not cut all your lovely long hair. This craze for bobbed hair is perfectly ludicrous. But you are really quite pretty, and with the right accoutrements—perhaps rouge, a very little, you are just a touch on the pale side, darling—'

Lulu stopped breathing. She felt as though a bolt of lightning had hurtled out of the skies and struck her a stunning blow. 'Mother. You cannot mean—I am not an asset!'

'Nonsense. With your good looks, cheerful demeanour, and superb pedigree, we shall be able to look very high indeed.'

'Look very high for what? A buyer for me?'

'A buyer! Honestly, Luna, I don't know where you got this taste for dramatics. It certainly did not come from me. No, darling, a husband. This will be the event of the season—everyone will want to see me, now that I'm back, and after so long away! I am excessively in demand, and there shall be several millionaires in attendance. Marry one of them, darling, and you shall be set for life, and then your husband may save Castle Drax. It's quite perfect.'

Lulu remembered to take a breath. Her bosom swelled; well. She had never felt rage before; not like this.

It was of no use to shout at Lady Vexx, however: her father had proved that, beyond all possible doubt.

It was of no use to reason with her, either, for the scheme was indeed an excellent one—if only Lulu did not mind being auctioned off, like a thoroughbred race-horse, or a priceless painting.

She did, though.

'Well then, Mama,' said Lulu, when she regained control of her voice. 'If I am to dazzle these gentlemen suitably, I ought to have the gown I prefer, oughtn't I? I shall feel awfully odd in this one—quite awkward.'

Her ladyship visibly winced. The word "awkward", used in conjunction with her magnificent soiree and her daughter, could only turn her pale with horror. 'You look delightful, Luna, there can be no question—'

'I shall wear the silver, or I shan't be attending.'

Avarice warred with vanity: Lady Vexx wavered.

Avarice won. 'Very well, darling. Silver was never quite my colour anyway; I look a fright in it.'

Lulu collected her gown. Victory felt cold and slippery in her hands. 'Silly Mama,' she said, smiling. 'As though you could look a fright in anything.'

Her mother patted her daughter's cheek, mollified. 'Now that's settled, I shall need you out in the gardens, darling. They simply must be in good order before the party. We have a duke coming, you know.'

Lulu turned cold again with horror. The "gardens", as they had once been termed, were in a state of extreme disorder: they were a thicket, in short, a snarled mess of ivy and brambles and thousands of weeds. 'I don't think—even with your help, we cannot possibly—'

'I have an urgent appointment in town, sweetheart, but I am sure you and Fane will make excellent progress. And there's that new fellow, isn't there? Stormdust? Three of you! You'll have it done in no time.'

Nothing would convince her of the absurdity of the task, Lulu knew: she didn't try. She swept out of her mother's rooms with her shimmering gown in her hands, forgetting to smile.

Lady Vexx's voice came floating after her. 'We really must do something about your manners, darling. You've become quite the savage.'

Lulu, incensed, ventured no response. It was only later, after a calming bout of bread-making with Magwell, that she realised: Lady Vexx had heard of their plans for the castle, even from the far side of Father's summoning-circle. How?

Her ladyship, realising Stormdust was wanted to drive the car for her, took him away early in the afternoon. Lulu and Fane took one long, doubtful look at the tangled forest lurking at the rear of the castle, to be cleared, somehow, with only two pairs of hands, and mutually declared themselves on an afternoon-spanning tea break.

Lulu took hers in the empty shell of the library, grateful for the peace and quiet, even if it was rather forlorn.

She'd got halfway down a cup of something green and fragrant when a dull *thud-thud* sounded at the door: Fane's best attempt at a polite knock.

'Yes?' she sang out.

Hinges creaked: Fane's long, pallid face appeared. 'Count Vexx would like to see you, Miss Lulu.'

'Then he may come down to the library. I am quite comfortable here, and so shall he be.'

Fane withdrew. Five minutes later, he was back. 'Begging your pardon, Miss Lulu, but Count Vexx says—'

'Oh, very well,' Lulu sighed, and chugged down the rest of her tea in two swallows. Parents were really a lot of work, what with one thing or another. She might have done better to tackle the garden, after all.

Lulu soldiered off to the west wing. Whether by accident or design, a single door granted access to the great, draughty space, with its twenty-three largely abandoned chambers. Lulu tapped upon this unpromising portal: it was gargantuan, hammered out of black oak and iron, its top peaking in a gothic arch that might, in any other door, have achieved elegance.

'Father,' Lulu called when no one answered. 'Are you still breathing? Mother has left the castle, and I cannot help thinking she may have left a trail of destruction behind her.'

Bolts scraped; a shattering clanking sound heralded the removal of a heavy barricade. A key turned in the lock, the latch rattled, and finally the door opened: Count Vexx glowered.

'Of course she has, but I remain intact—chiefly thanks to my fortress. Come in.'

'Well, I shall, but I do want to come out again later.' Lulu waited while her father replaced all his locks, bolts and barricades, then followed him into what was, apparently, the new library. It had the books, at least—many of them—and a familiar emerald-hued blaze flickered in the dark stone hearth. But it had the penetrating chill and musty aroma of a long-abandoned room, with such quantities of ancient dust that Lulu began at once to sneeze.

Count Vexx waved a hand, as though that might clear the air. 'Lulu. There's nothing for it. We shall have to sell Castle Drax after all, and your mother with it.'

Lulu stared. No, he did seem to be in his right mind: he looked normal, anyway, his silver hair in its usual sleek waves, his suit brushed and spotless, his green eyes gleaming, sharply, with a glowering humour.

'But we decided—'

'Yes, yes, I know. Nobody wants to leave the old place, and I shall have to make it up to Fane and Magwell somehow. But better that than see it remain in the hands of that woman!'

'That woman you voluntarily married, not all that long ago.'

'Positively eons ago.'

'Why did you marry her, come to think of it?'

Count Vexx's handsome mouth quirked in an expression Lulu couldn't quite read: it might have been mirth, liberally laced with disgust. 'She was the most ravishing creature I had ever beheld.'

'I suppose, she still is.' She was devastatingly beautiful, he was broodingly handsome—and titled. And, at that time, wealthy, or at least he had the trappings of it. A match made in Hell.

'We can't sell Castle Drax, Father. We agreed! And we promised! Fane will be devastated, and Magwell, and we can't do that to them. Or to ourselves.'

'She'll ruin us, Lulu. She already has.'

'Then you'll have to persuade her to leave.'

His lip curled: definitely disdain, there. 'I already have, once.'

'I'm not talking about sending her down to the cellar. I mean, persuade her. She doesn't really want this house, anyway. Mother wants somewhere newer, cleaner, shinier, grander.'

'If I had the money, I would gladly purchase a palace for her, and lock her in it. Sadly, I do not. She spent it all.'

'Bit of an irony, that,' Lulu agreed. 'Still, I may have an idea.'

'Oh?' Count Vexx brightened. 'My brilliant Luna, of course you do.'

'Well, hold on a minute. I have a question, first. How married are you and Mother, at present?'

'Marriage is not a state that occurs in degrees. One is either very, entirely, completely welded together for all eternity, or not even a little bit.'

'I know,' Lulu nodded, 'but if your wife is missing for many years, and presumed dead? Are you not deemed a widower, after a certain number of years?'

The Vexx countenance brightened further. 'I could certainly argue that I am. It might even hold up in court.'

'Perfect,' said Lulu, beaming. 'In that case, we shall have a delightful party.'

'The party! No! I won't have it.'

'But you must, and shall,' said Lulu firmly. 'Leave it with me, Father. One more excessively elaborate social event, and all will be well.'

He gave a sigh, but it wasn't his irate, obstinate, get-thee-gone exhalation. It was his mournful, slightly irritated, long-suffering sigh. 'Fine,' he said curtly. 'But I shall limit my appearance to half an hour.'

'Please do. And I have a specific task for you to do, while you're at it.'

Lady Vexx returned with her hair cut and styled, a necklace of polished sapphires around the slender, white column of her throat, and Stormdust in her train, carrying some eight or ten bags and boxes. Her ladyship's purchases, Lulu gathered.

'Darling! I've had a wonderful time.' She stopped in the centre of the great hall—arresting Lulu's progress across it, on her way down to the kitchens—and divested herself of her pretty ivory gloves, tugging daintily at one finger after another. 'I cannot think why I've stayed away so long. Motorcars, darling! Simply fabulous. And the fashions, I declare, I die for them.'

Lulu eyed her mother's formerly long and sweeping hair, now considerably shortened, and crimped into sleek, chic waves. 'So I see.'

'Take them up to my room, sweetheart. I shall want them presently.' This puzzled Lulu, until she realised it had been directed at Stormdust; he lumbered off up the stairs, hauling my lady's many acquisitions along with him.

'I adore him,' beamed Lady Vexx, waving him off with a flutter of her slender fingers. 'Sings like a dream.'

'Have you a prior acquaintance?' Lulu asked, bemused by these signs of favour.

'Don't be silly, darling. Of course we have. Now, about your gown. That old silver thing just wouldn't do for me at all, what was I thinking? So you may have it with my goodwill. I have got something a little better.'

At appalling cost, no doubt. 'Mother,' said Lulu quickly, arresting Lady Vexx's sashaying progress up the stairs. 'Were you—happy, all these years? You know. Over *there*.'

'Don't be ridiculous, Luna,' her ladyship snapped, without pausing her ascent.

'You were never happy here, though, were you?'

Lady Vexx stopped. 'My darling girl,' she said without turning around. 'Clearly you know nothing about married life.'

That was a no, Lulu thought, satisfied.

'You and Father are not married anymore,' Lulu ventured. 'Not really. He's been a widower a long time.'

'And I, a widow.'

Which made Lulu an orphan, in a manner of speaking; her smile came out a little twisted. 'Maybe it's time for you both to be happy, Mother.'

Lady Vexx turned her exquisite head, displaying her perfect profile. She paused there, thinking; 'Perhaps it is,' she said, and went on up to her boudoir.

Excellent. Lulu permitted herself a little skip of glee as she went on her way to the kitchens: everything was coming together nicely.

The day of the grand soiree arrived, and an army descended upon Castle Drax. A chef and his team of staff, to turn out canapes, aperitifs, confectionery, and patisserie; a sommelier, to arrange the champagne, the wine, and the brandy; a fleet of footmen, to serve and shepherd the guests; a string quartet and a jazz band, to entertain them; and an uncountable quantity of maids, hordes of them, to clean up after everybody.

Also a unit of gardeners, to Lulu's private satisfaction: they were set to clearing the thickets that surrounded Castle Drax, a job Lulu was profoundly grateful not to have to do herself.

She could worry later about how to pay them; Lady Vexx never would.

The lady herself directed her troops with the ruthless precision of a military general. By the waning of the sun, as eventide drew in, the castle stood transformed. If it hadn't quite metamorphosed into a glittering palace of dreams—such a transformation lay far outside even Lady Vexx's powers—it had become a sleek creature of dark and beguiling elegance, the perfect locale for a stylish soiree.

Never had Lulu dreamed that looming Castle Drax, empty, echoing and hollow for as long as she could remember, could bustle and teem with so much life. The halls rang with the sounds of busy industry: footsteps every which way, doors clattering, voices chattering, and the musicians tuning their instruments. She bumped into somebody everywhere she went: a footman dashing off downstairs, his hands full of silver in urgent need of buffing; maids swiping cloths and dusters over every dust-ridden surface; a violinist perched in a window-seat, playing some mournful dirge as he awaited his cue to begin. Lady Vexx might be an enchantress; with a wave of her wand, she'd filled the castle with magic.

Lulu found that she didn't altogether care for it.

She retreated to her own room for a breath or two of quiet, but found even there her sanctuary invaded: a dresser waited to tend to her, a stern, grey woman with a cool stare and an arsenal of accoutrements at her disposal.

'There you are, Miss Vexx,' said this lady. 'You are quite late. We shall scarcely have time to complete our preparations before your debut.'

'I am not making a debut,' Lulu objected, futilely. 'I am far too old to be launched into society, and I don't know what I would do with a husband if I had one.'

'It isn't so much what one does with a husband,' came the answer, 'but rather what a husband might be supposed to do for you. And one might accomplish rather a lot with a duke at one's disposal, no?'

Lulu did not want a duke at her disposal, nor did she suppose any such person would appreciate being milked of their resources for the improvement of Castle Drax. Well aware, though, that her views would be widely considered eccentric, she held her peace, and permitted herself to be sheathed in shimmering silver, her hair expertly arranged and ornamented with silver combs. Her dresser—Madame Avon—performed wonders with cosmetics, and by the time Lulu stood ready to descend, she might almost imagine herself capable of enchanting several dukes. She was a smoke-eyed, red-lipped siren, pale as the moon, and glittering.

She would fade to insignificance by her mother's side, which was as it should be. 'You are quite the magician, Madame,' Lulu praised, gently touching the smooth waves of her fair hair. 'I am sure I shall never look so magnificent again.'

'If all goes well, you won't have to,' said Madame Avon. 'Your manners are as much a part of your outfit as your shoes or your eye-shadow, mind. Use them well.'

'Oh, I certainly shall,' Lulu smiled. Her reflection seemed someone else entirely, lips red as blood, eyes agleam with purpose. Here was the face of a woman who could move mountains, if she wished to. Lulu only needed to move one.

'Ladies—and—Gentlemen!' The speaker was Count Vexx, the words uttered in a thundering, rolling boom pitched to carry over the hubbub of a hundred guests all chattering at once. They were spread across two of the finer drawing-rooms, and spilling into a third; the air was already thick with candle-smoke and perfume. Gold light from a hundred candles glinted softly off jewels enough to buy Castle Drax several times over.

'My wife and I are delighted to welcome you to our humble abode,' continued the Count. An airy gesture took in dark silk wallpaper, fine ebony furnishings, silver candlesticks, and a host of like sumptuary; in the soft can-dle-light, their state of general decrepitude went unno-ticed. A ripple of laughter rewarded this little jest, and the Count's handsome smile flashed.

They looked wonderful together, even Lulu thought so. Her father, impeccably dark-suited and brilliantined, devilishly good-looking; her mother, beautiful as an angel, a celestial creature robed in starlight. The stuff of dreams.

'We are also delighted to announce Lady Vexx's return!' boomed the Count. 'Here she is! I know many of you thought her dead and gone these many years. I, I admit, never lost hope.' A heartfelt sigh from several guests; someone threw a rose at the Countess's feet.

'And since those hopes have been sadly dashed,' Count Vexx went on, 'I am overjoyed to announce our permanent separation, her imminent departure, and our forthcoming divorce. Will that be all, dear?' This last to Lulu, who nodded. 'Tremendous. I'll be off, then.' He left without another word, already stripping himself of his velvet dinner jacket.

A bubble of befuddled chatter rose to a muted roar. In the midst of the turmoil, Lady Vexx stood tall, poised, and martyred, a tear glistening like dew upon her perfect cheek.

'Luna,' she hissed out of the corner of her mouth. 'I really think you might have warned me.'

'Sorry,' said Lulu mendaciously, her quick gaze scanning the crowd for the duke. There: already coming their way, and what a splendid specimen he was. He had height and breadth of shoulder; handsome features, and a noble mien; and youth enough to fall shatteringly in love with the perfect princess of melancholy poised in a halo of light at Lulu's elbow.

'Your Grace,' Lulu smiled, pointlessly: he was not looking at her. 'Permit me to introduce Elandria, Lady Vexx?'

'Elandria,' breathed the duke, as though the name itself had the power to enchant. He took up her hand, kissed it, gazed in adoration; the soon-to-be-former Lady Vexx gazed soulfully back at him.

Lulu left them to it. Her work was done, and perfectly; the rest would take care of itself. She swiped a macaron and a bonbon on her way through the throng, and ate them on her way back to bed.

9

Of Brains and Brawn

In the end, it was the smell that broke Miss Lulu.

The noise she could bear, for a little while longer; the bashing, the crashing, the deep, booming thunder. The black halls of Castle Drax reverberated with the sounds of busy—and heavy—industry, the very walls shaken with it. What their new lodger could possibly be doing down there in the dark and dank cellars, Lulu declined to imagine—especially once that *smell* came seeping up through the floors. Iron, sharp and metallic; the pungency of raw and *very* fresh meat.

And then, an odour of advanced decay. Sickly and rancid, a stench that climbed inside Lulu's head, and stayed.

She'd sat down in the dining-room with a plate of fresh bread, made with Magwell's considerable skill. Melting over its warm and white crumb was an oozing layer of salted butter; adjacent sat a hot and milky cup of tea, steaming. Luncheon. Lulu had brought a thick ledger with her, and an inkpot. A gold fountain pen took its turns with a butter knife; Lulu wielded both to excellent effect, absorbing sustenance even as she went over the quarterly accounts. A painful business, especially after her mother's grand event. They would be months recovering from it.

Her repast was but half gone when the stench overtook her. Something had *died*, and a while ago; the smell of freshly-butchered meat, penetrating for some time now, seemed a bouquet of roses in comparison.

The smell, somehow, grew worse. Lulu gagged, and set down her bread and her butter-smeared pen. Intolerable. What, in her wisdom, had Minerfa *done*?

She waited a moment, in case the stench might fade as quickly as it had emerged, but it didn't. Her half of a luncheon threatened to come up again; Lulu hastily rose, leaving her paraphernalia strewn over the gleaming black table.

She half ran into the hallway, and around to the cellar stairs. Her quick steps rang loudly on the black stone floors, prominent in the sudden cessation of clamour.

'Minerfa,' called Lulu, and went down a stone stair. 'Minerf—oh dear, what *have* you found to do down there?'

'Coming!' came Minerfa's deep-throated voice. Two minutes ticked past before she appeared, swathed from collar to shoes in a thick cotton overall liberally smeared with dark-stained—somethings. Her bruise-coloured face was half hidden behind an enormous pair of safety glasses, and a heavy cloth bound back her hair. 'It's going marvellously, Miss Lulu,' she announced. 'Have you come to help?'

A miasma of meat, fresh and rotten, surrounded the castle's lodger, laced with an acrid smell of hot iron. Lulu, half choked with it, shook her head furiously. 'No,' she croaked. 'I came to cry mercy. What is that *smell*?'

'It's the new heating system. I'm halfway through installation. It will pong a bit, but—'

'Not that, so much,' Lulu managed. 'The—rest of it.'

'The meat? Well, that's my luncheon. I need a lot of fuel, when I'm working.'

'But is something *rotting*?'

'Ahh.' Minerfa adjusted her glasses. 'That would be the corpses.'

'Corpses.' Lulu clutched at the door frame, her knees having weakened. 'Corpses? More than one dead body.'

'Yes, I found a few. Is that everything? I am rather busy—'

'What did you do with the bodies, Minerfa.'

'Oh! Well, I must have thrown them somewhere. Let me see.' She bustled off. More clanking sounds followed, and the shattering crash of something heavy breaking. 'Found them!' she called.

Lulu felt a powerful disinclination to investigate. Nothing but trouble awaited her down there in the dark; another calamity to complicate her already convoluted day.

Besides, she was a little afraid. Considering the overpowering stench of advancing decay, the bodies must have been dead for a few weeks. She could be sure, then, that none of them were the residents of Castle Drax. She had seen her father only this morning, pacing up and down the upper gallery with slow, forbidding steps, and muttering to himself. She had baked plaited loaves with Magwell late the previous evening; helped Fane polish the dinner-gong; sung a ditty with Stormdust as they buffed the gleaming bonnet of the family motorcar.

Still, just because all her nearest and most dear were accounted for, didn't mean the three corpses below couldn't be people she knew. In fact she had a strong premonition to the contrary.

She did not want to go down there, at all; wanted nothing more than to walk away, and pretend that this fresh catastrophe had not occurred at all. But there was nothing to be gained by dithering. She wrapped a length of her chiffon scarf over her nose and mouth, in the probably vain hope of stifling the smell, and followed Minerfa down the dark stairs and into the bowels of the cellars. If her knees shook a bit on the way down, nobody need know it but her.

Detritus lay everywhere. Lengths of partially assembled pipes, hammered out of blackened steel; shattered black floor tiles in little heaps, the casualties of some heavy object falling; Minerfa's collection of spanners and hammers and—oh dear, at least one barbarously sharp knife, copiously bloodied. A section of wall had come down halfway along a dark passage, strewing a rubble of tumbled black stones over the floor.

Minerfa dodged and hopped and sashayed her way around these various obstacles with perfect ease, scarcely noticing. Lulu, encumbered by a poor combination of ordinary human eyesight and a prevailing, almost uninterrupted gloom, picked her way more carefully.

'I may have encountered just one or two little difficulties with the installation,' Minerfa was saying, jumping lightly over a heap of half-molten iron. 'But I daresay I shall have it working directly.'

Lulu hoped so. To add to her general discomfort, the warren of passages and chambers below the castle proper—a damp, gloomy labyrinth never touched by sunlight or warmth—was utterly, shatteringly cold. Five minutes down there and she was shivering so hard she could no longer push any words past her clattering teeth. Those corpses had better be worth it.

At least they'd passed right by the room with her father's summoning-circle in. She'd had a moment's apprehension that Minerfa was going to stop *there*, that the mysterious bodies were something to do with that unhallowed space. Mercifully not.

The rotting aroma grew, abruptly, stronger. Like being punched in the face with a month-old fish, Lulu thought, retching.

'—problem is with the valves I want for the— oh, here we are.' Minerfa stopped. Cobwebs wreathed her sturdy form, and a thick quantity of ancient dust; she resembled an animated corpse herself. Lulu supposed she looked similar, after stumbling through so much muck and detritus. She sneezed.

A collapsed pile of dust-smothered lumber had been a large cupboard until recently. Someone had taken a hammer to it, by the looks of its splintered boards and twisted hinges. Probably one of Minerfa's massive steel hammers, one of which lay discarded nearby.

The contents of the erstwhile cupboard had come spilling out, and lay in three distinct heaps of foul-smelling flesh. Three corpses, some time dead.

Lulu recognised one at once: Mrs. Bell, the estate agent in charge of selling Castle Drax. Her dead face, rouged and rotting, stared accusingly at Lulu.

'I did wonder that I had not heard from Percy and Bell, lately,' she sighed. Actually, she had been counting her blessings over it; the problem of how to dispense with Mrs. Bell's services had been plaguing her for some time. They no longer wished to sell the castle, but Mrs. Bell certainly did; a large commission fee was at stake.

Murder would not have been her preferred solution, however. It would not have appeared in her top three favoured resolutions, even.

'What's that?' asked Minerfa, vaguely. She'd speedily lost interest in the dead, and gone back to tinkering with her gadgetry.

'This lady is Mrs. Bell. She was supposed to be selling the castle for us.'

'What?' Minerfa's head came up. 'Do not sell the castle, I pray you. I've only just settled. Do you have any idea how hard it is to find a good place to live?'

For Minerfa, Lulu could well understand that it might be. And who else considered Castle Drax a "good" place to live? Few indeed. 'We aren't selling it, anymore,' Lulu reassured her. 'Not that we had many takers.' She pinched her nostrils together, breathing through her mouth to lessen the smell. The three bodies were a nightmare of sagging, putrid, maggot-ridden flesh, and she would have to examine them: two remained unidentified, and she would need to glean some sort of clue as to the mode of their demise.

She bent over Mrs. Bell, first, and mercifully was not obliged to remain in the posture long. A purpling ring of bruises around the estate agent's throat clearly proclaimed that she had been strangled. With a length of rope, perhaps? Lulu moved hurriedly on to the next victim.

Another woman, dressed in exquisitely fine silk and tweed. She had not been young; the remains of her face were ravaged by time, her hair mostly grey. A string of lustrous pearls adorned her neck, and her fingers were thick with jewelled rings. Someone with wealth and status, then: that did not bode well. She, too, had been strangled.

The third corpse was male, and—Lulu blanched. She knew this man, too. Pale of face and hair and suit, though the former now bore the discolouration of death and the latter was begrimed from its sojourn in the dusty cupboard. He had been stuffy in life, colourless in manner, and not at all Lulu's favourite person.

How had it come about that both Mrs. Bell and Mr. Percy, estate agents, were lying dead under the vast bulk of the castle they had been attempting to sell?

That gave Lulu a bad feeling. She returned to the third corpse, the elderly lady. Sunken cheeks, ribbons of decayed skin, too-prominent teeth with the jaw falling apart around them—these features had obscured those that might have been immediately recognisable to Lulu. Upon closer inspection, she reconsidered. Elderly, expensively dressed, and last seen heading down into this very cellar in company with Mr. Percy—this was Lady Rondel, would-be purchaser of the castle.

'This is a disaster,' Lulu groaned.

Minerfa looked up, and smiled. 'Is it? Those are always diverting.'

'No, truly,' Lulu persisted. 'There can only be one motive for killing these particular people, all three of them together. *And* for hiding them down here, of all places.'

'They were untidy?' suggested Minerfa.

'No. That is, they were certainly inconvenient, but tidying them away into the summoning-circle was an effective enough solution. Why kill them?' She suffered a momentary doubt that Mr. Percy and Lady Rondel had ever gone into the circle, after all; perhaps they had merely been murdered. But, no. Their disappearance had occurred months ago; surely their bodies would exhibit far greater decay, were that the case. And she had seen Mrs. Bell relatively recently.

Mr. Percy and Lady Rondel had come back from wherever the circle had taken them. And someone had been anything but pleased to see them.

Lulu feared she knew who.

'Minerfa,' she said, struck by a stray thought. 'How came you to find these people? Was it the smell?'

'Oh! No. They fell out of the cupboard, when I smashed it.'

The destroyed remnants of the hapless cupboard looked as though a house had fallen on it. 'Why,' asked Lulu carefully, 'did you smash it?'

Minerfa picked up her discarded hammer, and swung it. A largely intact plank splintered into shards. 'I found it amusing,' she explained.

'I don't suppose you might find it amusing to convey these deceased persons upstairs, and out into the yard?' Lulu ventured.

'Not in the least.' Minerfa destroyed another plank, her great hammer landing with a thundering *crash*.

Fane would probably oblige. But first—Lulu left the pungent cellar behind, with feelings of profound relief, and went on up to the upper gallery, where she had last seen her father.

Count Vexx was still there. She heard his footsteps as she trudged up the dark-carpeted stairs, pacing. He'd stopped muttering, but she heard a lugubrious sigh.

She reached the landing, and paused. The upper gallery was a charming space, as Castle Drax went: a long, light, well-lit hall, its panelled walls hung with an eccentric array of oils on canvas. A long, deep-green carpet runner adorned the centre of the room, and Count Vexx was presently attempting to wear holes in it. He wore his black jacket unbuttoned, and his ordinarily sleek hair was a touch dishevelled. He looked up as Lulu appeared, showing her a handsome, chiselled countenance twisted with annoyance.

'Yes, what is it?' said he testily.

How did one gracefully enquire into the murderous habits of one's noble parent? It depended on the parent, really, and this one was Count Vexx.

'Father. Did you by any chance strangle a pair of estate agents and a potential purchaser of our home, and stuff their lifeless bodies into a cellar cupboard?'

'Not that I can recall,' he answered. 'And I do think I would remember that.' He smiled a little, his eyes faraway.

'Did you ask someone else to do it?' Lulu persevered. 'Fane, for example.'

'There can be no question that he would, if I asked him to. But I have issued no such order. Not recently...'

That Lulu had no desire to enquire into. 'The fact is, someone has slaughtered those most likely to effect the successful sale of our ancestral home,' she said, pointedly. 'And I can only imagine it must have been someone who despised the notion of giving the place up.'

'Fane would do no such thing, without orders.'

'Then it must have been you, Father.'

Count Vexx didn't answer, right away. He'd stopped pacing, and stood with his hands linked behind his back, eyes fixed on some faraway point, and thinking. Lulu waited.

'Strangled, you say,' her father mused. 'Were there finger marks? Hand prints, around the throat?'

'No. I assume something like a rope must have been used, though the marks left seem broader than a rope is likely to be.'

'Oh, well then. It assuredly was not me.' Count Vexx, vindicated, smiled, and paced a bit more, whistling.

'How do you figure that?' Lulu pressed, exasperated.

'Where did you get that scarf?' Count Vexx pointed a manicured finger at the azure chiffon confection knotted loosely around Lulu's neck.

Lulu threw up her hands. 'Father, stop changing the subject. This is important.'

'I'm not changing the subject. Answer the question.'

'From Mother's dressing-room, but—'

'There you are, then.'

'It—what? But...oh.' Lulu tightened the scarf around her own neck, twisting the delicate fabric into a thick, and surprisingly strong, rope. Yes; quite enough pressure to result in death, if one were determined.

Lulu hadn't considered Countess Vexx, probably because her mother's return to the castle had been very short-lived. But she had been appalled at the notion of the castle's sale; what was a great family without a grand estate to live upon? She'd hatched a scheme to marry her protesting daughter off to some wealthy gentleman, precisely to negate the necessity of it.

And she had returned to the castle the same way she'd left it—back through Father's dratted witch-circle. As had Mr. Percy, and Lady Rondel. A collision between *those* three had turned out very poorly indeed.

'Oh, Mother,' Lulu sighed. 'Are you sure, though? I know she can be difficult, but—'

Count Vexx's bark of laughter held a measure of despair. 'Difficult. Charmingly put, Lulu, and inadequate.'

'Surely she is not capable of triple murder.' Lulu thought of her mother's bright, blonde beauty; her vivacious manner, and winning smile; more compellingly, her fastidious devotion to correct etiquette and social success. This seemed out of keeping with those traits; these were brutal killings. Heartless.

But Count Vexx tapped his throat, indicating the scarf Lulu wore. 'Everyone is capable of murder, Lulu,' he told her. 'Some more so than others.'

'Including Mother?'

He made a careless gesture, and paced away from her. 'An attractive smile means nothing at all. The devastating Lady Vexx is a creature sculpted from solid ice.'

It was the scarf that convinced Lulu, a little against her hopes. She'd missed it before, in the pervasive gloom of the cellar: a gauzy thing, airy, once, and pretty, tinted the colour of lilac blossoms and stitched with silver leaves. Now it lay crumpled, and slightly torn, buried under splintered wood and the limbs of her ladyship's victims.

Lulu remembered that scarf, dimly. It had been a favourite of her mother's, prior to her disappearance; five-year-old Lulu had worn it herself once or twice, swanning in front of Mama's long mirrors and fancying herself very fine.

She hadn't seen it since—until today.

'Oh, Mama,' she sighed when she saw it, and drew it out from beneath Mrs. Bell's rotting legs.

'What's that?' asked Minerfa, vaguely interested.

'Evidence.' Lulu held it by a flimsy corner, her nose wrinkling. The scarf was ruined with rot, and it stank; she was tempted to burn it at once.

'Best to get rid of it, then,' said Minerfa wisely.

'What? Why?'

'Is that not what one usually does, with evidence?'

Lulu eyed her lodger, and said nothing: a rather awful silence.

Even Minerfa felt it. 'Oh. That isn't what one does with evidence?'

'Not here, at least,' said Lulu, striving to mean it: the desire to burn everything, all of it, and forget it ever happened, was almost overpowering.

'What, then?'

What indeed. The last Lulu had seen of her esteemed mother, she'd been sweeping away from the gloomy castle in the passenger seat of a very fine motorcar. Its owner, the duke, scarcely left her ladyship's side, a fact which caused Lulu a measure of guilt, now. It was at least a little bit her fault, after all—and she'd saddled the duke with a murderess.

No, she couldn't let Lady Vexx get away with it. Besides, Mr. Percy may not have been much regretted, but someone might mourn for Mrs. Bell. Maybe even the execrable Lady Rondel. One never knew; people were strange.

'What we do with evidence,' Lulu decided, 'is hand it over to the police.'

Minerfa's face fell. 'Oh, dear. I do not think that will be amusing at all.'

No one else did, either. Minerfa might continue her bashing about in the cellars; she was a paying resident, and bore no responsibility for the disasters that occurred around her. Count Vexx's total refusal to countenance a police visit, though, that was another matter. 'Over my dead body,' he said when Lulu floated the notion. 'And I rather think we have enough of those to be going on with, hm?'

'What then do you suggest?' said Lulu, with faint hope.

A witchfire burned in the upper gallery, lighting up the black hearth in lurid green. 'Cast the lot of them into the fire,' her father said, indicating this ice-cold blaze with a carelessly elegant sweep of his arm. 'And the scarf.'

'And then?'

'Then, what? It's done with.'

But it would not be. The town of Andirac must look askance at the vanishment of two of its citizens, and the world beyond must come in search of the Lady Rondel, eventually. They would be traced to Castle Drax in time, and then—trouble.

So Lulu went away from the gallery, leaving her father to his musings, and shut herself into the telephone closet in the great hall. The operator connected her to the police in no time; Lulu described the situation in brief terms, and fervently hoped she had chosen correctly in doing so.

She took the precaution of locking a particular cellar door, before the constables arrived. It wouldn't do to lose one or two of them to the summoning-circle, just yet.

The doorbell rang an hour later, thundering discordantly from cellar to attic. Lulu, lying in wait, threw open the heavy front door at once. Its ancient hinges groaned as it slowly swung wide, adding a shrieking counterpoint to the general cacophony of doom.

On the other side of it, wide-eyed and wary, a tall bulk of a man stood in a rather decent suit. He wore a dark fedora hat over the brilliantined black waves of his hair. A pair of bulky figures in constable's uniform hovered alertly behind him.

'Ah!' said Lulu, beaming. 'The police.'

'Detective Inspector Shah,' he introduced himself, eyeing Lulu as though she might, at any moment, transform into some devilish creature, and eviscerate him.

Lulu dimpled, and stepped back, with a gracious gesture of invitation. 'Do come in.'

'I suppose it's safe to?' said Inspector Shah, casting a wary glance up at the vast, looming bulk of the castle.

'Quite safe,' Lulu assured him. 'Dear Mama left a fortnight ago, and Father isn't at all in the mood for violence.'

The Inspector's brows rose. 'Reassuring,' he decided—Lulu suspected him of sarcasm, a little—and stepped inside. Two constables trailed after.

'Shall I offer you some tea?' Lulu enquired, hauling the heavy door shut again: it closed with a dull boom of finality. 'I hardly know what would be appropriate. We are not much in the habit of entertaining the police, you know.'

'I find that remarkable,' said the Inspector, a comprehensive glance taking in the excess of black marble, the awful, shadowed expanse of the ceiling, and the crackling emerald flames in the monstrously-sized hearth.

'Tea, then,' Lulu decided, and went down to fetch it herself. Fane and Stormdust had made themselves scarce, and Magwell had expressed a firm intention of remaining below, in the kitchen. Nobody could guess how a police officer might respond to the three; nobody wanted to find out, at least not today.

Minerfa was another matter. Unconcerned, and obliviously hammering about downstairs, she wouldn't interrupt her own work in favour of hiding herself away. But her unusual bruise-coloured countenance might occasion little remark, half-concealed as it was behind thick goggles, and a length of cloth over her mouth and nose. Besides that, the Inspector had enough to occupy him.

Lulu hastily constructed a respectable beverage, to be served in respectable crockery: a rose-painted teapot Lulu had found in the depths of a cupboard with a broken latch, part of a pile of dusty floral tableware. Probably Mother's. She whisked these delights away with a plate of Magwell's cardamom biscuits; if one was about to unleash the awful sight of the Draxian cellars upon the visitors, together with no fewer than three ageing corpses, it wouldn't hurt to put up a show of harmless hospitality first.

She found Inspector Shah on his knees in the hall before the great, frigid hearth, one hand held out to the green-glowing fire. 'I must say,' he remarked as she came in, 'this is possibly the strangest thing I have ever seen.'

'How kind,' Lulu beamed. 'Father's work. He'll be so pleased.'

Inspector Shah rose to his feet, examining his frost-wreathed hand with absorbed interest. 'Most interesting,' he said. 'I shall be speaking to Count Vexx, but first, we shall see the bodies, please.'

Lulu set down her tray atop a carved ebony chest, and took a biscuit for herself. 'I've left everything as it was,' she assured him. 'Except for the scarf, of course, but there was no help for that. I had to make sure.'

'Make sure of what?'

'That it was Mother's.' She led the way to the cellar stairs, nibbling cardamom crumbs. Magwell's baking had a way of settling her stomach.

'Do you tell me Lady Vexx killed three people?' The Inspector's voice held a note of incredulity: doubtless he had heard of Mama. Probably he'd seen her photograph in the society papers: gloriously blonde and coiffed, ravishingly smiling.

'And dumped their bodies in our cellar. Yes, it was most ill-judged of her.' Lulu spoke loudly, hoping to forewarn Minerfa. A dim clanking sound rattled through the floor, emanating from somewhere.

The corridors below seemed darker and colder than ever, which was odd. Lulu had never been especially disturbed by it, before, but with a suspicious detective inspector in tow, everything appeared subtly different. Shadowed, sinister, and shabby: the perfect lair for a ruthless killer, save that Mama had always hated everything about it.

It really was darker below, Lulu realised after a minute: Minerfa's lanterns, dim as their glow had been, were extinguished, all save one. Something else was missing, too—the stench. Nothing worse assaulted Lulu's senses than a smell of mildew, and stale air. 'Minerfa?' Lulu called, bewildered. No answer came.

'And who is Minerfa?' enquired the Inspector. He'd sent the two constables ahead, with their electric torches. Their hunched shoulders and dragging steps proclaimed their unease, but at least the cold, white glow of their torches kept the worst of the darkness at bay.

'Our lodger,' Lulu explained. 'She's been down here today working on a—project, and discovered the unfortunates when she was, ah, dismantling a closet—' Lulu came to an abrupt halt, for there lay the broken mass of oaken boards that had, so recently, been a large cupboard. Besides that, dust aplenty, thick enough to choke upon; ragged veils of spiders' webs hanging in gauzy swags from the stone ceiling; a stray length of piping, roughly hacked off, that Minerfa had left behind. No bodies, though. Not so much as a finger remained of Mrs. Bell, Mr. Percy, or Lady Rondel.

'Well,' murmured Lulu. 'This is rather awkward.'

'The bodies, ma'am?' Inspector Shah prompted, grown impatient with the long ramble through the castle's underbelly.

'That's just it,' said Lulu. 'I appear to have been—mistaken.'

The Inspector grew positively testy. 'How in the blazes can you be mistaken about a trio of corpses?'

'It does seem peculiar,' Lulu agreed.

He turned about, the skirts of his great-coat swirling through layers of dust. 'Do you mean that someone has removed them?'

'I hardly know.'

A sigh; he turned back to her, fixed her with a dark stare. 'Then there is no proof that any crime has been committed, is there? I have only your word for it.'

'And why would I invent such a tale?'

'I have *heard* that Lady Vexx—whom you accused of murder—has recently left here in a state of high dudgeon. That there is little love lost between her ladyship and the Count.'

'Read the Society papers, do you?' Lulu smiled.

The Inspector flushed. 'Is it the truth, however?'

'Largely,' Lulu admitted.

'If there is some quarrel between you and your mother, Miss Vexx, may I advise counselling as a preferable alternative to wild accusations of homicide?'

'Yes, I do seem to have wasted your time.' Lulu, quite aware how the thing looked, attempted a smile rather than a defence. 'Do have some biscuits before you leave, won't you? Our cook made them just this morning. They're really quite exquisite.'

'Wasting police time is an offence, Miss Vexx. '

'And I am most terribly sorry. Shall you arrest me, do you think?'

'Not this time.' With which dark pronouncement, the Inspector gathered his constables and withdrew, declining the biscuits.

Lulu collected the plate, and took it with her up three echoing staircases to Minerfa's room. A lantern stood outside Minerfa's firmly closed door, flickering green with witchfire. Lulu took that as an invitation. She knocked politely. 'Minerfa?'

The door flew open. Minerfa, divested of goggles and overalls, stared hard at Lulu. She had a quantity of cobweb draped over her dark hair. 'Yes?'

'Biscuit?' Lulu held out the plate.

Minerfa snatched three and crammed two into her mouth at once. An aroma of cardamom wafted up.

'I had thought we agreed we were not getting rid of the evidence?' Lulu suggested.

'I do not remember agreeing,' Minerfa replied.

Which, unfortunately, was true. 'One Detective Inspector Shah now thinks me entirely mad,' Lulu persevered.

'You probably are.'

Lulu handed over the plate, reserving one last biscuit for herself. 'Dinner's at seven,' she said, turning away. 'Magwell's making brain and brawn pie.'

A hoot of joy from Minerfa. 'My favourite,' she declared, and the door slammed.

'I know,' said Lulu, and went downstairs.

10

Gone Murdering

Once in a great while, there dawns a day so perfect, so prismatic, so balmily blue, even the hardest of hearts cannot help but lift their cold eyes to the sky, and smile, a very little.

How great, then, the delight of a Lulu Vexx, buoyant sort as she is. The sun shone, and so did she, whisking along the dank, dark corridors of her ancestral home with the brisk, bouncing step of a spring breeze herself. Summer hovered on the golden horizon; the temperature was so mild on this beautiful day, Lulu very almost wasn't even cold.

And what occupied her sometimes brilliant brain on this most delicious of days? What prospects, pregnant with hope and happiness, drifted behind her bright, green eyes?

Spring cleaning, for one; she is the chatelaine of Castle Drax, which is (to put it plainly) an unmitigated disaster.

And, for another: murder. An odd combination, and wildly mismatched, but parental influence must bear the blame.

It may seem surprising, considering her ancestry, but Lulu had never accounted homicide as a practical solution to any of life's little difficulties. The idea had never so much as entered her head.

The same had not proved true for others at Castle Drax. Lulu had long felt some vague suspicion as to her father's past escapades; he had, on more than one occasion, dropped dark hints of dark deeds, performed on some long-ago occasion, and Lulu had taken great care never to enquire.

But it wasn't he, probably, who had strangled three only somewhat offending individuals a few weeks prior, and hidden their decomposing bodies in a cupboard in the cellar. Probably.

The more likely culprit—if, in some respects, implausible—was Lady Vexx, the Count's esteemed wife and Lulu's magnificent mother. Ravishing, widely adored, and ruthless about one or two things—but a murderess?

The matter would not leave Lulu in peace. A week had passed since the discovery—and, shortly afterwards, disappearance—of the three victims, and Lulu had thought of little since, however glorious the weather.

On this day of beautiful days, she had a tour group to prepare for. Thirteen members of a ladies' landscape painting society proposed to be guided about the place, and subsequently to install themselves in the grounds, with their canvases and their paintboxes. They were paying for the privilege, mercifully—the castle swallowed money like a sinkhole swallowed houses—and Lulu dashed from corridor to stairs to drawing-rooms, attempting to impose an air of at least moderate respectability.

She found Minerfa in a bathroom on the first floor, drawing fiery runes onto the dim and wavering glass of the ancient, half-shattered mirror. The first—and, as yet, only—paying lodger at the castle, Minerfa had kept to her own rooms for her first fortnight in residence. Now, though, there was no telling where she might turn up, or for what purpose.

'While you are doing that,' said Lulu, knowing better than to remonstrate with her over the runes, 'might you perhaps take up this duster, and do something about those cobwebs in the corners? They are thicker than the lace on my mother's best ballgowns.'

Minerfa did not reply until she had completed, with great care, a final fire-licked rune, which shimmered strangely green. 'There. Be sure to trot your little group through here. They'll enjoy these.' She took up the proffered feather duster after that, and set to against the cobwebs with a vigorous will. Lulu did not trouble herself to disagree about the runes: Minerfa was probably right. And they might distract the ladies' attention from the sad, cracked state of the dark stone floor tiles, the permanently grimy windows (one boarded up), and the lion-footed bathtub, once rather fine, but now stained and marred with a great crack through its blackened enamel.

Lulu, then, said very little, which did not evade Minerfa's notice. 'You are not still in a stew about that little problem, are you?'

'If by "little problem" you mean a certain trio of dead people: yes,' Lulu replied, rolling up her frayed cotton sleeves and attacking the bathtub with a soapy sponge.

'Whatever for? I dealt with that difficulty superbly.'

'Yes, as to that,' Lulu remarked. 'What did you do with the bodies, exactly? Burned them?'

'Most impractical. No, I merely sent them back where we all came from.'

In other words, she had hurled them into Count Vexx's summoning-circle, whereupon they had duly vanished. Nothing had come out of it in response, it seemed, but then one offered live sacrifices, as a rule of courtesy. Dead ones were seen as gifts, belike. Tribute?

'Back where many of us came from,' Lulu corrected absently. 'Some of us did not.'

'Oh?' said Minerfa, devastating cobwebs with emphatic sweeps of her duster. 'Which few?'

'Well, me, for one, and Father.'

'Ahh,' said Minerfa, in a tone Lulu did not at all like. 'If you are sure.'

She had been, but now she was not. Lulu stifled a curse. 'One dreadful and macabre problem at a time, please, Minerfa.'

'Absolutely. Very sensible.'

Minerfa was amused, curse her. She knew something Lulu would—probably—-give a great deal never to learn; that being so, a return to the incidental problem of unexplained corpses did seem preferrable.

'The problem with your excellent solution,' Lulu persevered, 'is that it is temporary. The three people we found there must be missed, eventually, and at least two had known connections to this house. When their absence has been noted, that acid-tongued Detective Inspector will be back.'

'Mm,' said Minerfa (swipe-swipe-*swipe*). 'You had better do your hair, then.'

'What can my hair possibly have to do with anything?'

'Why, if he admires your hair he will forget all about the murders.'

Minerfa, without a doubt, came from *somewhere else*—whatever lay on the other side of Father's summoning-circle. There were times, such as these, where her grasp of local social customs might be termed eccentric.

Though, not without a kernel of truth.

'Well, I will,' said Lulu, for a well-groomed appearance could not hurt her, when there were monied visitors about the place. 'But I don't think it will help with *that* difficulty.'

'It will,' said Minerfa promptly, and without a trace of doubt. 'You'll see.'

Lulu took her bucket of grimy water and her sponges away, attempting no further argument. Minerfa would learn, sooner or later, and in the meantime, it *did* take a while to set the waves in the blonde bob of her hair. She'd better get started.

The ladies arrived in a succession of gleaming motorcars, and emerged clad in a parade of expensively tailored dresses and suits. They were groomed and styled and arrayed in gold and pearls; far better suited to a luncheon than a painting afternoon, or a tour around a grimy and dust-ridden castle. Lulu hoped Magwell's best efforts would satisfy their refined palates.

She herself had worn her best cream silk blouse with a good tweed skirt and jacket—stolen, as usual, from her mother's discarded articles. Lulu went among the chattering throng of disembarking visitors, welcoming, shaking hands, and attempting to emanate just such a chic graciousness as Lady Vexx might have done.

She had got most of the matrons and their daughters ushered into the cavernous black maw of the great hall when another motorcar drew slowly up, and disgorged a youngish lady arrayed in a jewel-blue sari. A latecomer, of course; Lulu trotted back down the wide stone steps to welcome her, and stopped short when the passenger side door swung open on the dark motorcar, and a man she recognised emerged.

'Ah, Miss Vexx,' said Detective Inspector Shah. 'We apologise for the lack of notice.'

Lulu, nonplussed, took a moment to recover from her surprise. 'Er, Inspector, how—nice to see you? How can we help?'

He smiled. She hadn't seen him do that before. 'My sister is a passionate painter, and when she heard of your afternoon event she was eager to participate. It is a little last minute, but I assured her she would find the chatelaine most gracious.'

Relief made Lulu emphatically gracious; this wasn't about the bodies, then. 'Naturally,' she answered, with a smile for the lady. 'Miss Shah is very welcome.'

'Call me Priya,' came the answer, warmly. 'How good of you! I told Ravi it would never do simply to show up, but how glad I am to be wrong.'

Lulu raised her brows at Detective Inspector Shah, who was obligingly retrieving an attractive, new-looking set of enamelled paint boxes from the motorcar. She had met him only recently; he had responded to her report of the corpses she'd found in the cellar, arriving with two constables in tow—and leaving again in high dudgeon, believing Lulu to have fabricated the whole. Now he stood smiling, in a good blue suit with a subtle pinstripe, his black locks impeccably groomed, and with a glamorous sister on his arm. What could he mean by it?

'Mr. Shah employs an unfair advantage,' she said mildly. 'One must think very carefully before offending an officer of the law.'

'Today he is only my brother,' said Priya, with a light laugh. 'He comes prepared to be sociable, and obliging. Your dark secrets are safe for now, Miss Vexx.'

'What a relief,' said Lulu, with perfect sincerity. 'Now, please, luncheon awaits us, and we should not let it get cold. Shall you be joining your sister, Inspector?'

'Naturally I would be delighted,' said the Inspector, and bowed.

'Naturally,' murmured Lulu. She had the sense that there were other passengers in the car; some vague shape indicated as much, through the darkened glass of the windows. But they were too deep-tinted for Lulu to see clearly, and the Shahs made no move to extract anybody else from the vehicle. Lulu concluded herself to be mistaken, and led the way inside.

To Lulu's surprise, Inspector Shah proved to be extremely sociable and obliging. She had described him as "acid-tongued" only that morning, but now he was full of bonhomie, regaling Lulu's guests with entertaining anecdotes of sleuthing, and soliciting an array of confidences and stories from the thirteen ladies of the landscape painting society. Priya, too, demonstrated a vivacity and ease in company that had Lulu almost envious—and, by the end of luncheon, a trifle suspicious. Without these impromptu guests, the conversation over the cheese-and-dill stuffed mushrooms, egg and bacon pie, and sticky treacle tart, would likely have proved rather sluggish. The siblings were exerting themselves to please; and why?

Her suspicions only grew over the course of the afternoon. Thirteen ladies—plus Priya—arranged themselves around the grounds with their easels and palettes, and serenely devoted themselves to the production of indifferent views of the ill-kept shrubbery ("charmingly natural"), the dark, tangled copse of yew trees beyond it ("very gothic, I should shudder to step into it!"), and of course the vast, hulking monstrosity that was the castle. Largely, Lulu left them to it, though she kept an eye on them from a discreet distance.

By three o'clock, Lulu knew for certain that Priya was no longer among them. Indeed, she was nowhere about the grounds; and her brother, too, was unaccounted for.

This, then, was why they had come, and why they had gone to such lengths to charm Lulu and her guests. There had been some objective, some mission they were minded to accomplish at Castle Drax, and which they could not—or would not—attempt openly.

In other words, the Vexxes were being covertly investigated, after all. Was the Inspector here about the murders again, or was it something else? Something *worse*?

Fane and Stormdust were keeping themselves aloof from the company, as they always did when there were guests. Lulu had no explanation for their oddities that would pass muster with a refined group of ladies, and Fane and Stormdust both preferred not to be gawked at, poked, and speculated over, in the same way as Grimspound's statuary, or Molly Stittlegarth's murals. Now, though, Lulu wended her way with quick steps up into the northwesterly wing of the castle, and a suite of chilly, sparsely furnished chambers on the top floor there, which Fane had long preferred as his own abode. What if some rumour of their presence at the castle—and some false notion of their purpose, their identity, or their good nature—had reached Inspector Shah's ears? What if he had seen something on his last visit, and had become suspicious? Lulu was responsible for the well-being of all the castle's residents (with the sole exception of Lady Vexx, when she chose to appear), and she had left two of her family at the possible mercy of the police.

Arrived at the towering and heavily barred portal that separated Fane's domain from the occasional bustle of the rest of the house, Lulu hammered smartly upon it; and when that proved productive of no response, took up the long-handled hammer that waited beside it for just such a purpose, should an emergency develop, and delivered herself of a heavy, ringing blow to the solid iron door. A dull *boom* echoed.

She waited, panting a little with effort, and mercifully the sound of rusted bolts pulling back and oaken bars being lifted occurred to gladden her ears. Hinges squealed; Fane's long, craggy face appeared, drawn and anxious. 'What is it?'

Lulu set down the hammer. 'Is everything well with you, Fane dear, and Stormdust?'

Fane opened the door wider, revealing Stormdust's large and rounded face smiling gently beyond it. He was wearing a sumptuous crimson silk robe, filched, probably, from Count Vexx's wardrobe (or, just as likely, gifted). 'We are the goodest of good, and the wellest of well,' Stormdust assured her.

Lulu sagged a little with relief. She had already ascertained that Magwell's kitchen fortress remained unassailed, and her father—well, Count Vexx could take care of himself.

'We have intruders on the loose, somewhere about the place,' Lulu told them. 'One Detective Inspector Shah, and his sister. I suspect them of skullduggery, and if it isn't you they are after then it must be—I fear they are gone down into the cellar.'

These were words to strike horror into the hearts of all Draxian folk (or glee, in some cases; circumstances do vary).

Lulu felt paralysed with horror, for a moment. She'd told Minerfa her disposal of her mother's victims would prove but a temporary solution, and she'd been right. Odd of him to bring his sister on such an errand, but what other explanation could there be? Inspector Shah had changed his mind, come to suspect foul play at Castle Drax after all. What would he do, when he discovered the source of Count Vexx's eldritch power?

Lulu was already pelting downstairs before she'd formed the thought, Fane and Stormdust close behind her. The way down and down was a long one, and winding; by the time Lulu clattered down the cold stone stairs to the cellar, she was sweating and gasping for breath.

A small part of her hoped—half expected—to find nothing amiss, the seemingly innocuous door to the summoning chamber untouched and unaltered. Of course not. It stood slightly ajar; Lulu heard voices coming from beyond it.

She shoved it open and hurtled inside, aware that if she hesitated she might lose her nerve altogether.

There stood Inspector Shah, and Priya. They were not smiling now, all their conviviality faded into an attitude of profound gravity. Oddly, a constable's helmet lay against one white-washed wall, as though it had rolled there.

The five-pointed star daubed into the stone floor in a dramatic hue of crimson appeared, to her expert eye, slightly smeared.

'Right,' said Lulu, breathlessly. 'It's true, I lied to you. Well—that isn't quite right, is it, I told you the truth, only you wouldn't believe me, so THEN I lied. We—we did send the bodies back through.' She paused for breath, her hands shaking. 'Nobody here killed them, though, I swear it.'

Inspector Shah heard this in silence, his dark gaze shifting to take in the presence of Fane and Stormdust behind her. His expression remained cool, unreadable: no shock, no horror. This could be a good thing, or very bad indeed.

Priya gave a soft little sound, rather like a sob. Yes: she was dabbing at her eyes with a lace-edged handkerchief.

'Oh, dear,' said Lulu, the rest of her speech deserting her. 'I suppose it is a little sad, though I assure you the only one of them worth regretting was Mrs. Bell, and not very much, at that.'

Inspector Shah paced to the wall, picked up the shiny blue constable's helmet, and quietly handed it to his sister. 'They'll be much happier, Pri, I promise.'

Priya gave a watery smile. 'I know. Only I will miss them so.'

'Me too,' agreed her brother, with a sigh.

Lulu heard all this with profound confusion. 'Terribly sorry,' she said after a moment. 'I don't seem to have the first idea what is going on.'

Priya collected herself. 'We do apologise, Miss Vexx. It was unconscionably rude of us to make use of your circle without asking, only it is such an awkward application to make. And then, you know, Ravi thought to do a little digging—'

Inspector Shah interrupted. 'I heard of the disappearance of Mrs. Bell, of Percy and Bell's,' he told her. 'And of the earlier disappearance of her partner, Mr. Percy, along with a prospective client of their agency, Lady Rondel—who was said to be on the point of purchasing Castle Drax at the time. I was wrong to accuse you of fabricating the existence of those three bodies.'

'Thank you?' said Lulu, uncertain whether this classified as an apology.

'Why exactly did you dispose of them?' He phrased the question mildly enough, but his stare was keen—hawkish.

'I didn't,' Lulu sighed. 'Our lodger thought it would be the best thing to do. She—is not from around here.'

'Ah,' he said. 'I see.' And it appeared that he did.

'Is that why they disappeared?' Priya interjected. 'Did they go *through*?'

'Mr. Percy and Lady Rondel did, yes,' Lulu answered. 'Some weeks ago. They were warned about the cellar, of course.'

'And these two gentlemen were the result.' Priya smiled at Fane and Stormdust with far more warmth than either were accustomed to eliciting, save from Lulu herself.

'Stormdust was. Fane has been with us for many years.' Now that Lulu had caught her breath, her mind was catching up, too. 'Your constables have gone through, have they? The two you brought with you before.' She'd not been introduced to the pair of silent, stoic officers, not even given their names. They had been hatted and suited, their coat collars buttoned high; Lulu, so distracted by the calamity of the three corpses, had scarcely glanced at them. But they were like Stormdust, and Fane; they had to be.

Inspector Shah nodded. 'They have wanted to go home for years, but we didn't have a way to send them. We couldn't find one, until last week.'

'But how could you possibly—?' said Lulu, perplexed. 'You never left my side.'

He smiled. 'You made me quite angry, Miss Vexx—and suspicious. I asked questions about your family.'

Lulu grimaced. She had no doubt he'd heard plenty of sinister reports of their misdeeds—one or two of which might even be true.

'I hope you are not about to arrest me for murder, then,' she sighed. 'Or poor Father, either. He was irritated by Percy and Bell, and that absurd Lady Rondel—and I own he does not at all want to sell the castle, least of all to so benighted a person! But he gave up homicide many years ago.'

Inspector Shah's brows rose. 'Reassuring,' he remarked. 'No, Miss Vexx. I suspect you of a variety of mildly nefarious arts, but not murder. I am inclined to credit what you say of your mother.'

'Yes, and whereabouts is she?' asked Priya, brightly; as though she were enquiring as to the current pursuits of some once-favourite niece.

'Gone murdering somewhere else, I presume,' Lulu replied. 'She left with the Duke of Albion, though I haven't a notion how long she will remain with him.'

'The Duke of Albion,' echoed Inspector Shah.

'I'm afraid it was my fault,' Lulu admitted. 'Poor boy.'

'This seems to be quite the story,' said Priya.

'Quite,' said Lulu. 'Shall I offer you some tea? And then I will tell you all about it.'

11

Bread Every Day

'The weather continues fine,' wrote Lulu to herself. *'Mother continues missing, and murderous. Maxwell's macarons were particularly fine this week—delicate as clouds, and strawberry flavoured. I have no idea how she contrives it; some eldritch force at work, no doubt. I shall take some down into town, for I am nearly out of red paint. Minerfa continues industrious, though the castle continues cold. Father hasn't left the library for three days.*

Really, everything has been rather peaceful.

Yours ever,

Luna Vexx

She set down her pen, and left the thick cream pages of her private journal open atop the antique escritoire in her chamber, so the ink would dry. Not that it mattered; no one would read her words. She'd write her missives on letter-paper, if she had anywhere to send them. Talking to herself was...well, it was talking.

Morning sunshine pooled like liquid gold over the dark, cold floor of her room, a shimmering spot of brightness amidst the pervading gloom. She adored this season, late spring and summer; only then did the clouds part over Castle Drax, and a glimmer of something like warmth penetrate into the chill, dark bones of her ancestral home.

One got used to shivering, after a while.

She snaffled another of Magwell's macarons—she'd unwisely left her box of them open at her elbow, where their soft, pink colour and sweet fragrance could tempt and tempt her. Last one, no more: Lulu slammed the lid on them, savouring the final burst of fruity sweetness on her tongue, and took herself out the door before she could fall upon the remainder. She had better uses for these.

She went first downstairs to the musty, dusty cloakroom, and the sole functional mirror left in the castle, however fogged its ancient surface. Her sleekly shingled hair fell in neat, blonde waves around her face: good. Respectable enough, for a foray beyond the gates. Her tweed had seen better days, and her skirt had a tea-stain on it, but nothing much to regard. Lulu donned her best, no-nonsense manner and a charming smile borrowed (perhaps surprisingly) from her father, the Count, and went out to the garage.

The sun beamed down upon her, and so did Stormdust, merrily engaged in buffing and rebuffing the gleaming, dark green bonnet of the Vexx family's sole vehicle. It had been a handsome motorcar, once, and in its heyday a luxurious equipage. Nowadays it was out-of-date, and its workings could be unreliable. But at least it did work, thanks to Stormdust, a new member of the strange castle family whose passion for cars rivalled his fondness for heart-rending ballads.

His smart white coat was neither smart, nor white any longer, being liberally smeared with motor oil and other less identifiable substances. This troubled him not at all; he wore it with unimpaired pride; and, spotting Lulu tottering over the gravel drive in her neatest pair of heels, welcomed her with a broad smile and a merry ditty, sung in his rich baritone.

'It is a delightful morning, isn't it?' Lulu agreed. 'Stormdust, if you aren't terribly busy, shall you mind running me into town? I have an errand or two.'

'I CAN THINK OF NOTHING I'D RATHER BE DOING!' Stormdust answered with shattering emphasis.

He probably meant it, for he enjoyed driving the car almost as much as he enjoyed polishing it. 'Super,' smiled Lulu. 'Just down the hill and onto the high street, please.'

He drove well, for all that he had only learned the art recently. Slowly, of course; nothing could be permitted to risk damage to the perfect bodywork of his precious project. Lulu could almost have got there faster by walking, but she didn't mind. There was a curious pleasure to swishing along at a sedate pace in a gleaming green car, running her slim fingers lightly over the glossy walnut fittings and black leather upholstery. Sunlight glittered off the clear windows; the engine sleekly purred.

It was too early to encounter many of the good citizens of Andirac. Only a few pedestrians turned to stare as the huge motorcar glided past, and hurried to get out of the way of its inexorable, if slow, progress. The roads of Andirac had not been built for motorcars—nor for horse-drawn carriages, either. An old town, its origins several hundred years in the past, it was a poky sort of place, its streets narrow and winding.

Stormdust drew to a majestic stop at the top of the high street. Lulu waited; he liked to get out, liked to caress the bronzed handle as he opened the shining door for Miss Lulu, and lovingly push it to again after her.

'I shan't be very long, I should think,' smiled Lulu, and he performed a creditable doff of his peaked chauffeur's cap, a recent acquisition that had, unaccountably, delighted him.

'I shall await!' he declared, performing a little skip as he got back into the driver's seat.

Lulu sauntered. There was no rushing and bustling, not on such a shimmering morning. She waltzed at her leisure past the bakery, inhaling tantalising aromas of fresh-baked bread as she passed its stone-linteled door. The hairdresser's was nearly empty, only a single customer seated inside, having her dark hair set in waves.

Lulu lingered in the window of the bookshop, tempted to step inside. There would be something to interest her father, doubtless, and perhaps he'd be pleased. But new books were expensive, too much so; her mother's ill-judged party, staged to impress the monied set, had put paid to all such purchases for some time to come. She stepped hastily on, and came to Miss Lamarre's arts and crafts shop, a tall, narrow building sandwiched between Mr. Brummel's bookshop on one side, and the Luttrells' grocery shop on the other. Local black lava stone made up the base of the sturdy buildings, hewn in great, inelegant slabs. The remainder was built from hand-pressed bricks, pale grey, as if to balance out the darkness of their foundations. Since the cobbled street bore a similar hue, with the sloping roofs all clad in black slate, Andirac was a magpie of a town, black and pale, a chessboard of a place.

Miss Lamarre, with her eye for aesthetics, had heightened the striking effect with a window full of black-and-white stationery sets, glass bottles filled with black ink flanked by white marble pens, reams of black craft paper with a hint of glitter in it. On the other side of the door—set invitingly open—an array of paintings sought to catch the eyes of passersby. One caught Lulu's attention: a local artist's rendition of Andirac, with its huddle of dark slate roofs and bland brick facades; and, looming above in lone splendour, the hulking, black shadow of Castle Drax, imaginative whorls of storm-clouds swirling around its towers.

Lulu stepped inside. Miss Lamarre was occupied with a customer. Lulu heard her thin, fluting voice the moment she crossed the threshold—'Sold out of the peacock-blue, ma'am, but more arriving next week—the lavender, now, there's some silk in it, very fine—and how is dear Bertie enjoying the new paintbox—?'

Lulu amused herself by drifting through the proffered landscapes. Most of them were not accomplished pieces—the work of local amateurs, hopeful of a sale. But there was another of the castle, painted, she thought, by the same hand as the one in the window. It depicted Castle Drax from rather closer by, omitting the town, and featuring instead the green expanse of the sunlit sea. No storm-clouds, here; it almost, really almost, made the castle look pleasant.

'That one!' uttered Miss Lamarre, coming up behind Lulu. 'Yes, it is rather lovely, isn't it? Terribly popular, these pieces. I can't keep them in stock.'

Patently untrue, since she had at least two in her possession. Exaggeration, though, was her nature, and sales her business. Lulu found a smile for her, and offered the sweet-smelling box.

'A little delivery,' she announced. 'Magwell's best yet, I do believe.'

Miss Lamarre was not elderly, not yet, but her body would catch up to her spirit soon enough. She held herself as though she were fragile, perhaps arthritic, and dressed in the loose, comfortable velvet gowns of a woman too old to care for fashion, and too eccentric to array herself in drab. A wide-brimmed hat, thick with blue glass beads, framed her narrow face; the straggling brown hair beneath it hadn't been brushed in days. 'Darling of you!' she trilled, taking the box. 'One of these days I shall coax your excellent Magwell out of that gloomy old place and have her come and live with me. See if I don't.'

'It may seem strange, but Magwell's devoted to the castle,' Lulu replied. 'It suits her very nicely.'

Miss Lamarre dismissed this improbable revelation with a disdainful sniff. 'Well, dear, what shall it be today? I have a lovely palette of blacks and greys just come in—'

'Red, please,' Lulu said quickly. 'Reds and pinks, if you have them.'

Miss Lamarre plainly considered Lulu incapable of comprehending colour, given her choice of abode, but she produced the red watercolours with only a moderate little show of surprise. 'I'll keep a good set of the black for you,' she promised, 'for the next time Magwell bakes.'

Lulu was polite enough to thank her for this, though without committing to the deal. 'Who paints those landscapes?' she asked, on the point of leaving. 'The ones with Castle Drax.'

'Interested, are you?' Miss Lamarre's eyes gleamed. 'They aren't cheap, dear, I must tell you.'

'I don't want to buy them,' Lulu interjected hastily. 'Well—that is, I daresay I should be happy to, whenever I am in funds, but at present I am merely—curious.' The two landscapes, besides being by far more competently painted than any other in the shop, had a flair to them, a bright spirit, that brought out the very best of her home, storm-clouds included.

'Truth to tell, I hardly know,' Miss Lamarre admitted. 'They're sent to me by post, and I pay for them the same way. I have never met the artist.'

Lulu pondered this. 'They sell for a lot, do they?'

'Oh, quite a pretty penny,' chuckled Miss Lamarre, and named a sum that raised Lulu's manicured eyebrows near into her hair.

'I don't suppose I could have the address, could I?' she ventured. 'I'd very much like to meet the person with such talent.'

'You aren't planning to poach my best painter away from me, I should hope?' Miss Lamarre's pleasantness dimmed, a hint of steel replacing the soft, fluting quality of her voice.

'Not at all,' Lulu assured her, hoping she spoke truly.

'Well, then.' Miss Lamarre went away, and returned a few minutes later with a square of paper in her long-fingered hands. An address was inscribed upon it in quite the most perfect calligraphy Lulu had ever seen.

'There you are, dear,' said the lady, nodding significantly as she handed it over. 'Calligraphy classes weekly, mornings or evenings, to suit your schedule.'

Lulu thanked her, remembering to exhibit just enough interest in the classes to be polite, but not enough to raise fixed expectations, and left.

Stormdust, true to his word, remained elegantly parked a short way up the street. He had attracted a gaggle of young boys and girls, all far too enchanted with the shining motorcar to feel any dismay at its driver's broad, odd face or unusual complexion. Stormdust had lent his peaked cap to a rotund child with a missing tooth proudly displayed by a wide, beaming smile.

The children scattered as Lulu approached, leaving her to consider this vision of herself as a far more alarming prospect than Stormdust.

'Got what you wanted, Miss?' asked Stormdust, settling his treasured black cap back onto his head.

'That, and more,' Lulu said, and handed him the note with the address. 'Do you think we could find this house? It could be important.'

Stormdust fingered the thick, textured paper, and smiled down at the sharp black lines of the text. 'Prettiest of pretties,' he noted.

'Yes, madam at the shop teaches calligraphy, if you're interested. But the address?'

'Calligraphy,' repeated Stormdust, rolling the syllables around his mouth. 'The address. Yes! Yes, the address.' He got back behind the wheel, then popped out again to open the door for Lulu. 'In a trice, nothing easier,' he assured her, which surprised her a little, for when had Stormdust had occasion to learn the layout of Andirac?

He hadn't, as it transpired. They veered ponderously about the narrow streets, scattering pedestrians and pigeons alike, until Lulu spoke up from the expansive back seat, 'Left there, I think.' Her hazy knowledge, plus an occasional smiling interrogation of a passerby, brought them at length to a street so cramped, Stormdust was obliged to park the unnecessarily large vehicle near the mouth of it, leaving Lulu to venture along it on foot.

Not among the more salubrious areas of the town, but Lulu was too accustomed to peeling paint, begrimed black stone, and the dirt of years crusted in filmy layers, to much regard the state of it. She went at a brisk pace, her heels ringing on the cobbles, ducking under overhanging garrets so low, and so closely crowded, as to virtually merge the opposing rows of houses. Aromas of fried cabbage and woodsmoke attended her as far as number 27, a cramped dwelling of grey brick streaked by rain and soot to a hue of near black.

Lulu rapped smartly on the knockerless front door, dislodging a wisp of faded blue paint. A heavy silence answered her, and lingered long after her second knock.

Her third prompted a shout from above. A square window banged open; there appeared in its aperture a face, thin as a rake, and flushed with annoyance. This upper storey hung so far over the street, Lulu could have handed the stranger a cup of tea without spilling a drop. 'No!' barked this incensed person. 'I don't have it!'

'What don't you have?' Lulu enquired mildly, mentally adjusting her expectations of Miss Lamarre's mysterious painter. The sharp-boned face was young, frightfully so, and framed by a tangled cloud of mouse-brown hair. The voice was light, youthful, feminine, and, under the annoyance, shrill with something like fear.

'The money!' the painter replied. A gust of wind clattered the weathered shutters, and blew her hair over her face; she left a streak of greyish paint behind when, with an impatient swipe, she shoved it out of her eyes. 'I don't know who it is you come from or what I owe you for, but I haven't got it. Go away.'

A novel approach to debt collectors; Lulu had never tried it. She wondered idly if it worked. 'I'm not here about a bill,' she said, holding up her empty hands to demonstrate a lack of sinister papers. 'My name is Lulu Vexx and I am here about your paintings.'

'My...paintings.'

'You are the one who painted such exquisite views of the castle, aren't you?' In case of any possible confusion, Lulu pointed upwards and behind herself, where the monstrous shadow that was Castle Drax eternally loomed.

'Exquisite?' The girl seemed speechless, if only for a moment. Then her hard little eyes narrowed. 'What did you say your name was?'

'Luna Vexx. Lulu.'

'Very funny.' Before Lulu could stop her, the girl slammed shut her window. A rain of ancient paint drifted down in flakes.

Lulu, unaccustomed to having doors—or windows—shut in her face (except by her father, of course) lingered a moment in the street, nonplussed. She was unused to going unrecognised, either; to be sure, the Vexxes did not often venture out of their ferocious abode, but they had been haunting the town of Andirac for generations. Besides, Lulu's face and profile had been liberally circulated through a number of local papers and magazines, not so long ago. She'd made sure of it.

'If you'd like to hear my proposition,' she finally called, 'come up to the castle, anytime.' She knocked what she hoped was a cheery farewell upon the shabby front door, and went away to her car.

Stormdust regarded her gravely as he held the door for her. 'Madam, you appear quite put out,' he observed. 'And you have blue dust in your hair.'

'Paint,' Lulu sighed. 'Someone slammed a window on me, and it was shedding like a dog.' She was feeling rather put out, now that he mentioned it; why? The girl owed her nothing. Lulu shook it off, and retrieved her smile. She instantly felt better.

'You will carry your point,' offered Stormdust as he started up the car. 'It is the most certain of certainties.'

Perhaps she would; but first she would have to determine what her point was going to be.

The new red paint glided over Lulu's reclaimed canvas like satin over skin. Finer quality than any she had yet owned; its value must exceed that of a box of macarons, however good the confectionery may be. She was fortunate that Miss Lamarre possessed a sweet tooth.

She had got some of it on the tatty cotton lawn of her painting smock already, wasting it. Too good for that. Lulu slowed her hand, outlining her imagined sunset in streaks of coquelicot and raspberry. Lurid, no matter how carefully she daubed the whorls of colour—and anyway, it clashed with the emerald waves of her wind-tossed sea. She sighed, and dropped her paintbrush into the water jar. She did so love to paint, and yet her hands and her eyes could not muster between them a modicum of the skill she would like to command. What was it that had so enlivened the compositions she'd seen at the arts and crafts shop? Some elusive quality, forever beyond her.

A sharp wind whistled through the absent panes of the windows, and Lulu shivered in her thin smock. Aunt Maud had painted up here every day of her short life, turning out imagined (and often horrifying) tableaus as inferior in quality as Lulu's. The brisk flow of air had inspired her, perhaps, for the missing panes had never been replaced, or boarded up. The light, at least, was good, though Maud's creations remained impenetrably dark. They languished, now, in a great iron-bound trunk in the attic, locked out of sight and mind both. 'I had to put up with her nonsense in life,' Count Vexx had once declared. 'I'll be damned if I'll put up with it after she's dead, too.' Lulu's paintings would suffer no such ignominious fate, she knew; her fond parent would, in all probability, throw them straight onto his beloved acid-green witchfire.

She was halfway out of her smock when the cacophonous tones of the lugubrious doorbell thundered through the floor. That was the trouble with hauling the castle out of the past; it had been a lot quieter, before.

Lulu clattered downstairs, tugging the flapping sleeves of an ancient cardigan over her arms as she ran. She had paint on her face; she could feel it, a dry, crusty spot on her cheek. She was still rubbing at it when she arrived in the great hall, and found Fane towering over whoever had been so unwise as to call.

'There is a person here, Miss Lulu,' he announced, pronouncing the word "person" with awful emphasis. 'To see you, Miss.'

Dwarfed by the soaring arch of the massive front door, and by the unusual height of the butler who'd opened it, stood Lulu's acquaintance from Andirac. Her eyes were very wide and she stood still as a rock—perhaps because the discordant tones of the doorbell's grand fanfare had yet to quite die away.

'You really are a Vexx,' said the girl, without seeming either pleased or otherwise by the idea.

'A meagre specimen of the breed,' Lulu agreed, smiling. 'How do you do?'

'You've got paint on your face.'

Lulu scrubbed at her cheek again. "I was painting. Trying to. Won't you come in?'

The girl lingered on the wide black stone of the doorstep—one might even say she skulked, warily. Lulu plainly read unease in the bony angles of her body.

'We won't eat you,' Lulu assured her. 'Shall you, Fane?'

'I never eat young ladies, Miss. Certainly not before luncheon.'

'Do you think you might contrive to rustle up some more macarons?' Lulu ventured. Noting the increase of interest in her guest—and the hungry lines of her fine-boned face—Lulu amended, 'And sandwiches? Plenty of them.'

'Magwell's just bringing out a batch of fresh rolls,' said Fane, smiling—perhaps unwisely—at the young lady. 'And the hens have laid well this week. Egg sandwiches, young miss, and speedily.' Fane performed his most elegant bow and lumbered away, leaving the young miss in question staring after him.

'And you *live* here?' she said, shrill with incredulity.

'It really isn't as bad as all that,' Lulu replied. 'There are moments where it's even quite pleasant.'

The girl extended one scuffed boot, and, with the air of a person waiting, at any moment, to be savaged, she stepped over the threshold. When moments ticked by and nothing untoward occurred, her shoulders marginally relaxed. 'So,' she said, drifting over to the massive black marble hearth, and the blaze that roared, invitingly, greenishly, within it, 'What am I doing here?'

'Well,' Lulu began, 'I was hoping you might—'

'This isn't even warm,' interrupted the girl, snatching back the hands she'd held out towards the fire. 'It's freezing. What kind of a place is this?'

'The Seventh Circle of Hell,' said Lulu. 'A small adjunct.'

'No. I mean really.'

Lulu shrugged. 'It's Castle Drax. The sandwiches are this way.' Hunger defeated curiosity; the indignant girl, blowing frostbite from her fingertips, followed in Lulu's wake.

Fane had taken a shine to their unusual visitor. This was clear from the statuesque proportions of the sandwich platter he brought in, stacked almost as tall as she was with still-steaming rolls. He brought strawberry macarons, too, and a large porcelain jug brimming with milk.

Their guest—Cleo, she thickly revealed around a mouthful of egg—ate her own weight in bread and sweets, and gulped at least half of the milk. Lulu watched her bolting food, intrigued and increasingly puzzled. Hadn't Miss Lamarre said her paintings sold for a high price?

'If this is about my work,' said Cleo when she had, at last, sated herself, 'I can't help you. I have an—(she belched)—agreement with a prestigious vendor.'

'The arts and crafts shop,' Lulu nodded. 'That's where I saw your paintings.'

Cleo scowled. 'Well? What, then?'

'I was hoping,' Lulu said, feeling a strange stab of diffidence, 'that you might teach me.'

Cleo, distracted by a stray strawberry-flavoured crumb, crunched through the words: 'What? Teach you what?'

'To paint. As well as you do.'

Large, famished eyes met hers. Cleo considered her, sizing up Miss Vexx as though she was a cow she was thinking of buying. 'Why?'

'Because I love to do it,' Lulu replied.

'And?'

'Cannot I engage in art merely for the love of it?'

'Not with a castle the size of a small town falling down around your ears.'

She was astute, this one. Lulu's smile was rueful. 'Very well. I might also have hopes of being able, some-day, to sell some of my work.'

'It won't pay for this place.' Cleo's thin mouth twist-ed. 'Won't even feed you, most like.'

'Miss Lamarre led me to believe your paintings command good prices?'

'She was having you on. Or she's swindling me.' Cleo gnawed on a ragged fingernail. 'Do you suppose she's swindling me? The rat.'

Lulu thought of Miss Lamarre's mild, if odd, manner, and the inflection of her words. 'I think it more likely she was trying to fleece me,' Lulu decided. 'One would expect a chatelaine to have money to spare.'

Cleo snorted. 'She hasn't been paying much attention then, has she.'

'But you have.'

'I like the castle.' Cleo's tone turned defensive. 'Purely artistically, I mean.'

'So do I.' Lulu turned the tarnished silver platter, offering Cleo the dregs of the sandwich tower. 'Here's my offer. Teach me to paint, and in return you may have room here, and board.'

Cleo snatched a sandwich. 'Bread every day?'

'Magwell bakes every morning.'

'Eggs and fancy pastries?'

'Not every day, but sometimes.'

'Horrifying green ice-fire all my own?'

'I'd have to ask Father about that, but I daresay—'

'I'm joking. I'm not *crazy*.' She thrust out her jaw, as pugnacious as a competitive boxer. 'I can't think of anything I'd like more.'

Lulu waited. The words were positive, but an oceans-deep anger laced the words; had she misstepped? Painting aside, she had no desire to send this bruised and half-starved child back to her comfortless berth, not if she could prevent it.

'Would you...like to see your rooms?' Lulu ventured, after a long silence.

Cleo stared at her, blank-faced. 'Rooms? Plural?'

Lulu gestured, vaguely, the sweep of her hand taking in the entirety of the vast bulk that was Castle Drax. 'We are not overwhelmed with advantages, at present,' she said, 'but we do have rather a lot of space.'

Adding Cleo to the ragtag muddle of Draxian residents proved so simple a process, Lulu's heart sagged like a wet paper bag. She had almost nothing to retrieve from the crooked little house in town; her stock of garments filled scarcely half of the portmanteau Lulu gave her to carry them, and her paintbrushes, palettes, and precious stock of canvas, frame wood, and pigments took up the rest. She had nothing else worth the salvaging.

Lulu gave her a suite of four connecting chambers in the east wing. Cleo liked to paint in the mornings, so the light would be ideal, and she'd chosen rooms with long, wide windows and high ceilings. True, they remained drafty, icy, and black as the depths of Hell, but Cleo took to them—and a small wardrobe of Lady Vexx's outdated but sound dresses—like a proverbial duck to a pond full of breadcrumbs.

It took a week for Miss Lamarre to learn of this development. A note then arrived for "Miss Luna Vexx", perfectly inscribed on lavender paper emanating a delicate scent of lilac.

It would pain me to discover that the promises of the Honourable are anything but, she had written. *Pray unhand my star painter, kindest regards, Avril Lamarre.*

Lulu penned an exquisite reply on thick ivory parchment embellished with painstakingly inked stars:

Castle Drax's painting salons require a reliable supplier of canvas, paint, brushes, and accoutrements, can we interest you?

PS Magwell is looking for a sophisticated outlet for her new line of patisserie. Someone with prominent premises in Andirac, perhaps?

12

Melancholia

Perhaps it was a consequence of a change in the weather, which had manifested an iron-dark sky and frankly excessive quantity of thunderous rain clouds. Perhaps it was the result of Count Vexx's own mental furniture, which despite its various brilliances possessed a strong tendency towards melancholy.

Perhaps it was something else entirely, beyond Lulu's capacity to understand or anticipate; regardless of the cause, her noble father was patently *in a mood*, and the plaintive strains of wailing, woeful jazz reverberated around Castle Drax to prove it. He'd taken to the gramophone again.

The lachrymose tones emanated from the other side of the emphatically closed library door, a soft emerald glow shining, green and strange, through the arched fanlight. Lulu found myriad reasons to pass down the corridor, in case the sound of her brisk footsteps might put her father in mind of anything he might need. Fane had a similar idea;

he had stationed his towering self to the left of the door, his long, lined face grave as a vicar at a funeral.

Lulu, passing for the fifth time with (on this occasion) an armful of darned linens urgently requiring relocation, paused at the door and listened.

Besides the mournful notes of a clarinet and the slow thud of drums, nothing: from the Count, a sepulchral silence.

Lulu exchanged a glance with Fane. Concern lurked in his pale, rheumy eyes, echoing her own.

'I hardly know what to do for him,' she murmured.

Fane shook his grey head. 'Nothing to be done, Miss, but wait.'

He spoke the truth. To suffer alone was her father's way, impatiently repelling any and all attempts at comfort or commiseration. He would emerge later, or tomorrow, his mask of smooth unconcern restored, mildly irascible in his customary fashion, and resistant to any reference to his indisposition.

Until then, a pall of palpable gloom would linger in the hallways of Castle Drax. Already shadows roiled in the corners and coiled about the polished black banisters; no light could dispel them, however bright or enthusiastically wielded. When Lady Vexx had left, the castle had been plunged into near total darkness; after Lulu's third tumble down one staircase or another, she had gone about for weeks with Magwell's apron-strings tied into the sash of her floral dresses, without which she would likely have broken her infant neck.

It had never got so bad as that again; and yet Lulu feared that this spell of misery had much to do with her mother, once again. She hesitated, lifted her knuckles, almost went so far as to knock—

Fane shook his head, his mouth a thin line. 'Best not to, Miss.'

Lulu permitted herself a small sigh. In all probability, however, the Count would soon recover, and so would the castle; cheered by the thought, she hefted her stack of ancient sheets and turned—

'Luna.' The Count's voice, pitched low. 'I don't know what you intend by dancing about in front of my library, but you may either go away or come in.'

Come in! No gracious invitation, but an invitation nonetheless. Lulu handed her linens to Fane, who instinctively caught them in his large, gnarled hands, and turned the doorknob directly.

The library lay shrouded in dense shadow, broken only by the eerie, green glimmer of a witchfire in the hearth. The hundreds of leather-bound volumes in their neat rows were a hypothetical presence; nothing could be seen of the silver-gilded bookshelves, and the black-gleaming tiles of the floor melded seamlessly with the gloom. It was like falling into a bank of stygian fog, Count Vexx's pale face floating in the midst as though severed from all bodily concerns. He was scowling.

'Hello, Father,' said Lulu, stepping carefully through the murk. 'Is there anything I can do to improve what I perceive to be a difficult mood?'

'You may leave me in peace,' he replied coolly. 'And quiet.'

'That doesn't appear to be helping. At this rate, half the castle will be shadow-drowned.'

'What of that? The damned place is black as your mother's heart as it is.'

'I thought this was about Mother,' said Lulu. 'I am certain she isn't worth this much regret.'

'Who said anything about regret? I couldn't be happier she's gone.'

'If only she hadn't left with a rich, handsome, and much younger man, leaving three fresh corpses behind her?' Lulu guessed.

The Count maintained a lofty silence.

'Come, Father. No one could be more sympathetic to your feelings than me—'

'I have no feelings,' interjected Count Vexx.

'—But this wallowing isn't at all good for you, nor is it good for the castle. I can hear the walls weeping from here.'

The Count sat up in a rustle of dark cloth. The pallid moon of his face dimly registered resolve. 'You're right,' he declared, to her speechless surprise. 'I should do something productive about it.'

Conscious of a sinking feeling of nameless dread, Lulu mustered her wits. 'What do you have in mind?' she said cautiously. 'The weather continues favourable; perhaps a walk in the grounds—'

'I shall go and find her.'

'What? Father, you cannot possibly want her back,' Lulu blurted, all thought of diplomacy lost to shock.

'Of course not.' He was recovering his spirits rapidly; Lulu read it in the crisp coolness of his tone, not to mention a noticeable reduction in the hellish black shroud. A book or two emerged from the fog, and traces of silver gilt.

So why then did she feel that everything had just got significantly worse?

'Then why do you want to find Mother?' she ventured.

'So I can kill her.'

Lulu's heart plummeted into her shoes. 'Father, no. Vengeance is never the answer—'

'Some might term it justice,' he returned, out of his tall, dark chair and smoothing the rumpled folds of his suit.

'Justice is the province of the police,' she tried. 'And I might remind you that we already have an inconveniently sharp Detective Inspector in pursuit. He will certainly find you out—'

'Then I will deal with him, too. Pray do not pester me with trifles; I have far too much to do.' The fog was rolling away in waves now, permitting Lulu all too clear a view of her noble parent's visage. She might, if pressed, term his expression "diabolically gleeful".

'You gave up homicide! It's terribly bad for your health!'

'On the contrary, it is excellent exercise, and thoroughly invigorating. Just the ticket to perk me up, I should say.' He grinned at his daughter, fiendish in aspect, and before she could muster any further remonstrance he had gone out of the room.

Lulu trailed after. Fane, taken by surprise, lingered still by the door, staring after the suddenly ambulatory count with palpable shock. 'Very well done, Miss Lulu!' he told her. 'Very well done, indeed!'

'No,' Lulu sighed, and slumped against the bone-chillingly cold, black wall. 'I've made everything much worse.'

Lulu had wild thoughts of speeding after her father and arresting, somehow, his determined hunt of her mother. She might be able to persuade him—no, nothing could change his mind once he got into this stubborn state of resolve. She could sabotage the motorcar in some fashion? Or, more likely, persuade Stormdust to do it, for she knew little about motors, and must—for practicality's sake—draw a line at carving holes in the tires. She could—well, she could possibly...

No. There was nothing she could do here to avert disaster. Her father, once roused, was a force of nature; nothing would stop him now save a similar power raised against him. Lulu had no such pretensions.

She attempted instead to put the matter out of her mind, and returned to her work. Magwell had spent two days in her kitchen, turning out macarons and madeleines of exquisite delicacy. Lulu had already lent a hand in measuring, mixing, piping, and baking; she went back into Magwell's territory now, leaving Fane keeping solitary vigil by the arched and massive front door, against her father's possible return.

Magwell did not labour alone. Cleo and, to Lulu's particular surprise, Minerfa bent over the huge oaken table, carefully lowering lavender-scented macarons and the fragile fan-shapes of madeleines into petite cardboard boxes. Minerfa, for all her facility with the tools of heavy utility, possessed a deft touch with a length of ribbon; she was finishing each pretty package with gracefully twisted bows. Cleo, stacking macarons, surreptitiously filched one, and scoffed it. Lulu let it pass. The girl had been famished for months, if not years; it would take some time before a glow of health softened the bones of her sharp-featured face.

'Everything going well here, I hope?' said Lulu, with a lightness she didn't quite feel. *Please* let everything be going well *somewhere*.

Dora, one of Magwell's neat, black hens, lifted her beak and clucked confirmation. She lay near the blazing stove, her dark feathers partially covered by a thick jacket hand-knitted in crimson yarn.

'Good,' sighed Lulu in relief.

Magwell looked up from a sheaf of papers. She wore a stained apron over the rotund bulk of her belly, her brass-framed pince-nez pinching the bridge of her broad nose. 'Something the matter, lovie?' she rumbled.

'Not a thing,' Lulu answered brightly, unwilling to spread her hopefully baseless unease to this tranquil group. 'What's that you've got there?'

Magwell scratched a few figures into the paper before her, the nib of her pencil squeaking. 'I'm reckoning costs. They are steep, I must tell you.'

Fashioning perfect delicacies and presenting them attractively was no cheap endeavour, Lulu well knew. She'd got the boxes and ribbon from Miss Lamarre, who would also employ her delectable calligraphy skills to inscribe labels for the goods. Lulu had instructed her to title them "Draxian Delights". In exchange for these things—and the use of her premises in Andirac to sell them—the owner of the town's arts and crafts shop would receive twenty percent of receipts.

The remainder would have to cover the costs of all the fine-milled flour, highly refined sugar, ground almonds, fresh lemons, good quality butter and extra eggs for the making of the sweets. Some of the eggs had been contributed by Magwell's hens, at least, and Lulu had gathered all of the lavender from the shambles once known as the shrubbery.

She was hoping for a reasonable profit, but that would require setting high prices. It was a gamble, one that may or may not pay off.

'Miss Lamarre has doubled my proposed prices,' Lulu offered. 'She knows her market, so I am hopeful.'

Cleo snorted. Some of her own paintings had been sold by that same lady; the two had an ongoing disagreement as to their value. 'Careful she don't swindle you,' she said.

'I shall require a meticulous accounting,' Lulu replied. 'And I shall check on the boxes myself, next week. Can I help?'

'Oh, no. We don't need you at all,' said Minerfa, completing another bow with a flourish.

'Please give me something simple to do,' Lulu begged. She didn't want to be left rattling about the castle alone, fretting over her father's antics. She had far rather remain in the warm and cosy kitchen, among the comforting presence of the other women, deedily occupied.

Magwell gave her a sharp look through the thick glass of her lenses, but made no further enquiry. 'You can start on the pastry for dinner, if you like,' and she indicated a covered ceramic bowl waiting at the far end of the table. It was filled with white flour. A smaller sorceldish sat next to it, heaped with yellow cubes of butter. The frigid green flames of witchfire coiled up the dish's silver sides, leaving an intricate pattern of frost.

'I've already put the salt in,' said Magwell, and went back to her reckoning.

Lulu scrubbed her hands, then dug them gratefully into a mess of butter and flour. She felt soothed, at least for now. Knowing Count Vexx, he would not permit her to languish long in so tranquil a state.

A week passed, and the master of Castle Drax did not return. Lulu's state of palpitating apprehension dissipated after a day or two, when no fresh calamity occurred. She had far too many claims on her attention to continue squandering it on her father's doings; there were the beribboned boxes to be delivered to the arts and crafts shop, fresh foragings to be gleaned from the wilds surrounding the house, an endless deluge of cleaning, mopping, dusting, and mending to undertake, and schemes for the financial salvation of the castle to dream up.

Three days after the Count's departure, Minerfa, in the midst of her interminable attempts to manufacture a heating system, contrived to flood the cellars (somehow). The rest of the day was spent in mopping up swathes of brackish water, smelling, faintly and ominously, of sulphur.

After several more days spent in similar frantic fashion, Lulu had almost forgotten about her father's homicidal mission. She was reminded of it, abruptly and horribly, when Fane came thundering down the staircase to the kitchen—recognisable by his galumphing and irregular tread—and burst into the midst of a cosy, if brisk, construction party turning mounds of sweet pastry and frangipane into tartlets.

'The Master's back,' Fane gasped, purple with exertion. 'But he's got—he's with—' The overextended butler lost the power of speech, and doubled over in a wheezing attempt to regain it.

Lulu didn't wait. Who could her father possibly be with that had prompted such an extraordinary reaction from the mild and mellow Fane? Her thoughts flew to her mother; her stomach flipped accordingly. She dropped her ball of pastry dough into a dusting of flour, scrubbed her hands on the voluminous apron she'd borrowed from Magwell, and hurtled up the stairs.

She heard Count Vexx's voice before she reached the great hall. '—Good of you to escort me, I daresay, but I require nothing further. Do have a safe journey back to the precinct, won't you?' Bitingly cold and dripping with sarcasm: his lordship, at least, was hale. But the precinct...?

Lulu burst in just as Inspector Shah replied: 'Not an escort, I'm afraid, and I won't be going anywhere just yet. I did mention you are liable to be arrested?'

Count Vexx beheld his daughter's arrival with a cool lack of interest, though the tightness in his sculpted face relaxed a fraction: what passed for a welcome, with him. 'Ah, Lulu. Pray deal with this fellow, if you please? I have urgent business to attend to.'

He'd said "please", a fact which rather deepened than assuaged Lulu's feelings of foreboding. He looked dishevelled, which enhanced the general effect; his hair hadn't been oiled lately, or even brushed, and his dark suit bore the stains of several days' wear. The "urgent business" in question likely meant a bath and a change of clothing.

Inspector Shah, by contrast, was a pinstriped paragon of excellent male grooming, and glowering at her from beneath the dark blue brim of his fedora. 'Miss Vexx. I am sorry to inform you that your father was discovered breaking into private premises—'

'An absurd misunderstanding,' Count Vexx interrupted.

'—With, I have reason to believe, the settled intention of causing severe bodily harm to its residents.'

'I have no idea why you should imagine any such thing,' returned the Count in freezing tones.

'You climbed over a wall into the Duke of Albion's gardens and were intercepted with several knives about your person.'

'Oh, Father,' Lulu sighed.

'That may be true, but there wasn't the smallest chance of my using them.' Count Vexx bristled with indignation, though whether at the notion of his descending to such vulgarities as to stab a person to death with his own hands, or from some other cause, was unclear.

'And why was that?' pressed Inspector Shah.

'Because,' bit out the Count, 'she wasn't there.' With which words he stalked off, ascending the wide stone steps of the grand staircase with an implacable resolve to escape. His footsteps split the air like the strokes of an axe.

'I believe he speaks truly, for what it is worth,' Lulu offered. 'He was never going to hurt the Duke, or any of his family or staff.'

'Then whom did he mean by "she"?' demanded the Inspector, his dark eyes glinting with the kind of impatient fury the Count so often inspired.

'Well,' Lulu hesitated. 'I think if he committed no crime then I ought not to say anything more.'

'He committed the crime of trespass,' Shah corrected her. 'And he clearly planned to hurt *someone*.'

'I do not believe that it is considered a crime to *want* to hurt someone,' Lulu countered. 'Or a great many of us would be guilty of a felony every time we lost our temper.'

'Oh?' Shah's face softened, slightly, as he considered hers. 'Have *you* experienced such urges often?' His tone patently expressed disbelief in the very idea.

Lulu smiled winningly. 'Frequently,' she assured him. 'But then, I am a Vexx.'

'So you are,' he murmured. 'And so is your mother, whom I collect is the target of the Count's present anger.'

'She did behave rather badly,' Lulu admitted. 'Even for a Vexx.'

'Her whereabouts is, at present, unknown,' said the Inspector. 'Unfortunately. If you should hear of anything—'

'Are you asking me to turn my own mother over to the police?' Lulu interposed, assembling her features, as best she could, into an expression of outrage.

'Yes,' came the implacable reply.

Lulu's indignation dissolved into a sigh. 'Yes, I suppose I shall.'

'Better that than permit your father to take matters into his own hands,' Shah pointed out.

'I cannot disagree there.'

'I am sympathetic to the difficulty,' Shah said, surprising her. 'Family matters are complicated, are they not?' He didn't wait for her reply, merely doffed his fedora and took his leave. Lulu heard the purr of a motor and the scrunch of tires as he drove away.

She knew better than to bother her father, just yet. He wouldn't be approachable until he'd bathed, at the very least, and fresh arranged his hair. But she went into the library and plumped up the velvet cushions that padded his favourite, high-backed chair; summoned the cold, green witchfire back to blazing life with a flick of her long fingers; and collected a trail of discarded books into a neat stack atop the ebony table beside the chair. She would send Fane in with a hot beverage, shortly, and a meal of the simple foods her father preferred. After all that, he'd be human again, she hoped. More or less.

Prepared for a return of the all-encompassing gloom, Lulu was pleasantly surprised to wake to a castle only partially shrouded in shadow. She could see her way along the high-ceilinged corridor from her own room to the stairs, and stood in no danger of falling down the latter, for there they all were, black as pitch but no more than usual. A few umbral tendrils coiled about the banisters and writhed about the floor, but nothing to give her any alarm. Her father's melancholia abated then, somewhat. Another day, and he would be quite back to normal—and he hadn't even had to slaughter anybody for it. Lulu clattered down to the kitchens in buoyant spirits, and carolled her greeting to Magwell, who was already taking a batch of steaming loaves out of the great oven, in jubilant tones.

'What's got you so cheerful, then?' said Magwell, setting her neatly plaited loaves side-by-side on a wire rack, to cool. Lulu breathed in a lungful of their fresh-baked aroma, smiling.

'Oh, I have been terribly anxious about Father, but he's getting much better.'

Magwell stared meaningfully at a boiling mass of gnarly shadow, disporting itself under the massive oaken table.

Lulu bent to survey it, dubious. 'Well, he is not entirely recovered yet, to be sure, but they do seem much diminished since yesterday?'

'It's more that they seem unusually lively.' Magwell covered her loaves with a blue cotton tea towel, and began breaking fresh eggs into a jug.

They did, now that Lulu came to think about it. Usually her father's shadows sulked rather than writhed, shifting and drifting with the slow roil of a fog bank. These had more the energy of storm clouds preparing to let loose.

Lulu's cheerful mood dissipated like mist in a brisk wind. She paused with one rubber boot on, half out the door to feed the chickens. 'I had better check on him,' she decided, and kicked the boot off again. 'Have you seen him this morning?'

Magwell shook her head. 'Take a loaf,' she said, pointing with a fork. 'One with raisins in.'

Lulu scooped up a warm and fragrant plait of bread, breaking off a small bit for herself as she barrelled back up the stairs; she was famished. Magwell hadn't spared the butter in these; the bread melted in her mouth, rich and golden and fruity. If that couldn't please her father, he had gone beyond the power of anything edible to recall him.

She pushed through the door into the library, already talking. 'Father, good morning! Magwell sends you a loaf and her best love, and I—' She stopped, for he wasn't there. The hearth lay dark and empty, the dark floor untouched by so much as a lick of frost. Books lay scattered about the half-shadowed floor, as though he had hurled them there in a fit of frustration.

'Father?' she called, in case he had, by some means, evaded her notice. But no one answered, and she left the room again at a near run.

He was not up in his preferred gallery, pacing; nor in his rooms, still asleep. He wasn't in the cellar, hammering at something with Minerfa, nor out in the garage with Stormdust, buffing up his motorcar. Cleo, painting in her atelier, protested against having seen him in days, and poor Fane—

'There's something badly wrong in all this, Miss,' said the steady old butler, exhibiting an unusual degree of perturbation.

They searched every inch of Castle Drax, the six of them, a process requiring some hours to complete. After that, the grounds, as best they could; some of it remained too thick with ivy and brambles to penetrate, but the same obstacle would have prevented Count Vexx.

By the time the sun set over Andirac, the Count's total absence could no longer be denied. The family collected miserably in the kitchen, clinging to warmth and company alike.

Minerfa, untouched—but appreciative of Magwell's loaves—said with unimpaired cheer, 'I am sure there is no need for all this concern. In all probability he is already dead, and it is far too late to be worrying about it now.'

Cleo snatched the bread out of her hands, and slathered cherry jam on it. 'How very reassuring,' she said, around an oozing mouthful.

'Yes,' answered Minerfa, taking another roll. 'I was always accounted rather good at that.'

Fane had no appetite, not even for Magwell's baking. Nor did Lulu. Even Stormdust made a subdued figure, perched atop a stool in a corner far from the stove, with a black fog curling around his shoes. He had not driven the Count anywhere, Lulu knew; not since his return to the castle by Inspector Shah. If Count Vexx had left, he had done so on foot, and at night. Such behaviour was so utterly out of character for him that Lulu could hardly suppose it possible.

That left only one plausible option, however unlikely it may be. She and Fane and Magwell knew it—Stormdust too, probably. She read it in their studious avoidance of the subject, no matter how many times the question of the Count's absence was rehashed.

Lulu, slumped in a weary heap over an untouched plate of fruit bread, finally roused herself. 'It's no use,' she said, and got down from the stool she'd drawn up to the scrubbed oak table. 'Avoiding the truth cannot alter it.' She went out of the room as she spoke, for now that she had mustered her resolve she would not permit herself to stop. Not until she knew.

Fane came behind her, his long, slow stride a comforting accompaniment to her own, light step. 'I'll go with you, Miss,' he said gravely, and Lulu managed a smile for him.

She took an old oil lamp from a atop a dusty chest of drawers, and carried it, lit and pungent, down into the darkness of the cellar. She rarely came down here, and never at night, for the impenetrable darkness smothered her, and the cold bore the bitter, brutal edge of deep winter. She pressed on regardless, her lamp's wavering flame holding back the shadows, just enough.

On into the dark room with the star etched into the floor. The red gleam of its paint was dull in the darkness, like old blood, and Lulu shivered.

'There—' she said, and started forward. Stormdust had been the one to check the room, sometime before; he'd returned with fresh reports of her father's absence, and hadn't noticed—or realised the significance of—the one thing that had changed.

A gramophone sat poised at one of the star's five points, glinting dull gold in the lamplight. It was the one that usually loitered in the library; Lulu hadn't registered that it was missing. A disc sat ready.

Lulu heard Fane's long, sorry sigh as she set the needle to the record, and waited. It wasn't music that emerged from the gramophone's soundbox, but her father's voice.

'I owe you an apology,' he said crisply, loud in the stillness of the cellar. 'In wedding your mother, I burdened you with the worst of parents. I sought to resolve this by encouraging certain of her...ambitions, the result of which was her departure Below. Perhaps I hoped...well, regardless, her sojourn there has in no way improved her temper. She is worse than ever, and it is my own doing.

'I'm going through. We all do, you know, sooner or later. I am leaving Castle Drax in safe hands, Lulu: yours. I know you won't be so foolish as to regret my absence.'

There followed a pause, so long that Lulu decided the recording must be over. But as she reached for the gramophone, her father's voice continued: 'She will want to return, eventually. She belongs there. And when she does, I'll—'

Nothing followed, though Lulu waited for some minutes. The record ended in unbroken silence.

Lulu had little trouble filling in the gap in her father's narrative. By "she", he must again be referring to her mother. And if he encountered her beyond the borders of Lulu's world, well...

Nobody spoke for some time. Then, at length, Fane drew himself up and, to her horror, bowed low to her. 'Countess Vexx,' he addressed her. 'The stewardship of Castle Drax is yours.'

Something formal rang in his words, something deep and dark and grave: Lulu shivered.

'No,' she said, firmly, though a slight quaver betrayed her. 'My father is still the Master of Castle Drax. He will come back through.'

Fane's rheumy eyes were kind, and sad. 'They never do,' he said gently. 'Not for long.'

She did not ask how he knew, just how long he had been serving the Counts Vexx. It didn't matter. He was wrong about her father, he had to be.

Lulu lifted her chin, and swept out of the dank and freezing summoning-chamber. 'Come on, Fane,' she told him, crisply. 'We have work to do.'

13

Surely Hell Itself

A fortnight passed, blazing by in a breezy bustle of activity. Fourteen days, crammed full with groups of visitors, conducted diligently over the halls of Castle Drax by Lulu Vexx herself; with bouts of baking and confectionery-making, batches of treats and sweets shipped off in boxes to the high street of Andirac; with keeping Cleo supplied with pigments and fresh bread, Minerfa with metals and tools and an occasional hand applying one to the other; with sweeping and dusting and mopping the gleaming black marble-and-stone surfaces of the castle's walls, floors, and furniture.

Fourteen nights spent snatching sleep in bits and pieces, whiling away long, wakeful hours with books, if they proved diverting. When they didn't, chilly treks from bedchamber to turret-top, torch in hand, shiveringly applying soft waves of colour to thick paper in a vain attempt to improve the skill of her hands and eyes.

A fortnight thus, since Count Vexx had stepped into his own summoning-circle in the cellar, and disappeared. A fortnight since, and he had not come out again.

Neither had anyone else.

This last troubled Lulu almost as much as her father's abrupt departure. That wasn't the way of things. It was a summoning-circle after all, not a doorway, or a portal. People went in, occasionally, by way of an offering to—well, the Beyond; whatever it was that lurked on the other side. And the Other Side gifted a denizen of its own, in return. Fane and Magwell and Stormdust had found their way to the castle by way of the cellar, and stayed; changed places with a few souls unwary enough, or stubborn enough, or foolish enough to stray into danger.

But no one had changed places with Count Vexx. No one had emerged to take up the vacant space he had for so long occupied, in the dark castle on the edge of a cliff. Two others had lately gone through, with similar result: Inspector Shah's constables, natives of that dim and distant Other place, keen to go home. There need be no trade, for that, or so it seemed.

What that implied about her father, Lulu did not much wish to consider. What it suggested about the Vexxes, likewise. Many generations had lived, loved, and died between those cold, black walls; a family, like any other. Ordinary, in spite of all their oddities. Weren't they?

These were the thoughts that kept her wakeful, long hours into the night. She scoured her father's beloved, but abandoned library, for volumes that might cast some light upon the nature of that pentagram below, and whatever lay beyond (without success). Her landscapes, daubed in watery green and blue, sprouted implausible shadows whenever she became distracted—knots of writhing darkness, like those that clung into the corners of the castle's dark passages, and gathered, thick and seething, in the maze of rooms below. She'd ruined a batch of Magwell's white rolls, her mind wandering, and been banished from the kitchen for two days.

She'd gone down to the summoning-chamber every day of that fortnight, and listened again to her father's message of farewell. *I am going through. We all do, you know, eventually.*

He would come back someday, she was sure of it. He must.

I leave the castle in capable hands, Lulu. Yours.

Castle Drax, mired in debt, crumbling more by the year, and beyond saving, one would think. Lulu certainly thought it, though she tried not to, for with her father gone there was no one but her to preserve it. Fane, Magwell and Stormdust were counting on her. Minerfa and Cleo, too, her lodgers, with nowhere else to go.

And she with no thought in her head but to bake their way out of penury; to stave off total ruin with bonbons, and macarons.

No, it wouldn't do.

At the close of this first fortnight of her father's absence, the newly (and resentfully) installed Countess Vexx shut herself into the telephone cabinet beneath the grand, sweeping staircase, and asked the operator to connect her to the police.

'Your father has been missing for two weeks?' Detective Inspector Shah had an emphatic way of frowning, Lulu found. Quite forbidding, his black brows thunderously contracted, his near-black eyes flashing annoyance. She felt an impulse to pacify him, and stifled it: he wasn't here to be pleased.

'Yes,' she confirmed. 'In a manner of speaking.'

The frown, improbably, deepened. 'Is he missing or not?'

Lulu had brought him into the library, where her father had last been seen. To her, his high-backed chair gaped emptily, his absence from it a constant reminder of the choice he had made. To the Inspector, though, the room exhibited its usual signs of recent habitation: a cushion dislodged, a stack or two of books here and there, one lying open with a pentagram scrawled in its margin.

'He is gone, and—well, I believe I know where, to an extent, but—'

'Miss Vexx. You reported a man missing, and requested my personal attention to the matter. If he isn't in fact missing, merely stepped out somewhere, then I cannot help you.'

'It's more complicated than that,' sighed Lulu. 'Shall I just show you?'

'You may have ten more minutes of my day,' said Shah, consulting a sleek wrist-watch with an irritated curl of his handsome mouth. 'I have other, pressing cases to attend to.'

Lulu nodded, and led the way at once downstairs into the cellars. She took up her old oil-lamp along the way, and lit it, but the thin glow could do little to repel the thickening shadows that writhed over the cold stone floor, and twisted up the walls. She went slowly, therefore, and kept close to the Inspector.

'Is this normal?' Shah enquired, halfway along a passage near totally shadow-drowned.

'No,' said Lulu. 'It began shortly before my father—left, and has not improved since.'

Shah said nothing more, but followed in silence as Lulu groped and stumbled her way back to the summoning-chamber, with its livid-red pentagram marking the dark floor. The shadows there were so thick, so tempestuous, Lulu could no longer make out the brassy glint of the gramophone Count Vexx had left there.

'Ah,' said Inspector Shah, in a tone of sudden enlightenment. Lulu waited while he took in the scene, then ventured forth with the oil lamp until its yellow glow caught a glitter of bronze. She played her father's recorded message yet again, alert for every slight shift in his tone, every pause or hesitation. Each time she heard the words, they seemed to say something slightly different.

'Miss Vexx,' said the Inspector, when her father's voice had trailed, once more, into silence. 'It appears—'

'Lulu, please,' she interrupted.

He considered her for a moment in silence. 'Very well, Lulu. It seems that your father went willingly, and as such, this is no matter for the police.'

The frown had smoothed from his features, at least, and he spoke with some sympathy. Nonetheless, her heart sank at his words. 'He was not in his right mind,' she said. 'He fell into such melancholy after mother's—escapade, and I fear he was acting on some unsound impression—'

Inspector Shah shook his head; he was turning away. 'Still not a matter for the police,' he told her. 'No crime has been committed.'

Lulu took a breath. 'Inspector, please. I requested you personally because you are—no ordinary detective. Are you?'

He paused, and turned back to her. The lamplight turned his brown skin bronze, and caused his eyes to glimmer eerily in the darkness. 'Why do you say that?'

'Your constables,' Lulu said. 'You brought them here in order to send them home. You know something.'

'About what?'

'About—' Lulu waved a hand, vaguely, at the star-pointed circle. 'About whatever lies on the other side of *that*.'

Inspector Shah said nothing, only studied her face. Finally he said: 'How much do you know of it?'

'We are a part of Hell's Seventh Circle,' said Lulu in a rush, heart thumping. 'This is Castle Drax's Andirac side; there's another. And this—' Another sweeping gesture at the crimson pentagram '—is a pact between the two. A deal, of sorts. We owe them souls, Father once said.' He had been telling Lulu all this since she was a small child, and her mother had gone one day down into the cellar, and never come back. She hadn't believed him; not until much later.

The Inspector's face was dark, unreadable. 'And in return for these souls, you get...?'

'Someone comes through. We don't own them: they stay if they wish to. And Father never sent anyone through against their will. He always warned them, and if they went anyway—' She shrugged.

'Like your mother.'

Lulu nodded.

Shah rubbed at the beginnings of a short, black beard: he had been too busy lately even to shave, it seemed. 'I don't think I have any information that is likely to help you.'

Lulu's hopes crumpled; she shifted the lamp, so he wouldn't read it in her face. 'I see.'

'It certainly won't bring your father back.'

'It might,' Lulu insisted fiercely. 'And if it doesn't, at least I will know what's become of him.' Whether he's happy there, she thought but didn't say. One didn't propose or anticipate happiness for a denizen of the Seventh Circle of Hell; not to a sensible man like Shah, at any rate.

He sighed, a slightly harassed sound. 'Very well. I truly am very busy, but if you can meet me in town later tonight, I can spare you an hour.'

Joy surged; Lulu forgot herself so far as to perform a gleeful little bounce. 'Thank you.'

'I'll tell you everything I can. What you do with it is up to you.' He tipped his dark fedora to her, and turned towards the door. 'Now please, get me out of this dungeon. I'm not ordinarily afraid of the dark, but this...'

Lulu shuddered. 'It is a bit too much, isn't it?'

'Another five minutes here and I shall be hurling myself through that circle. Anything to get away.'

'Surely Hell itself can't be worse,' Lulu agreed, hurrying forward with the lamp. She felt Shah's fingers curl into the sash of her dress as she led the way back into the passage, and he maintained his grip until they had both emerged into the relative light and comfort of the first floor. Then at last he let go; Lulu witnessed a strong shudder shake his tall frame as he stepped back. 'Eight o'clock at the Drake?' he proposed.

Lulu knew of the premier pub in Andirac, though she had never gone in. 'I shall be there,' she assured him.

'Marvellous.' And he strode away, offering her only the most perfunctory bow as he went.

'Thank you!' Lulu called after him.

He waved a hand vaguely in acknowledgement, and then he was gone.

Lulu only belatedly remembered that she had meant to enquire for Priya. Ah well. Save that for the Drake; in the meantime, Lulu had cleaning to do.

She was late getting to the pub, as it transpired. She had been on the point of dashing out of her front door at quarter to eight, only to discover—by way of a brief glance in the cloakroom's mirror—that she had a filmy veil of cobwebs clinging to the blonde waves of her hair, a smudge of something black and indeterminate along one cheekbone, and a small tear in her green silk blouse, through which a pale glimmer of skin showed. Perhaps it didn't matter how she appeared; Shah certainly would care nothing for the neatness of her clothes, or the arrangement of her hair. But she was the Countess Vexx, now, at least for the moment, and she could not show her face at the Drake for the first time looking like an ill-kempt housemaid.

Stormdust would not hurry his glacial pace, not even for an important meeting. He drove her down into Andirac at a speed only slightly faster than walking, and parked with the utmost care opposite the pub before he deigned to let

Lulu out. It was twenty-five past eight; Lulu hurried across the street, mentally rehearsing her apologies.

The Drake was a substantial building, three tall storeys of grey brick and black stone shimmering with mullioned windows. A green-lettered sign bore a painted image of a sinuous dragon, its tail coiling around the pub's name. As Lulu hauled open the heavy brass-handled door, a roar of noise billowed out, and an aroma of beer, and roast meat.

Shah sat alone in a snug corner, a little removed from the other, crowded tables. He was comfortably ensconced on a bench upholstered in shiny green leather, and a tall glass sat atop the lacquered oak table before him, empty save for a lingering film of froth.

'Inspector Shah, I'm so sorry for my lateness,' she said as she slid into a seat opposite him. 'You see—'

'You may as well call me Ravi,' he said, tapping his fingertips lightly upon the tabletop. 'At least while we are here. This isn't a business call.'

'Ravi. Thank you for coming. Oh! Before I forget, do you think your sister might like to attend a watercolour salon?'

Ravi blinked at her. 'What? Priya?'

'Yes. I'm organising a series of salons and workshops, you see, and perhaps an art show, and she did seem to enjoy the last one—'

'An art show? While your father's missing?'

A short, balding man in a dark blue apron appeared, and set a fresh glass of foaming beer before the Inspector. He produced a glass of chilled white wine for Lulu, and bustled away again. Lulu hadn't noticed Ravi order. 'Yes, it isn't ideal,' she agreed. 'But he left the castle to me, and there's—oh goodness, so much to do. I cannot simply abandon everything until we get Father back, much as I might wish to.' She sipped her wine; the cold, crisp beverage slid smoothly down her throat, soothing.

Ravi's mouth quirked in an expression she couldn't decipher. 'The curse of a great estate,' he said. 'I'm sure it's very difficult.'

Ah, that's what it was: sardonic. 'It isn't a great estate,' Lulu replied coolly. 'We don't own much land and whatever fortune there once was is all gone. Castle Drax is broke. If I can't find a way to generate some income, we will have to sell it.'

His dark eyes, fixed on her, lost some of their stoniness. 'I see,' he said neutrally. 'Would that be so bad?'

'It's my home.' Lulu blinked back a sudden welling of tears; where had they come from? 'And my father's, and—and Magwell and Stormdust and Fane. Cleo and Minerfa. There's nowhere most of us could go where we would be—' She searched for the right word. Safe? Welcomed?

'How many of you are—' Ravi paused. 'From—'

'Beyond the summoning-circle? Four. I think. I'm not quite certain about Minerfa—I haven't asked.' She didn't offer her new and unsettling doubts about her father's antecedents, and therefore, her own. She hadn't decided how she felt about that, yet.

'So they could just—go back.' Ravi had a way of studying her face, intent, focused; it made her uneasy, when she couldn't tell what he was thinking.

'They could. Would, if they had to. But their home is here. With us.'

'They don't want to go?'

Lulu shook her head, gulping wine. 'Unlike your constables, I gather.'

Ravi nodded, and at last relaxed his scrutiny of her face. 'But they never...they didn't find a home here, on this side. Their command of the language was never very good, and without a safe harbour—well, they were arrested for theft. Imprisoned. I think they were just trying to survive, although they may simply never have understood the concept of private ownership and personal property. When their sentence was up, they had nowhere to go.' He shrugged and returned to his beer, as though there was nothing else to say.

'How did they come to be working for the police?' Lulu prompted.

'They weren't. They were working for me, unofficially. I've been searching for a way to send them home.'

Lulu digested that in momentary silence. 'Why didn't you just tell me that before? Why sneak them in? I'd have given you access to the circle, no question.' He'd shown up with his sister, and a pretense of attending one of Lulu's watercolour painting events. Only belatedly had she discovered the Shah siblings' real purpose at Castle Drax that afternoon.

'I wasn't sure,' said Ravi abruptly.

'About?' said Lulu, when he fell silent again.

'About you. I realised what kind of staff you had, but I couldn't tell whether they were there by choice or—not.'

He hadn't wanted to entrust his constables' safety to Lulu if he wasn't certain that she would see them as people, and free. She wanted to take offence, but couldn't: he was right to be concerned. 'They aren't staff,' she replied. 'Not exactly. They're family. But Magwell loves to cook, so she gradually took over the kitchen. Fane's rather sociable—and very nosy, if truth be told—so he took to answering the door, and attending upon guests, when we have any. And since he also has an excellent nose for wine, he functions more or less as a butler. And Stormdust? I was hoping he might have a flair for cleaning—Gods know I could use the help—but he has a passion for the motorcar, and spends most of his time out in the garage.'

A smile lurked around Ravi's expressive mouth. 'What about Minerfa?'

'She came to us a different way. I don't know how or why she crossed over from—from over there, but she's here as a lodger. She's building a heating system, I'm told, though I have no idea why, as she seems to like the cold.'

Ravi drained his glass, and set it down with a snap. 'Well, I can see that I erred in not discussing my constables' situation with you. Who knows but that they might have chosen to stay at the castle, with you.'

'I can understand why you didn't.'

Ravi gave a half-shrug. 'Excess of caution. Hazard of the job.'

'But how did you know where they'd come from? How to send them home?'

'I didn't, for a time. But I could see they were—different. I had heard before of—well, the police files are full of odd cases, reports from the public most people wouldn't credit, or have any idea what to do with. I was able to track down one or two knowledgeable people, who gave me some hints; then I did some research—' He did his half-shrug again. 'A long and tedious trail, in truth.'

Lulu, following her own train of thought, mused: 'I wonder how many more there are? Adrift somewhere, I mean, and in need of help.'

'Shall you adopt them all?' The words were coolly said, but Ravi was smiling a little.

'Oh, goodness.' Lulu rubbed at her forehead, noticing at last a throbbing headache. 'I should like to, if they need asylum, but I cannot deny it would be a strain on our already stretched resources.'

'Hence the painting salons.'

Lulu sighed. 'It seems absurd, doesn't it? A few painting salons for ladies, a few boxes of meringues, and I expect to save an entire castle from ruin.'

'You're doing what you can,' said Ravi.

'I'm trying everything. Anything. We have some small profits coming in from Magwell's confectionery, so far, and I'm hoping an art show might be productive of something. Maybe it could be a yearly event; it might even grow quite big, if we get it right. Then there's the lodgers, of course. We don't charge a lot for rooms, but it at least covers board and a little more—' She broke off, flushing. 'Sorry. You aren't here to be rambled at about my problems.'

Ravi shook his head. 'It's relevant. I'll make sure Priya joins you for the next salon.'

Lulu felt suddenly awkward; vaguely guilty. 'Only if she wants to. Perhaps she was only pretending an interest in painting.'

'Not at all. She's an enthusiastic amateur at a great many things, including watercolour painting. Also, painting in oils. Playing the harp, and the pianoforte. Several modern languages, and at least two extinct ones—it was she who worked out how to communicate with my constables, after a fashion. Couture, patisserie, embroidery, flower-arranging...'

Lulu couldn't help laughing. 'She sounds thoroughly accomplished. I shall be quite intimidated, next time I meet her.'

'She is burdened with such an abundance of intellect and talent, she hardly knows what to do with it all.'

'Burdened? Surely that is a blessing.'

Ravi smiled. 'Sometimes. But if she hasn't anything sufficiently interesting to do, she'll grow ferociously bored. It can take five minutes. She and I will both be delighted if you can contrive to occupy her, for a time.' He glanced at his wrist-watch, and sighed. 'I should get back. I have a mountain of paperwork waiting for me.'

'Surely a Detective Inspector has assistants, to do that for him?' Lulu ventured.

'Not at all. At least half the job is filing reports, and I usually do that in the evenings.'

Lulu bowed her head. 'Then I shan't keep you from it any longer. Thank you for sparing time to meet with me.'

Ravi nodded, and rose. 'It was a pleasure, ma'am,' he said with sudden formality, and offered her a half-bow.

'It was, wasn't it?' Lulu agreed. 'Ah, Inspector—'

'Ravi.'

'Ravi. If you come across any more... lost souls, do bring them to me.'

He smiled down at her, and nodded. 'I shall.'

Later, Lulu could only curse her own foolishness in not thinking of it before. Minerfa! Why hadn't she put to *her* the question of how, or where, she had come through? Perhaps she might have gleaned something new, something that might help her retrieve her father.

It was the awkwardness of the application that had prevented her. Minerfa had never really spoken of her previous home, her origins, her race, and it could only be impossibly rude to make enquiries into any of those things without an invitation to do so.

How to make such an application without hurting her guest occupied Lulu for some time, without much result. In the end, she decided to apply first to Fane, Magwell, and Stormdust. They might have a great deal to tell her, if she would but ask, and in their case she had less fear of erring, or offending.

Less did not quite equal none, however.

Lulu began with Fane. She found him with a set of chamois leather cloths in hand, the sleeves of his frayed black jacket rolled up, and the big, brass dinner gong dismantled into pieces before him. A strong, acrid scent of salted lemon juice and white vinegar filled the crooked antechamber. He was cleaning it with gentle hands, lovingly buffing it back to a golden shimmer.

'Fane,' said Lulu. 'You said—you said they never come back, once they've gone through. What did you mean?'

Fane stopped polishing, and looked in silence at Lulu. 'I meant the Counts Vexx, Miss,' he replied, cautiously, as though he expected some adverse response.

'They...all go through? Hasn't any one of them ever died peacefully abed?'

'Not to my knowledge, Miss. And I have been here for a very long time.' He took up his cloth and his leather again, and resumed polishing.

Lulu sank into the beckoning arms of a threadbare green velvet chair. A sigh escaped her, of dismay, perhaps; the implications of Fane's revelation did not bode well. 'And why, Fane? Why do they all leave the castle for—' Hell, she was going to say, but something stopped her. A hooded look in Fane's eyes, a stillness about him.

He didn't answer for some time. Lulu waited, and finally he said: 'They are not going through so much as they are going back.'

'Oh.'

Fane nodded.

'Oh, dear.'

Silence again, as Lulu strove to absorb this new and unwelcome idea. Her mind reeled with it, fitting it like jig-saw-pieces against every other sign, every small, odd thread of information she'd picked up over the years. The picture it all made was frightfully clear.

'It can be hard,' Fane said suddenly. 'It *is* hard, to make the change. From there, to here. Many of us never adjust.'

Lulu pictured her father: his sleek handsomeness, his agelessness, his acerbic distaste for, seemingly, everything beyond the walls of the castle (and much within them).

He had never been a happy man, not in all the years Lulu could remember. Was that how it had been with him? Had he been—homesick? Adrift? Lost?

And she sought to drag him straight back again.

'Do you know why Father left, Fane?' Lulu asked.

Fane shook his grey head. 'His sentence was completed years ago—'

'Sentence?'

Fane's pale lips stretched in an expression that wasn't truly a smile. 'It is a punishment, Miss, for most. Exile. Servitude, in one form or another.'

Lulu stared, aghast. 'Fane. Do not tell me all your long years with us have been a punishment?'

'Oh no, Miss. At first, perhaps, but I...I came to prefer it, here. I've stayed because I wish to.'

'But Father stayed for me. Was that it?'

'Your mother, first,' Fane answered with cold disapproval. 'And then for you.'

Lulu reflected, with an odd detachment, on the neatness of the arrangement. If her mother had gone through the summoning-circle, it had been a punishment for her, too; exile. But why would her father have chosen that, if he had been yearning for his old home? Why send her through, when he could have gone himself? Lulu couldn't make sense of it.

She shied away from the looming question of her own nature, her own origins. Time enough to grapple with that horrifying prospect later.

'I don't know what to do for Father,' Lulu admitted. 'Did he leave because he was unhappy here, or because he expected to be more so there? His message...' There had been so much bitter self-reproach in it, Lulu could not help thinking he hadn't been returning from exile so much as entering it.

'He did not confide in me, Miss,' said Fane quietly. 'I don't know what he intended.'

'If he needs help, he must have it.' Lulu gnawed on a fingernail in frustration. 'If only I could talk to him.'

'Only way to do that is to—' Fane stopped himself, with a sideways glance at her, and shook his head.

'No telephone will reach so far, I suppose?' Lulu supplied. 'I'd have to go myself.'

'I do not advise it, Miss Lulu.'

The prospect did not appeal to Lulu, either. She didn't want to visit Hell Proper, didn't want to know, in any detail, what it was like on the other side. She might not be able to return. And what had her father stayed so long for, if not to raise and prepare her as chatelaine? *I leave the castle in capable hands, Lulu.*

Fane was hesitating over something. 'If I were to go,' he said at length, 'I should certainly not be permitted to return here again. Nor would Magwell, or, I believe, Stormdust.'

'And they would regret the loss of the castle.'

Fane nodded. 'Greatly.'

'I shall never ask it of any of you,' Lulu promised. Nor of Minerfa, either, for surely some similar conditions must apply to her.

No. It must be Lulu, or nobody. And how could she go? Whom could she leave in charge?

'Could you manage without me for a—a time, Fane? You and Magwell and Stormdust.'

Fane abandoned the gong. 'I really do not advise it,' he said with uncharacteristic urgency. 'You wouldn't *like* it there.'

'I don't have to like it; I shan't intend to stay. I only want to find Father, and if he wishes it, bring him back.'

Fane, deeply troubled, only stared at her, shaking and shaking his head. 'Oh, no, Miss Lulu. Pray don't.'

'I fear I must.' She couldn't just abandon her father to whatever fate awaited him in a home he hadn't seen in decades—how many years, she did not even know.

But nor could she abandon the castle. A conundrum she didn't know how to solve.

'There may...there may be a way to send a missive,' Fane ventured. 'It would be very unorthodox, but it might, perhaps, be managed.'

It would cost him something to do it; Lulu read that plainly in his hesitance, his gravity. 'How might we do that?'

'We'd make a pact, Miss. With someone—or something—that's going through.'

Lulu thought of Inspector Shah's constables, with a stab of regret. They might have carried a letter, if they hadn't already gone beyond recall. 'Do you know anyone who might wish to go?' she asked Fane.

'No,' he said gravely. 'But I could summon...something.'

Not someone. Something. Lulu knew enough of the process to realise it would come at a price. 'Well, then,' she said, rising. 'How can I help?'

The blood streaming from a slash on Fane's arm was a deep, dark blue, though it was a little hard to tell; all the lamps and lanterns Lulu had brought below flared with a crystalline-green light, and the glow about the dark cellar room was lurid.

Three o'clock had just chimed upon the sluggish, out-of-sync clocks above, staggered over several minutes. The thin, distant tones of the last were dying away as blood dripped and pooled in the centre of Count Vexx's summoning-circle.

Lulu had seen more of three a.m. lately than in the whole course of her life before. At least this was in a good cause. She was there to witness, and dictate her message to her father. Fane had not permitted her to participate in the pact.

Fane was speaking, but in no words Lulu could decipher. One of the tongues of Hell, she supposed, though the rich, fluid language hardly sounded like it. Fane's voice rose to a commanding, thundering bellow; the emerald flames flared high; somewhere close by a window shattered.

The witchfires dissipated the shadows far more effectively than anything else had done. For now, the room was largely clear and bright, save a deep cloud swirling in the heart of the crimson pentagram. Fane's blood dripped into it, sending up wisps of acrid black smoke.

Something else was moving in there, Lulu perceived; something dark-shimmering, scaled, taloned...

The creature erupted, claws flashing, black beak gaping in a scream of fury. Its hide had the dark iridescence of spilled oil; its wings, webbed like a bat's, were dark as the night itself. Those wings were beating frantically, waves of smoke and black fog beaten into a whirling tempest around it.

Fane thundered something, and clenched his outstretched fist. The creature screeched, then quieted, setting its two clawed feet to the green-lit floor and bowing its long-necked head. That head, Lulu saw with incredulity, was that of a cockerel.

'Tell it what you wish conveyed,' Fane instructed her.

Lulu regarded the cockatrice doubtfully. It resented Fane's commands, that much she could clearly see. A cold light of barely-restrained rage flickered in the gleaming black eyes, and the long lines of its muscles coiled with tension. However diminutive its size—and it stood not much taller than a chicken—she did not doubt its capacity to cause her serious injury, if she displeased it.

'Quickly,' Fane prompted, and Lulu jumped to obey.

'Yes. Sorry. I wish for you to bear a message to my father, the current Count Vexx, from his daughter Luna. Tell him...' she hesitated. The thorny question of how precisely to enquire into his state of being, his intentions, his wants, remained unresolved. He had resented all such enquiries even before he'd retired from his life at the castle; she could hardly suppose he would welcome such an intrusion now that he had severed himself from them all.

'Tell him we miss him,' she said simply. 'That his place with us remains unchanged, and—'

The cockatrice coughed, and spat a black ball of smoking something onto the floor. 'Pathetic,' it uttered in forbidding tones. 'I shall carry no such mewling words to His Greatness.'

His Greatness? Lulu glanced at Fane, whose face demonstrated a total unwillingness to engage with the subject of Count Vexx's status elsewhere. 'Well then, what should I say?'

'You are Mistress here, are you?' said the cockatrice, glaring at her. She hoped uneasily that its mythical ability to turn flesh to stone with a glance would prove exaggerated.

'I am,' said Lulu, as sturdily as she could manage.

'THEN YOU COMMAND!' roared the cockatrice, wings flaring.

'Fine!' Lulu howled back. 'Tell my snivelling excuse for a parent that it was the very heights of cowardice to abandon us like that, and if he doesn't bring his lily-livered carcass back to Castle Drax post-haste I shall go down there and drag him back myself! By. The. Hair.' She drew herself up to her fullest and moderately terrible height, and loomed awfully over the creature at her feet. Count Vexx couldn't have done a better job of it himself.

The cockatrice clucked and cackled, oozing smoke. 'Beautiful,' it said, and vanished in a whirl of black fog.

Nobody spoke for a time. Fane avoided her eye, occupied with winding a clean length of bandage around his bleeding arm.

'That was surprisingly satisfying,' Lulu ventured.

Fane, surprisingly, grinned. 'The Count will be proud,' he told her.

'Really?'

Fane nodded. 'He won't come back, but he'll be properly chuffed.'

The old butler was right, as it soon proved. Three o'clock struck the following morning, and Lulu was in her turret-top atelier, toying with a paintbrush. She was shivering too hard to wield it with any precision, the night wind chilling her to the bone. She'd slept for two or three hours, then lain wide awake, reliving every syllable of the message she had conveyed to her father.

She felt bad about it, now. What had possessed her to show such anger? Where had all that rage been lurking? No trace of it remained, that she could sense; she was weary, worried, and irritable, and she wanted nothing more than for the sun to rise, and dispel the night and her dark thoughts both.

'MADAM!' roared a terrible voice. Lulu jumped, the paintbrush in her hand splattering black paint over the bare stone wall. 'I BRING WORDS FROM HIS GREATNESS.'

Lulu hastily set down her brush. 'Well? What are they?'

The cockatrice folded its dark, webbed wings, and set-tled into a comfortable crouch. 'No,' it said.

Lulu waited, but nothing else was forthcoming. 'That isn't words, that's one word,' she pointed out.

'True,' conceded the cockatrice.

'That cannot be it, surely?'

'That's it.' The cockatrice fluffed its wings, tucked in its beak, and emitted a soft, clucking snore.

'No? That's all he has to say to me? NO?' There was the rage, roaring back in a torrent; Lulu was shaking still, but she was no longer cold.

The cockatrice made no answer, save for another snore.

'And what are you doing?' Lulu demanded. 'Sleeping? Go back to Hell, if you want to do that.'

'Certainly,' it said. 'In ninety-nine years.'

'What?'

A gleaming black eye opened, and fixed her with a glare. 'Those were your terms. I carry a message to His Greatness, and in return I am permitted to sojourn abroad for no less a period than ninety-nine of your years.' The eye closed; the lines of its shining black beak set in a smug smile. 'I am, of course, confined to the environs of your charming castle, unless given explicit permission to go beyond its boundaries.'

'Of course,' Lulu echoed, conscious of a growing feeling of hollow despair. 'And what exactly am I supposed to do with you for ninety-nine years?'

'Feed me,' answered the cockatrice. 'Unless you would prefer for me to hunt for my own sustenance. I'm told there are small creatures aplenty, quite tasty. If you should prefer to cater my meals yourself, be advised that I enjoy fresh meat, full-fat cream, and those pastry tarts with the black cherries in.'

Lulu, bereft of words, could only stare. What had Fane—why had he—how was she supposed to—

'Catering it is, then,' said the cockatrice, beaming. 'Breakfast at eight?'

14

That Damned Chicken

A sleepless night landed Lulu in the dining-room before five o'clock in the morning, with a cup of tea and a bread roll snatched from the kitchen, and her accounts book and pen. She'd grown used to going over the castle's financial affairs while she ate, and she usually had the huge, echoing chamber and long, polished table to herself.

Not today, despite the early hour.

'Oh! Excellent,' said Minerfa at quarter-past five, striding into the dining-room with her clattering, steel-toed tread. She was already clad in her oil-begrimed overalls, and swinging a hammer in one hand. 'Good morning, Lulu.'

'Good morning,' Lulu answered with an absent smile, scrawling numbers in her neat columns.

'I need two tons of steel, welding equipment, a large quantity of raw beef, and a much larger hammer.'

'Mm?' Lulu said, and then her lodger's words sank in. 'I—I beg your pardon? You need what?'

Minerfa waved her hammer illustratively. 'This one's pathetic. Look at it! I could scarcely kill a cat with it.'

'Don't kill anything with—two tonnes of steel! Whatever for?'

'For making pipes, of course.' Minerfa dropped heavily into an elegant ebony-veneered chair, and slung the reviled hammer onto the gleaming surface of the dining table. Its solid steel head landed with an ominous *thunk*.

Lulu winced. There weren't many good features left to the decayed Castle Drax, but the exquisite dining table was one of them.

'Please be careful with the—pipes for? Oh, this is for your heating system—'

'No,' replied Minerfa sternly. 'This is for *your* heating system.'

'Yes, of course.' Lulu set down her pen, and applied her fingertips to her temples, where the beginnings of a headache throbbed. Barely five-thirty, and already she desperately wanted to go back to bed. Not that any real repose awaited her there, if she did; perhaps her father had had the right idea in fleeing the castle. 'Minerfa, while I appreciate your efforts greatly, I do not think we have the resources to purchase so many materials and tools. Perhaps it could be somewhat—condensed?'

Minerfa's dark gaze dropped to the rows of figures in Lulu's account book. 'Ah. They cost money, do they? Hmm. I suppose we could get them some other way?'

'Such as?' Lulu hardly dared ask. Minerfa's ideas frequently bore little relation to reality.

'Somebody must have some to spare. We could…ask.' Minerfa smiled, proud of her notion.

'Ask someone to hand us two tons of steel? For free?'

'Take it, then, secretly.'

'That is theft.'

'Yes?'

Lulu took up her pen again, and drew a raincloud, complete with thunderclap, in the margin of her page. 'We won't be stealing anything,' she said, as patiently as she could manage. 'I am afraid there's no way to get hold of so much steel. I'm sorry. Besides, I still can't fathom how you'd need so much.'

'It takes a lot of pipes,' Minerfa said mulishly.

'What does, exactly?'

'Channelling Hellfire. I know Hell isn't *that* far away from Drax, but still it must be conveyed, and over a difficult border—'

'What? No.' Lulu set down her pen. 'We are not heating this castle with the fires of Hell.'

'Whyever not? It isn't as though they'd miss it. There's really quite a lot of it over there.'

Lulu thought of her father's cold, green witchfires, and wondered. If he was, in truth, a native of Hell, is that why he liked the frost fire? He was accustomed to an excess of heat, and enjoyed the contrast.

She shook off the thought, forcing her weary and wandering mind back to the problem of Minerfa's...well, of Minerfa. 'It doesn't seem safe,' she said firmly. 'And it is certainly far too expensive.'

'Where am I meant to get enough heat to warm a gigantic pile of stone if I can't use Hell?'

'That,' said Lulu dryly, 'is exactly the problem.' She smiled an apology, for Minerfa's enthusiasm was valuable, even if her ideas were not. 'We are tolerably resigned to the cold, by now.'

Minerfa gazed sadly at the hammer she'd thrown down. 'Oh, well.' She shrugged, hauled herself out of her elegant chair—which creaked and groaned alarmingly—and stormed out, leaving her hammer abandoned atop the table.

Lulu sighed, smothering a twinge of guilt. The Vexxes had been ludicrously wealthy, once; they had to have been, to build Castle Drax. If only some part of that shining fortune remained. Naught but a miserable trickle of income was left to the estate, and it would never stretch to cover miles of steel pipes and a first-rate Hellfire-fuelled heating system. She couldn't even get the roof repaired, and the water damage in the observatory was approaching irreparable.

Minerfa was a lodger, Lulu reminded herself. She paid to live at Castle Drax, that was all. Lulu was not liable to satisfy her every whim, even when she was trying, in her own way, to contribute to the running of the household.

Still. Guilt gnawed at her anyway, and when a commotion of clucking and shouting broke out somewhere above, Lulu was, on some level, grateful for the distraction.

She bolted down passageways and up a spiralling staircase, following the furious sounds of Cleo's shrill bellow. Her rooms lay above the dining-room, four decently-lit chambers closed behind a stout, and lockable, door. How the cockatrice had contrived to get in, then, proved a mystery, but it *had*; it came galloping out as Lulu approached and sped past her legs, all but knocking her over.

'Runrunrunrunrunrunrun,' chortled the cockatrice, clucking, and vanished around a corner. A trail of bright green paint and shining black scales marked its passage.

Cleo appeared at her door, her thin face livid. She, too, wore a quantity of green paint splattered over her painting smock. 'What,' she bellowed, 'is that damned chicken doing in my rooms?'

'Not a chicken,' came the cockatrice's voice, floating on some malevolent echo.

'I am sorry,' Lulu said. 'Was your door locked? I can't think how it came to get in.'

'It's upset three pots of paint,' Cleo went on, furious. 'Ruined one of my canvases—'

'Contributed to it,' said the cockatrice. 'With visionary skill, and you are welcome.'

Cleo growled. 'Stamped all over it with its big chicken feet, and now it's useless.'

'Oh, dear,' Lulu sighed. 'I'll talk to it.'

'If I catch it in here again,' Cleo said ominously, 'We'll be having fried chicken for dinner.' She slammed her door.

Lulu drifted back around the corner. The cockatrice sat just out of sight, its black beak set in a broad smile.

'You really mustn't,' Lulu remonstrated, mentally cursing Fane yet again for saddling her with the beast. 'Her paintings are important.'

'I'm not a chicken,' answered the cockatrice. 'She does understand that, yes?'

'I don't know.'

'I would not taste good, fried. Fricasseed, perhaps, with a generous quantity of garlic butter...'

'Perhaps if you left her rooms alone?' Lulu suggested. 'There's a whole castle to run about in.'

'Yes, but most of it is not at all entertaining.'

Fair enough; most of it was empty, draughty, and echoing. 'And what do you find entertaining?' Lulu persevered.

'Painting.' The cockatrice clucked. 'And...breaking and entering.'

'How about I give you your own rooms? Then you need not be infiltrating other people's.'

The cockatrice's cockerel head tilted; its beak snapped. 'Why not...both?'

'Your own paints and paper, then. You can paint, but without damaging Cleo's work.'

'I prefer hers.'

'Her what? Her paints?'

The beaky smile broadened. 'Her work.'

Lulu folded her arms. 'All right. What will it take to get you to stop bothering Cleo?'

'Cherry pies,' said the cockatrice promptly. 'Two.'

'Just two? That's it?'

'Two per day. You may deliver them to my room.'

'Can't do that,' Lulu retorted. 'Sorry. Cherries are expensive. Two cherry pies a week, best I can do.'

The cockatrice's leathery wings flared with irritation, its gaze turning stony. 'Very well. Two cherry pies a week, my own room, a supply of pigments and paper, and room service.'

'And in return,' Lulu began.

'In return, I leave the little paintress alone.'

'In return for your room and board,' Lulu persisted. 'You'll bring me any scales you shed.'

The cockatrice hissed.

'You're a lodger,' Lulu told it without sympathy. 'This is not a free hotel.'

The long, thin tail lashed, hitting the stone floor with a sound like a dropped saucepan. 'You will pay for this,' growled the cockatrice.

'The idea is that you will,' Lulu returned. 'It's scales, or you carry another message to my father for me.'

'Those were not the terms of our deal. I agreed to convey *a* message—'

'It's a long message,' said Lulu. 'Composed of several parts, and I imagine the next one will be ready to dispatch any moment now.'

The cockatrice's serpentine neck sagged, its head drooping.

Lulu took this for agreement. 'Come on, then. I'll show you to your room.'

The cockatrice scuttled after Lulu in offended silence, its talons clacking like knives over the night-black stone of the castle's cold floors. She led it a considerable distance, choosing to put several rooms and corridors and staircases in between the troublesome beast and the rest of the castle's residents.

She stopped at last at the door to the observatory, at the top of a long-abandoned turret. The stone steps sagged in the centre, smooth craters worn by the passage of centuries of feet: the observatory had been the pride of Castle Drax, once.

Now it was empty, and choked with dust. Lulu flung open the door, and regarded, in dismayed silence, the black mould creeping over the rain-damaged walls; a litter of crumbled plaster over the cracked stone tiles of the floor; the shattered or missing panes of glass in the mullioned windows. At least the great telescope was intact, however grimy its once-shining brass.

'Hm,' said Lulu doubtfully. 'We'd better clean this up a bit.'

But the cockatrice toddled in peaceably, and poked its black beak into the cracks in the floor; then, to Lulu's horror, into a film of cushiony black mould covering one dark wall. The beak clicked; the creature swallowed. 'Nicely aged,' it said. 'Deep, rich flavour. Very fine.'

'You're eating...mould.'

'Fungi is nutritious.' The cockatrice's wings flared importantly, its head nodding in appreciation. 'An underrated food group, but some of us possess the palate to appreciate it.'

'Oh,' said Lulu. 'You're—you're right. Fungi is wonderful. We have a great deal of it, if you're interested.'

'Strange place,' mused the cockatrice. 'Black cherries, rarefied and strictly rationed. But exquisite delicacies such as this! Plentiful.' It absorbed another beakful of mould, and sighed with profound satisfaction. 'I accept.'

Lulu shook her head. Strange place, indeed. 'One question,' she said. 'I never caught your name.' She couldn't keep calling it "the cockatrice", not if they were going to be co-habiting for a hundred years, nearly.

'I have transcended such meaningless considerations,' came the answer.

'Have you though? What about my father, His Greatness? That's a name, isn't it?'

'It is a title. A grand and noble title, of impeccable dignity, and—'

Lulu left the observatory, closing the door softly behind her. The cockatrice continued to chunter away, unmoved by her departure; its gravelly, snarling voice faded slowly away as she went back down the stairs.

Sleep favoured her, the following night, at least a little. She lay awake until the early hours past midnight, and fell asleep at last, to dream of acres of steel pipes brimful of Hellfire, and a tide of black mould swamping the flailing, decrepit castle.

She woke with a start, some appalling clamour having lacerated her gentle bubble of slumber.

'   S   K   K   R   -REEKAKA-SKKKREEEKAKAKAAKAA-KAAAH!'

Lulu rocketed out of bed and stumbled to her door, flinging it open. 'What—' she began, but the racket started up again, drowning her out.

'SKREEEEEEK—'

'WILL SOMEBODY SHUT THAT DAMNED CHICKEN UP.' The words were delivered at a battleground roar, and it wasn't Cleo. Lulu, on her way post-haste to the observatory, encountered Minerfa, wrapped in a bed-sheet and purple (more so than usual) with rage.

'It's dawn,' she groaned. 'It's crowing.'

'Then it shall stop,' snarled Minerfa. 'Or it shall have its neck wrung.'

Lulu began to run.

Not that the prospect of wringing that damned chicken's neck didn't appeal greatly to her, in that moment. The first sleep of several hours together she'd managed all week, and then—

'Stop it!' she pleaded, barging through the cockatrice's door, and into the frigid observatory. 'We're awake. Everyone's awake already, you can stop.'

The cockatrice, posed with neck stretched and wings outspread in the centre of its new domain, beamed at her. 'I did say you'd pay.'

'Oh, for goodness' sake. Please, stop.' She was begging, which was impolitic, but she couldn't help it.

The damned chicken radiated smugness. 'I am bored.'

'Then find something inoffensive to do.'

'Inoffensive.' The cockatrice rolled the word around its thin black tongue as though it had never encountered it before. 'No,' it decided, with a terse finality as elegant as it was abominable.

Lulu stared at the beast in utter despair. She was too long accustomed to dealing with her father not to recognise that her protests were functioning more as encouragement than deterrent. She was also familiar with the consequences of leaving a lively mind and a refined taste with nothing to do, and as much as it galled her to admit it, the cockatrice obviously possessed both.

'Black cherry pies,' said Lulu.

The cockatrice regarded her gravely. 'Madam, you have my attention.'

'I might be able to go as high as three per week.'

'If?' prompted the cockatrice.

'If you agree to spend two hours of every day down in the kitchens assisting Magwell.'

If the cockatrice had possessed feathers, every one of them would have bristled with indignation. 'I am no lackey, madam. A being of my exquisite sensibilities—'

'Exactly,' Lulu interrupted. 'You shall assist as taster and refiner of our signature recipes. I am sure a being of such exquisite sensibilities can manage that?'

The beaky smile returned. 'I shall consider your offer.'

Lulu waited.

'I expect to find it broadly acceptable.'

'Broadly?'

'Four black cherry pies a week.'

'Three and a half,' Lulu countered.

The cockatrice sighed. 'Done.'

Cockatrices did not shed scales at any great rate, Lulu discovered. By the end of the creature's first week at Castle Drax, Lulu had only two to add to her stash. She stored them carefully in a gilded box lined with velvet, in which she also kept her mother's pearls, a silk handkerchief Magwell had embroidered with her initials, L.V., and a pin in the shape of a swan her father had once, rather uncharacteristically, bestowed upon her.

The scales were monstrous pretty, she found, upon close inspection. Pretty, in that they were a glossy black, like onyx, but sheened with a faint iridescence. Monstrous, in that they were quite unlike any other material known to man or beast, outside of Hell. Hence, she thought, their value.

She had been so cowardly as to avoid the kitchen for the few days since she had concluded her arrangement with the cockatrice. That could not continue. As the week drew to a close, Lulu descended into Magwell's domain directly before luncheon, steeling herself to encounter a deal of discontent.

In which expectation, she was not disappointed. No sooner did Magwell catch sight of Lulu than she swelled with rage, and pointed her wicked-sharp chef's knife at Lulu's face.

'That!' she said.

Lulu blinked.

'Damned chicken.'

The infernal chicken in question lounged at its ease before the stove, emphatically in the way of anybody who wished to use it. It was, as usual, beaming. 'Just a touch more cinnamon,' it said. 'The balance of fruit to flavouring is very nearly there, Magwell, I congratulate you.'

'That,' said Lulu, 'is aggravating beyond belief and a curse upon all mankind, yet it does, I believe, know what it's talking about when it comes to cuisine.'

'Thank you,' said the cockatrice gravely. 'You may stay.'

'That?' echoed Magwell. 'A peculiar name, but then—' and now the knife shifted to point most ominously at the beast in question '—that is a peculiar beast.'

Lulu opened her mouth to correct Magwell, but decided against it. 'Its manner may be obnoxious, but is its advice wide of the mark?' She meant the question sincerely; more than once had she doubted her decision to dispatch to the kitchens a creature who considered creeping black mould a great delicacy.

Magwell glowered. 'No,' she admitted. 'That is what's so annoying about it.'

'You are most welcome,' said That, beaming. 'Now, I believe it is past time for my fourth cherry pie of the week?'

'The agreement was for three and a half?' Lulu said.

'Very well. My half. One of you may be so honoured as to consume my leavings.'

Magwell placed a delicate, lattice-topped pie onto her slab of a cutting board, and chopped it in two with one great, loud, emphatic sweep of her knife. 'There,' she said ungraciously, and took half for herself, cramming it into her mouth in one go. Comfort food. She'd earned it.

'No, no,' said the cockatrice, graciously. 'It absolutely isn't necessary to bring it to me! I shan't even insist on a silver platter.'

Lulu swiped the cockatrice's half of the pie, before Magwell, displaying an ugly glint in her usually mild eye, could throw it at him.

She presented it on the palm of her hand. 'Listen,' she said. 'You may antagonise, if you must, but you must not seriously upset Magwell.'

'Or what?' said the cockatrice, and took a morsel of sweet pastry with a snap of its black beak.

'Or I shall haul you back to the depths of Hell with my own hands, and leave you there.' Lulu was proud of the way she'd said it: her voice barely shook.

The cockatrice smiled, and, with unusual delicacy, devoured the rest of the pie. 'Bravo, Madam,' it said, beaming. 'You have learned to command.'

15

The Curse of Castle Drax

The hens were getting into everything, now.

They *had* been quiet enough creatures, contented with the salubrious henhouse Fane and Magwell had built for them near the rear door to the kitchen. Fed upon crumbs of Magwell's finest pastry, given the run of the garden (and, occasionally, the kitchen), they had been the cook at Castle Drax's boon companions these many years.

All a thing of the past, now.

'What *is* that?' asked Cleo, bending to scrutinise a fine point of detail upon Lulu's developing watercolour painting. A lesson was in progress, held in Lulu's painting turret at an early hour; the vivid spring sunshine bathed the draughty, dark stone room in a helpfully dazzling light.

'Well, it's...' Lulu groped for an answer, uncertain herself just what had emerged from her paintbrush while her thoughts had been wandering. 'It's a... plant? A foxglove, I daresay.'

Cleo rejected this suggestion with spirit. Seventeen years old, accustomed to neglect, and concealing a profound uncertainty under a brash manner, the authority of the role of *teacher* had perhaps gone to her head a little. 'Balderdash,' she pronounced heartily, shoving wisps of brown hair out of her eyes (and adding a bright smear of azure-blue to the medley of colours streaking her thin face). 'Those are eyes.'

They were, Lulu admitted sadly. And it wasn't even the first time she'd absently painted a malevolent and (in this case) violently green gaze into an otherwise serene landscape. She was crafting a summery, rustic scene, featuring the feathery tops of Fane's carrot crop bursting forth from damp, dark earth, with the rear façade of Castle Drax rising, sun-dewed and gleaming-black, behind them.

And yet, there they were: eyes as green as Count Vexx's witchfires, glaring with sinister intent from the midst of an artistically placed hydrangea bush.

'It's one of the Ladies,' Lulu acknowledged. 'I can't tell if it's Vera or Cora.'

'Doesn't matter,' said Cleo, with perfect justice. 'Paint them out.'

She'd produced an accurate enough representation of life at Castle Drax, Lulu considered, intentionally or otherwise. The formerly docile hens were forever lurking in dark corners and under bushes, staring out at their fellow residents with those unsettling fiery eyes. They were spying, most likely, enlisted by that damned chicken, though to what end she couldn't say.

'I think I will leave them there,' Lulu decided. 'I'm painting Castle Drax, after all, not some mere ordinary spot.'

Cleo shrugged. 'It's your art.' She said this in the same way one might observe *it's your funeral*.

Lulu felt a momentary compulsion to bow to her teacher's criticism, and erase the eyes. She stifled it. It was indeed *her* art; in fact it was *her* castle, now, since her father had gone.

Horrifying thought. The guilt melted into a spasm of alarm, and she hastily reapplied herself to her watercolours. Painting was calm. Painting was peace and creativity and—eyes, eyes *everywhere*, watching all that she did—

'That damned *chicken*,' Lulu sighed, and put down her paintbrush.

'You are rude,' answered a low voice, silky with satisfaction.

Lulu jumped, and spun. The cockatrice skulked under a low chaise longue, whose faded brocade upholstery had frequently embraced Lulu in her woeful moments.

Unthinking, Lulu hurled her paintbrush at it, splattering black paint over the scratched ebony wood. The cockatrice cackled and fled, its absurdly feathered head bobbing.

Cleo improved the thought by chucking her besmeared paint palette after it, and then a jar of mud-hued water, too. The latter bounced off the cockatrice's black-scaled hide, drenching it in cold water and old paint.

'Well! I call that poor hospitality,' it spat, shaking itself. 'I have half a mind to complain to the management.'

'I am the management,' said Lulu through gritted teeth.

'Go away, then,' said Cleo at the same time. 'No one wants you here, anyway.'

This was a little cruel, to Lulu's mind, even if it was perfectly true. She opened her mouth to say something conciliating, until the cockatrice, haring wildly about shaking water from its scales, barrelled into the legs of her easel. It toppled, taking her painting with it.

The cockatrice, mercifully, fled the room, clucking in glee or alarm (Lulu couldn't tell). It left large, splattersome, three-toed footprints all over her half-finished landscape in the process.

'Why don't you get rid of that thing?' asked Cleo, scooping up her palette and her water-jar.

Lulu considered salvaging her painting, and decided against it. The creation was ruined. 'Unfortunately I cannot. There was a pact made, you see.'

'So?'

'So, a pact is a solemn promise. Both sides are bound to perform whatever it is they agreed to.'

'But you didn't agree.' Cleo's mouth set in a thin line. 'Neither did we.'

'Fane promised for us.' He'd enlisted the cockatrice to carry a message to Count Vexx, wherever he now was. In return, he had agreed to host the creature at Castle Drax for—Lulu shuddered to think of it—ninety-nine years thereafter.

He'd been swindled, of course, but that was the nature of hell-beasts. Fane might be Hellspawn himself, but he was a gentle soul, not at all cut out to deal with the likes of that damned chicken.

Which was why he so badly needed Castle Drax, of course. They all did.

'Things will settle down,' Lulu offered, without believing it.

Cleo merely grunted, and returned to her own easel. 'You'd better feed them,' she observed. 'They're beastly when they're hungry.'

This was the problem with bribery as a tactic; one was obliged to maintain a programme of ever-increasing largesse. The Ladies and the cockatrice grew more demanding by the week.

'I'll speak to Magwell,' Lulu capitulated, and went out, following a trail of wet cockatrice prints down the spiralling stairs.

She trod carefully, for the dark staircases, lit only by thin arrow-slit windows, were blackened further by the roiling shadows creeping inexorably over the castle. The large windows and vibrant sunlight of the turret deterred them, for they rarely crossed that threshold. Elsewhere, though, the castle was sinking ever further into pronounced gloom. Lulu had initially attributed the effect to her father's melancholy mood, which had a pervasive way about it. But he had now been gone some weeks, and the shadows roiled ever more fiercely in the darkest corners of the castle. The cellars were bordering upon impassable. This ranked among the more pressing of Lulu's problems, save that she had not the smallest idea what to do about it.

'No!' said Magwell, the moment she saw Lulu. Her comfortable bulk reposed in her favoured rocking-chair, poised by the only fire in the castle that burned red and hot. Her pince-nez lurked upon her broad nose, and she had her ledger upon her lap. She pointed her pen at Lulu and said, with unwonted severity, 'I know what you are going to say. They are not to be fed again for at least two more hours! They've already had half a pound of pastry between them.'

'You're right,' said Lulu, 'but—'

'No buts, lovie,' said Magwell, returning to her figures. 'It is maddening, I know, but they mustn't be allowed to terrorise us all.'

One of the tyrants in question lurked by the hearth, her crimson beak set in a smug smile eerily reminiscent of the cockatrice's. Vera. 'They are already terrorising us all,' Lulu said with her best attempt at sternness, and even glowered at the hen, a little. 'Nothing can appease them but food.'

'And that is precisely why it must be carefully rationed,' replied Magwell without looking up.

Lulu couldn't argue, not when she was so perfectly correct.

'One of these days we'll be having chicken for dinner,' she muttered in futile rebellion.

Magwell nodded her head, whether at Lulu's words or at the contents of her ledger, Lulu didn't know. 'I should put them to use, if I were you,' she said, a trifle absently. 'Good, honest labour keeps a body out of mischief.'

The very notion that the cockatrice might submit to anything remotely resembling honest labour was perfectly fantastical; Lulu couldn't help laughing.

Then she stopped laughing, for a thought occurred. The cockatrice *was* here for a purpose, after all, whether it felt any enthusiasm for performing it or not.

'Hm,' she uttered, and decided. 'Yes. Where has that damned chicken got to now?'

The observatory lay abandoned and empty; its usual state, of course, prior to the cockatrice's arrival. The once-splendid room was half derelict now, its glass-domed ceiling hopelessly blackened with grime, and half the glass gone from the wide mullioned windows. She'd made it over to the cockatrice's use in the faint, and ultimately unsuccessful, hope that it would stay up there, and out of the way.

In the end, she found the bothersome creature out in the henhouse, enthroned in its upper storey. It had turned the snug little construct into a cosy palace for itself, occupying the uppermost floor in solitary splendour; the Ladies, evicted to the lower levels, had submitted to the change with a passivity which Lulu could only wonder at.

Still, she well knew how impossible the creature was to reason with. Supposing they even wished to, which seemed doubtful.

'There you are,' said Lulu, tearing open the scarlet-painted doors.

A baleful black glare greeted her. 'Madam, I am busy.'

'You are about to be much busier,' said Lulu firmly. 'The next part of my message to my father needs to be delivered.'

'You may make an appointment with one of my secretaries,' the cockatrice replied. 'I may have an opening for you next week. Shall we say Thursday?'

'Now,' Lulu countered.

The cockatrice fluffed its wings; they clacked ominously. 'And what do you offer in exchange for such...promptitude?'

'You are already getting ninety-nine years of housing and food, not to mention truly excellent service.'

'Am I?'

'A personal chef, butler and chauffeur; a chatelaine at your beck and call, however begrudgingly; *three* personal minions—'

'Madam, you bore me. I leave at once.'

Lulu resolved to be insufferably boring much more often. 'Excellent,' she said crisply. 'Pray be swift. The matter is urgent.'

'It always is,' said the cockatrice with supreme indifference. 'And what is the message?'

'Dear Father,' Lulu dictated. 'The weather continues fine, and the tide of shadows obstructive. Pray explain the latter at your earliest convenience. Fondest love, Lulu.'

'That is no way to address your loving parent,' said the cockatrice.

'I daresay I would know that, if I'd ever had one,' Lulu returned. 'Off you go.'

The cockatrice, surprisingly, grinned, and vanished in an acrid cloud of lurid green smoke. Wisps of singed straw smouldered feebly in its wake.

Lulu took advantage of its absence to plunder the henhouse. A riffle through the packed layers of straw—perfectly arranged for both comfort and aesthetic appeal, likely by the Ladies—produced a cache of three green-speckled eggs, likely thieved, and a bumper crop of shiny black scales. The eggs she delivered to Magwell, and the scales went into her treasure box for future use.

After which, feeling pleasantly as though she had got the better of the cockatrice, for once, Lulu fetched a mop and went to swab the floor of the dining room.

Miss Lamarre of the Arts and Crafts shop arrived promptly at noon, for luncheon. A combination of mild snobbery and, Lulu suspected, a secret loneliness, brought her up to the castle at any time Lulu cared to extend an invitation—and, occasionally, when she hadn't. Today's was a working luncheon, but Lulu knew better than to attempt to discuss business before Magwell's array of delicacies had been devoured.

'Miss Dephane popped in this week,' she revealed, halfway through a leek and brie quiche. 'Wanting accessories for the wedding, of course. There will be the event of the summer, you mark my words. I pressed a box of the rose macarons on her as she left, and she was so good as to say there is little she loves better than a well-baked macaron. No saying what may come of it, but catering *that* event—well! Very prestigious, Miss Vexx. Very prestigious indeed.' She paused to demolish three cress and cucumber sandwiches, and an iced lemon bun. 'Now, I *did* hear that Lady Debenham is returned from abroad. What a charming woman! She used to come in with her daughter, you know, near every week...'

Lulu let her talk without interruption—Miss Lamarre seldom required much response, in one of her expansive frames of mind. When naught remained of the repast but a meagre scattering of crumbs over the elegant porcelain platters, and Miss Lamarre's flow of gossip had at last dwindled to nothing, Lulu opened up her treasure box, and poured a glittering stream of cockatrice scales onto the damask tablecloth.

Miss Lamarre stopped short in the midst of her treatise on Miss Dephane's peach chiffon wedding gown. 'What,' she breathed, 'are they?'

'Cockatrice scales. Exceedingly rare.'

'I should think so.' Miss Lamarre's faded blue eyes lit with avarice. 'My dear Miss Vexx! Where can you possibly have acquired such a thing?'

'That's not important,' said Lulu quickly. 'Now, if these were to be fashioned into an accessory—a clutch purse, say, or a fascinator—do you think—?'

'I *do* think,' said Miss Lamarre. 'It will be a sensation—'

'Perhaps Lady Debenham...?'

'No no, not her ladyship, she is quite without the resources to—but Miss Dephane? The wedding—'

'Not at all suitable with the peach chiffon—'

'Oh no, frightful prospect, but for such a treasure as this—not too late to change the gown, not at all too late—leave it to me, Miss Vexx.'

'I shall need a high price,' Lulu cautioned. 'The roof repairs really won't wait much longer.'

'And my commission?'

'Fifteen percent.'

'Twenty.'

'Eighteen.'

Miss Lamarre inclined her head in gracious acceptance. 'I shall begin at once! There is no time at all to lose—' She gathered her embroidered cloth bag and her hand-crocheted shawl and bustled out, which was fortunate because a strong stench of sulphur warned Lulu of incoming trouble.

Trouble duly appeared, in the form of a smoke-wreathed cockatrice in a roar of emerald flame.

'I shall require a warm bath, a silk pillow of no less than five hundred thread count, *and* a saucer of Chateau de Paye '28, not too cold.' It coughed violently, and retched up a small nugget of smouldering coal. '*Disgusting,*' it rasped.

Lulu closed up her treasure box. 'Most people consider it a punishment to be sent here,' she informed it. 'Or so I am told.'

The cockatrice kicked a taloned foot at the expectorated coal. It flew across the polished floor, and clattered into a corner. 'Most people,' said the cockatrice, 'are idiots.'

Lulu found herself unable to disagree. 'Did you find my father?'

The cockatrice hunched itself into a miserable, sulphurous ball, its feathery plumes bristling with disgust. 'You are favoured,' it answered shortly. 'His Greatness deigns to reply.'

'Let's have it, then.'

The cockatrice stretched its long neck, and cleared its throat. 'Just the curse,' it intoned. 'Nothing to worry about.'

'The curse,' Lulu repeated.

'You may deliver my pillow and wine to the henhouse,' said the cockatrice, and stalked away.

'Wait,' Lulu said, scrambling out of her chair. 'The curse? What curse? Surely there was more?'

'Not a syllable.' The cockatrice picked up its three-toed feet and ran, leaving Lulu behind.

Lulu trailed along the passage to the hall, suffering from a profound bitterness of spirit. Trust the Count to disappear and leave her with a curse to deal with! And no information whatsoever! That was the trouble with parents. The moment there was anything unpleasant going on, off they went, without so much as a by-your-leave, or any apology, or anything.

She was stamping in her slippers, which was both unlike her and quite useless. She obliged herself to take a slow breath, and mustered up her smile from wherever it had gone. For every problem, there must be a solution; this one would prove no different, surely.

A curse lay upon the castle. All things considered, this came as little surprise; she rather wondered that it had never been mentioned to her before. But how long had it persisted? What else would it *do*, besides shrouding the castle in ever deepening shadow?

How to lift it off altogether? There must be information—

Her thoughts went at once to the library. For the first time it occurred to her to wonder whether there had been something in particular her father was looking for, during his many lonely hours perusing the books. She had long accepted him as a dedicated scholar, without having much idea what it was he studied; and he had certainly never invited her to discuss any of it with him. She hadn't cared, and only now did she wish that she had.

Her steps followed her train of thought, until she pushed past the creaking door and stood in the centre of the library itself. Few had entered since Count Vexx had gone, and a thickening layer of dust lay heavy over the tall back of her father's chair, and the books still waiting atop the handsome ebony table poised alongside. A tall glass stood empty of wine, stained with the dregs of the Count's last vintage.

Lulu swallowed a sudden lump in her throat. Foolish; her father was only absent, not *dead*. She stepped quickly to the long window and pulled back the velvet drapes, letting the sunlight filter through the murky diamond panes. The atmosphere of woe lessened, and she could turn her attention to the contents of the dusty onyx shelves.

Which were considerable in quantity, density, and grandeur. Hundreds, if not thousands; when she looked upon them with the eyes of a potential scholar, they seemed to have proliferated to an impossible number. She was not bookish herself; this was one taste of her father's (among many) she had never shared. The prospect of searching through so many thick, leather-bound volumes, crusted with dust and gilding, caused her heart to sink. She could spend months at such a task, without discovering anything to the purpose.

She sank into her father's chair, stretching her stockinged feet towards the cold and empty grate. How dark, how dismal the room seemed without the cheerful green blaze of witchfire! This, too, was an art she had never cared to master. She could revive a fire recently extinguished, but could set no fresh blaze. She picked up some of the books upon the table at her elbow, leafed through them. Natural philosophy; history of architecture; a book, most improbably, of sermons...nothing of relevance. Perhaps her father had not been working on anything relating to the curse. Perhaps he'd simply accepted it, as a fact of life at Castle Drax. Perhaps he'd given up.

Then again. Where might he keep those few books of particular note—of special relevance to their situation? Would they be shelved in the library, positioned prominently upon the shelves for anyone to see? Or would her father, secretive to his last breath, have removed them to somewhere more private?

Were that so, there could be only one place in the castle Lulu might find such a cache.

Count Vexx occupied a suite of rooms in the west wing, high up in the castle. He preferred to keep his feet out of the mud, he said, which Lulu took to mean his mind out of the mundane; up in the heights of the building, he was removed, physically and mentally, from all the toilsome day-to-day business of castle life. Lulu ascended entirely too many stairs and arrived, hot and out of breath, at the forbidding onyx-black portal that walled her father's domain away from all his nearest and dearest. Her heart drummed with exertion and a kind of trepidation. She had climbed these stairs before, presented herself at the massive door, but she had never gone *in*. The private residence of the Master of Castle Drax remained shrouded in secrecy, and eternally inviolate.

Fane stood outside the door.

'Miss Lulu,' he said, with his sweet, horrible smile. 'Is it lunch time?'

'Not yet, Fane,' Lulu answered, breathless. 'Soon.' She paused to gulp air. The passage here was narrow, dark, and comfortless, only a solitary green-lit sconce chasing away the writhing shadows. Fane's pallid, faintly green countenance glowed greener still in such light, sculpted by darkness into a mask of sharp angles. He seemed taller than ever. 'Are you standing guard?' she asked, doubtfully, for he loomed so imposingly she could think of no other construction to place upon his presence.

'Yes, Miss,' he replied. 'The Master bade me do so.'

'I see.'

'Not against you, of course.' Fane smiled again.

'Oh! Then I may go in?'

'Of course. *You* can only have just cause for doing so, I don't doubt.'

Since Lulu had no way of knowing what her father might consider just cause, she accepted this, and waited with tolerable patience while Fane deployed a collection of heavy iron keys across three different locks, each of which screamed in protest.

At last, the door swung open, ponderous and eerily silent, after the clatter the keys had made. Beyond, a blank blackness yawned; a mass of roiling shadows boiled over the threshold.

Lulu felt reluctant to enter, and cursed herself for a fool. What, was she afraid of a room? In her own home? The same room her father had dwelt in for all the decades of his life? Preposterous. She stepped in directly.

Lights flared, brilliant and emerald-green and so sudden, Lulu screamed.

Fane thundered into the room. 'What is it?'

'Nothing,' Lulu said quickly. 'I was just—startled.' She felt all the more absurd for her fear, for now that she was over the sacred threshold and could see about herself, the chamber proved mundane. She had stepped into a sitting-room, with a set of bulky, stuffed armchairs upholstered in mulberry-red, matching curtains at the three long windows, and embroidered carpets mitigating the chill of the marble floor. An enormous mantelpiece surrounded the hearth, its black marble contours embellished with carvings both elegant and slightly grotesque. A stack of books on a low table proved to be a collection of novels, all of recent publication.

A brief tour of the remainder of the suite revealed a comfortable bedchamber, plush and habitable despite the absurd grandeur of its four-poster bed, swathed in black brocade hangings; a dressing-closet, containing an unreasonably large quantity of expensive, mostly-black suits; a sumptuous bathroom, complete with a marble, claw-footed tub and polished bronze taps; and—yes!—a private library.

'Was there something in particular you was wanting, Miss?' Fane ventured to enquire, when Lulu fell upon this fresh collection of tomes with unwonted glee.

'All this time, Fane,' said Lulu, pulling books off narrow, dark shelves with a haste her father would doubtless consider highly disrespectful. 'We have been labouring under a curse. And I didn't even know!'

'Ah,' said Fane, with such a marked lack of surprise that Lulu abandoned the books.

'What—did *you* know?' she asked, thunderstruck.

'The Master told me of it long ago, Miss,' said Fane, head bowed, in vague understanding that Lulu was not pleased.

'He told you, but kept it from me! Whyever would he do so?'

'I believe he wanted to protect you from it, Miss.' Fane swayed from side to side, as he always did when he felt distressed. 'He used to say that *one* person in this infernal wreck should have a normal life.' He coughed, and added, 'His words, that.'

Lulu had decided feelings about that, but now was not the time to explore them. She was the chatelaine of a cursed castle, and she, too, had a family to protect. '*Why* are we under a curse, Fane?'

'Something to do with the old Count, the first one. He offended someone high and mighty, if you know what I mean.' Fane illustrated this point with a significant look downwards, towards the cellar, and the summoning-circle. 'And so he was sent into exile out here, and he and all his line tasked with, um. With administrating the gate, so to speak. Keeping an eye on it.'

Lulu stared. 'You are telling me my ancestor was cursed with a management job.'

'For all eternity. Yes, Miss.' Fane nodded emphatically.

'And this castle exists purely to house the gate.'

Fane nodded again. 'That's about the size of it, Miss. It was a mausoleum, to begin with,' he added helpfully.

'And I suppose you are cursed with—what role exactly? Doorman to the Gates of Hell?'

Fane performed an odd shuffle of shy discomfort. 'Well—it was that way to begin with, Miss, but I have come to rather like it.'

Lulu's brain reeled. Her father, manager of Hell's Gate-house. Magwell, cursed to the kitchens of Castle Drax for all of time. Stormdust, condemned to spend eternity driving Vexxes around. She'd always thought they had chosen their roles at the castle because they suited their interests, their talents.

'As curses go,' Lulu said with tentative hope, 'it doesn't seem all that bad...? I mean, I have heard of *worse*.' Magwell ensconced in her beloved kitchen was a vision of contentment, not torment. Stormdust couldn't adore his mechanical charge more if he'd given birth to it. Fane was patently truthful when he claimed to love his life at the castle; he'd broken his Hell-spawned heart at the prospect of leaving.

Her father...well.

Fane's silence began to seem ominous. 'It... it isn't that bad, is it?' Lulu ventured. 'That *is* all there is to the curse?'

Fane swayed like a tall tree in a brisk wind. 'Ah...the Master did make me promise never to show you—'

'Fane,' said Lulu firmly. 'I am the Master now.'

'True.' The old retainer's head bobbed with emphatic agreement, and possibly relief: clear directions to follow. He bustled away into the Count's sitting room. Lulu, following, found him poised before the hearth, thrusting his gnarled hands into the blazing heart of a frosty emerald fire. When he withdrew them, he held the most enormous book Lulu had ever seen. When he delivered this into her hands, she almost dropped it, such was the weight of the thing.

It was as black and polished as the castle itself, its covers limned in vivid green flames that flared with the same chill, heatless flame as the fire it had been drawn from. Four deeply-graven characters marched across the front, shadowed and ominous: V.E.X.X.

Lulu discovered her hands had gone tremulous; the tome shook in her grip. Steeling herself, she opened it to the first page.

An inscription, scrawled there in midnight ink, flared with an eerie green light as she read it.

Hieronymus Vexx

Is hereby

CURSED

By my will

There followed a signature Lulu could make no sense of, and then, by way of a postscript,

Let the following Curses attach to all who bear his Name, his Blood, and his Perfidy.

Lulu did not at all like the appearance of the plural *curses*. She liked it even less as she turned pages, and found a succession of detailed illustrations inked in shimmering colour. A parade of faces, most of them male, one or two female; twelve dark-haired, green-eyed lords and ladies, varied as to complexion and skin colour, but with a noticeable similarity of feature. Twelve Counts and Countesses Vexx. Their names appeared under their portraits: Hieronymus, Aimery, Wymond, Amphelise, Dragomir, Una, Jurian, Cornelius, Valentine, Kresimir, Ludovit, and the twelfth, her father Constantine.

Each also bore a further annotation: a single word. *Anger. Lust. Pride. Sloth. Greed. Selfishness. Jealousy. Arrogance. Vanity. Sadism. Cruelty.*

Her father's: *Melancholy.*

Lulu was unsurprised to turn a final page and find her own features, her own sleek waves of fair hair and wide green eyes.

Luna. Cowardice.

'Ah,' she said and closed the book, holding it blindly out to Fane.

He took it from her gently. 'All will be well, Miss.'

Lulu, tear-blinded, did not see him restore the hateful book to its fiery hiding-place. Melancholy. Had her father ever managed to overcome the curse of his own nature? The castle, wreathed in the shadows that ever clouded his mind, bore mute testimony to the hopelessness of even attempting it.

Cowardice. Was that the truth of her? Was it bound to be so, for always?

She would not weep; that only seemed to prove the wretched book right. She mustered her better spirits, straightened her shoulders, and mopped at her cheeks with a sleeve of her cardigan. There: almost as though it had never happened. 'Right,' she said, with a ghost of a sigh. 'One more question, Fane. I have asked it before, but—why did my father leave? Was it because he couldn't bear it here anymore? Or did he go through in order to—do something?'

Fane watched her with grave kindness, but he was already shaking his head. 'I don't know, Miss. He did not confide in me, and that's the truth.'

Her father's motives were inscrutable as always. She knew better than to send the cockatrice with the question: the Count would answer it as unsatisfactorily as he had her first two missives.

Was there a way to break the curse of House Vexx? Or had her ancestors simply set themselves to learning to tolerate it?

Curse or not, the castle was still her home—and Fane's, Magwell's, Stormdust's. She still loved it, doomed as it may be, and so did they.

And meanwhile, there were stairs to sweep, linens to launder, and accessories to design. Life at Castle Drax went on after its own, odd fashion. Lulu pulled herself together, and wandered off to get on with it.

16

Devilled Eggs

I t was not the customary aroma of fresh-baked bread or strong-brewed coffee that drew Lulu, irresistibly, down to the kitchens one morning. No sweet fragrances of pastry or marzipan, no airy cakes coming, piping-hot, out of the oven. It was not even the hearty scent of bacon frying, or baked kippers. It was an overpowering reek of rotten eggs, as sulphurous and suffocating as Andirac's hot-water springs.

There was no getting away from it. The stench had woken Lulu—had, more rightly, hauled her bodily out of her hazy dreams and welcomed her awake with a reeking thunderclap. She followed the smell down the many stairs to the kitchens, and swiftly regretted it.

'Magwell,' she gasped, retching. 'What in the world—'

Magwell, stout and unsmiling, presided over a large ceramic bowl set atop the great, scrubbed oak table. It was full of eggs, sulking in their black shells in the wan, grey light of dawn. Another bowl held water; Magwell tossed a succession of eggs into the bath, and fished them out again when, one after another, they floated. 'That damned chicken,' she said in answer to Lulu. 'Ask *That*.'

'My terms are eminently reasonable,' boomed the cockatrice from under the table. 'The cessation of hostilities lies in your capable hands.'

Magwell's response to this was to scoop up three reject-ed eggs and fire them in quick succession in the direction of that low, lugubrious voice. They splashed wetly; the cockatrice hared away in a fresh explosion of stench.

Lulu, shivering in her threadbare dressing-gown, gagged. 'Hostilities?' she gasped, covering her mouth and nose with a fold of her robe. 'What terms?'

The cockatrice flapped its black-scaled wings, sending a wave of stink over Lulu, and drifting up the stairs. 'Have mercy,' Lulu croaked, gritting her teeth against a strong urge to vomit.

'It has subverted my chickens!' Magwell shrieked. 'My poor ladies! They are laying at a frantic pace, and all their eggs are rotten. Not a single one I can use!' She hurled another reject at the culprit, which dodged; the egg burst over Lulu's foot.

That made an appalling sort of sense. No ordinary egg, however rotten, could muster so profound a stench; it was a reek befitting the very depths of Hell itself. Of course it was the cockatrice's doing. 'You mean,' said Lulu, hastily removing herself from the line of fire, 'It is holding our egg supply hostage.'

The cockatrice laughed horribly. 'Precisely, Madam.'

A fiendishly clever maneouvre, Lulu had to admit. Eggs were central to the household at Castle Drax, and not only for feeding the family. All of the baked goods they sold at Miss Lamarre's arts and crafts shop required eggs to make; even Cleo's paints were sometimes mixed up with egg yolk. Their income, such as it was, must be compromised by such a move, and their lodgers inconvenienced.

Wretched, wretched creature. 'And what,' said she wearily, 'are the terms of surrender?'

'The present accommodations in the henhouse are an insult,' said the cockatrice promptly. 'We require new, greatly enlarged premises, appropriately furnished. That means silk cushions, soft rugs, and fashionable curtains. We also demand an allowance of three macarons each per day, to start with, and an option to increase the quantity at our discretion.'

'Fine,' said Lulu, profoundly tired, and turned to go back to bed.

'Furthermore, there shall be a regular supply of fresh, sparkling wine delivered in suitable glassware.'

'As supplies allow,' Lulu conceded. The henhouse could be enlarged with reclaimed wood, and some acceptable silk might be rustled up from around the castle. But sparkling wine?

'And,' added the cockatrice, 'a bassoon for Vera.'

Lulu stopped. 'A bassoon.'

The cockatrice cackled hellishly. 'I just wanted to know if you were weak enough to agree to anything.'

'Lulu,' Magwell remonstrated. 'You cannot simply give it everything it wants! There will never be an end to this nonsense.'

She was right, of course. There would be a hostage situation every week, with freshly outrageous demands, and no end in sight. This, she realised with dim dismay, was her curse in operation: to cave to such tactics was cowardly, wasn't it?

'But—' she began.

'No buts!' bellowed Magwell, and threw another egg. 'If it is dissatisfied with its accommodation, it may go back to Hell.' This was said with all the grim severity of a displeased headmistress, but upon the cockatrice it had no effect whatsoever. The creature merely purred, 'Make that four macarons,' and grinned.

If only it would go back to Hell, thought Lulu despairingly. But a pact was a pact, and couldn't be broken without consequence. Would those consequences be worse than the cockatrice's continued residence? Could anything be?

Yes, they could. She swallowed her wistful dreams of marching the creature down into the cellar and hurling it back through the circle, and considered instead what might best be done.

'Magwell, I perfectly understand your feelings, but please stop throwing eggs,' Lulu entreated. 'The smell is overwhelming.'

Magwell snarled something incomprehensible, but certainly filthy, and satisfied herself with chucking one last missile at the skulking cockatrice. It hit.

'There,' she said with satisfaction. 'Now I will stop.'

The cockarice fled, shaking foul-smelling slime from its feathers. 'I await your capitulation!' it called as it went.

'They really could do with a larger henhouse—' Lulu tried.

Magwell's answering look was flinty. 'Yes,' she conceded. 'But not at THAT creature's say-so.'

'Fair enough.' Lulu drooped. 'Have we no eggs we can use?'

'Not a one. And there's all the frangipanes to do for Miss Lamarre's, and the breakfast to be got. And tomorrow I'll need to make a start on the custards—'

'Right.' Lulu tried to convince herself there might be money enough to purchase some more. They did bolster their own supply by such means, at times; but if they had to start buying all the eggs they needed, the profits from cake sales would diminish rapidly.

'I will deal with it,' Lulu promised, stoutly enough, but felt compelled in all honesty to add, 'Though I have no idea how.'

'You must find something it wants.' Magwell took a cloth, and began cleaning the spilled egg from the table's scrubbed oaken surface.

'We know what it wants,' Lulu pointed out. 'It has told us. A new henhouse, silk cushions—'

'Yes, yes. I speak of leverage.' Magwell, still incensed, slammed her wadded cloth into the dripping pools of egg with unusual violence. 'At present it is holding all the cards. It has something we need, and it has the power to keep it from us.'

Lulu nodded. They couldn't break the cockatrice's scheme by removing its power over their egg supply—not without incurring unsustainable expense—but perhaps they could exert an alternative influence...

'An exchange of hostages, you mean,' Lulu concluded.

'Exactly.'

Lulu nodded thoughtfully, and drifted away. Trading something of value to the cockatrice in exchange for the return of their eggs: an excellent scheme, for it must deter the creature from adopting similar methods in future. But how to accomplish it? All the cockatrice seemed to care about were good silks and better wine. Black cherry pies, and macarons.

And the Ladies.

'You know that cockatrice brains are considered a delicacy in at least four circles of Hell,' remarked Minerfa at luncheon, paused with a forkful of fresh, minced venison on its way to her lips. 'Also in Banberre,' she added, 'And the city of Liev.'

That explained why the cockatrice had been so desirous of leaving Hell, and for so significant a period as ninety-nine years. 'I have attempted to brain it, recently,' Lulu answered. 'Without success, but I continue to try.' A dreamy golden sunlight filtered into the dining room, a beam of warmth and hope amidst the bleak, black gloom. Ordinarily it would lift Lulu's spirits, but today she eyed it with baleful lack of interest. Castle Drax, besieged with problems; its chatelaine, quite ineffectual at solving them.

She almost wished, just for a moment, that her mother were here. The cockatrice would be no match for her.

'That is right,' nodded Minerfa. 'It is important not to give up, when faced with some insignificant obstacle.'

The cockatrice's desire to retain the full use of its brains was no insignificant obstacle, and it was equipped with talons as long as her fingers.

'I don't suppose you happen to have a taste for cockatrice brains?' Lulu enquired.

'Not especially.' Minerfa absorbed a nugget of venison with palpable relish. 'I might perhaps make an exception, in an emergency.'

Her tone did not encourage Lulu to consider the present situation as a qualifying emergency. 'I suppose violence is never the best way to resolve a problem,' Lulu conceded.

Minerfa looked at her strangely. 'And the noble Vexxes hail from—where was it, exactly?'

'The Seventh Circle of—ah. Never mind.'

Minerfa nodded. 'There is a certain efficiency to simply bashing the creature on the head, but you are a gentle soul, aren't you.' She spoke with a trace of pity.

Gentle, and cowardly: both poor qualities for a proud Vexx. Lulu toyed with a crust leftover from her cress-and-egg sandwiches, avoiding Minerfa's eye. 'I prefer a solution with some finesse,' she said with dignity. 'What is the point of being a woman of intellect if I never use it?'

'Quite right.' Minerfa completed her repast with a pint of milk, noisily gulped down, and rose from the polished table. 'I'll be in my library,' she said by way of farewell, and left Lulu alone in the dining room.

In the Count's absence, she had rather taken over the library. What she found to read about for so many hours in there, Lulu didn't know, but it was nice that someone continued to value the Count's abandoned books.

She regretted her airy words of a moment ago, now. As a woman of intellect, she ought to be able to come up with a clever way of dealing with the cockatrice, oughtn't she? And quickly, too. But her mind remained blank of ideas, and she went away, disconsolate, to clean the scullery.

'Nothing like painting to make you feel better,' Cleo said later, setting a fresh sheet of thick paper in front of Lulu. The golden afternoon light was richer still in the girl's sitting-room, pouring through the large windows in shimmering waves; it couldn't have been more perfect for painting.

'I suppose so,' said Lulu, doubting. She did not feel at all in the mood for painting fields of sunflowers, or tranquil sun-bathed lakes, or any other landscape the season might inspire.

'Whatever's bothering you,' said Cleo wisely, 'paint it.' She jabbed her own paintbrush towards Lulu's waiting paper in emphasis, then returned to her own easel, upon which a length of stretched canvas was gradually acquiring an intricate scene in oils. 'Don't think about it too much!' Cleo barked, when Lulu didn't move. 'Just paint.' She patently followed her own advice, swathed as she was in a painting smock so smeared with myriad colours its original white was a distant memory.

Lulu dipped her paintbrush into her black pigment, and began at once to paint. The wobbly outline of a chicken's head emerged, bristling with black feathers; then a black-scaled body, and talons of exaggerated length... 'That damned chicken,' Lulu sighed. 'I swear it gets every-where.'

'That, or its little spies,' Cleo agreed, scowling. She ap-plied a streak of azure paint to her canvas with a flourish, and added, 'I don't even know how they keep getting in!'

Spies. Yes. Lulu drew a black chicken, a tiny, stout shape trailing with lamentable loyalty after its beloved leader. She gave it a crimson beak—that was Vera—then added Dora and Cora, a trio of lurking shadows with flaring green eyes. They had been docile creatures, once. Now, they were the minions of pure evil.

Lulu paused with her brush to the paper, ruining her painting with a spreading splodge of paint. Minions. The cockatrice utilised them mercilessly, for every one of its schemes—including the egg debacle. Supposing it were to be deprived of the hens?

An exchange of hostages indeed. Lulu laughed at her own obtuseness, and painted out all three of the Ladies, leaving the cockatrice in isolation. It didn't look so intimidating, like that.

'What's funny?' Cleo demanded, glancing at Lulu's paper. 'You've painted a...black blob. Brilliant.'

'It's a—'

'Oh, it's one of those stupid shadows. Never mind the cockatrice; I wish *those* would go away. I near fell down the stairs yesterday, couldn't see where I was putting my feet. Here, you can add texture and depth like this—'

Lulu did not correct her; indeed she hardly absorbed Cleo's lesson. Her mind had wandered along another train of thought, for Cleo was right: the shadows were a danger, and growing thicker by the week. Soon, if they were not stopped, the castle would grow virtually impassable.

Her father's absence wasn't helping. She had begun to wonder whether it mightn't be making it worse. He was the Master of Castle Drax. He was supposed to be here, and he wasn't.

Curses upon curses.

Another idea formed, one that made her heart pound with wild terror and her hand shake such that she couldn't hold her brush steady; she set it down.

'What?' said Cleo, breaking off in the middle of a monologue about use of light and shadow. 'What is it?'

'What if I could get rid of them *all*?' Lulu said.

'All what?'

'The shadows. And the cockatrice.'

'Impossible. Nothing short of death itself will get rid of that creature.'

'Death, or a higher duty.'

Cleo scoffed. 'Duty? That thing knows nothing of duty.'

'No; but it knows obligation.' Lulu stripped off her stained smock and threw it aside. 'I have to go.'

Cleo shrugged, and returned to her own painting. 'Next lesson's Tuesday.'

'I don't think I'll make it.'

Lulu tracked Stormdust down on the terrace at the rear of the castle. He sat in a begrimed chair on the edge of the wildly overgrown shrubbery, contemplating its tangle of ivy and brambles and singing a soft song to himself (or perhaps to the rampant verdure, who could say). He greeted Lulu with a smile of such delighted welcome, Lulu's heart stabbed at her a little.

'Lo, Her Greatness!' beamed he. 'Pretty as a picture, she is.'

Lulu beamed too; she couldn't help it. 'Hullo, Stormdust. I have an odd request to make of you, if I may.'

He jumped up at once, and bowed. 'Any mission you like! Tell me.'

'Well—will you be so good as to take the Ladies down to Miss Lamarre's?'

'Going visiting, are they? Delightful! Charmingest of ladies they are. We'll leave at once.' Stormdust accepted this without further question, and went to fetch his peaked chauffeur's cap, without which he could not be prevailed upon to drive, even if his passengers were a trio of hens.

It fell to Lulu and Magwell to round up the three hens for dispatch, no easy task. They were stationed around the castle and grounds in positions of some advantage, and objected strenuously to being removed from their posts. Magwell bribed them with madeleines, or they would never have been prevailed upon to move; even so, Lulu came away from the escapade badly scratched about her hands and arms.

Mercifully, Stormdust proved to have a way with them. His deep, baritone voice had a soporific effect; he pulled away crooning, while Vera, Dora and Cora dozed peacefully in the back of the car.

Lulu held out little hope that they would remain with Miss Lamarre for long. They would certainly come back in search of their unholy messiah. By the time they made it back up the long slope of the hill, Lulu trusted that it would be too late.

She composed a note for Fane, which she left propped upon her own dressing-table.

Then she returned to her chores, and waited.

The cockatrice found her within an hour of the chickens' departure. She would have preferred to receive it enthroned in some grand way, poised like a queen upon a high pedestal, and wreathed in an aura of terrible power. In the event, she was engaged in dusting the books in the library, and was covered in it, from head to toe. Her first utterance upon her supplicant's appearance was a violent sneeze.

'Madam,' thundered the cockatrice, stalking into the library in a cloud of wrath. 'Unhand my secretaries.'

Lulu restored a heavy folio to its shelf with an emphatic thump. 'Unfortunately I cannot,' she said without turning.

'Of course you can,' answered the cockatrice testily. 'You merely refuse to oblige me. I am unaccustomed to being gainsaid.'

'They are not your secretaries. They *were* our egg-layers, and since they are no longer fit for the purpose, they have left the castle. You will have to manage without sycophants.'

Silence. Lulu resisted the urge to turn about, and survey the effects of her gambit upon her opponent. She continued dusting her father's tomes, affecting an air of placid unconcern.

At last, the cockatrice spoke. 'Touché, madam. I shall unhand your egg supply.'

'In which case, the hens may return. But any further interference with them and I shall ensure their permanent departure.' She did turn, then, and fixed the cockatrice with a gimlet stare to rival its own. 'Are we agreed?'

The cockatrice bowed its feathered head, though it smirked. 'I concede defeat,' it proclaimed. 'This time.'

'Excellent.' Lulu beamed. 'Then there is just one further request I shall make of you.'

'I owe you no further favours, madam.'

'Ah, but you do. Quite apart from the sheer havoc you have caused about the castle since your arrival, which merits some recompense, there is the matter of your side of the pact. Your duties are as yet incomplete.'

The cockatrice's head drooped, its smirk gone. 'And what is the message this time?' it grumbled.

Lulu replaced a final book, dropped her dusting-cloth upon the little ebony table, and took a deep, steadying breath. *Cowardice.* That was only true as long as she kept running away, wasn't it? If she didn't run, she wasn't a coward. She was only afraid. 'Me,' she told it. 'I am the message.'

'Unthinkable. This is most irregular.'

'Non-negotiable,' Lulu replied. 'Take me to my father.'

The cockatrice hissed, and spread its batlike wings to their fullest extent. Something dark glowed in its eyes, and for the first time Lulu felt a flicker of genuine fear of the creature. 'Madam, you fail to understand. It is forbidden.'

'So was devilling all of my eggs, and that did not prevent you, did it?'

'It is a matter of consequences,' said the cockatrice lofti-ly. 'You are not in the smallest degree terrifying.'

Lulu made a private note to work on that. 'You may blame me, unreservedly,' she said, before she had time to consider what horrors she might be volunteering herself for. 'The consequences shall be mine to bear.'

'I do not think you understand the workings of Hell, madam.'

That was too unquestionably true for denial. 'Do this for me, and your side of the pact shall be considered ful-filled,' she offered. 'You may live out the remainder of your ninety-nine years here at the castle, without further demands made upon you.'

The cockatrice's head twitched. 'An attractive prospect,' it conceded.

'Wonderful,' said Lulu. 'Then we are agreed—'

She had no time for further words, had she chosen to utter any. The cockatrice crowed some deep, dark, terrible syllable; dived at her with its wings spread, a wave of roiling shadow surging around it; and in an instant—without time to think, to doubt, to prepare—Lulu fell into a sea of green fire, and was gone.

Well, thought Lulu, somewhere in the heart of the tem-pest. *Too late to think better of it now.*

Dearest Fane,

I know you say the Counts Vexx never come back, but I will. I swear it.

I must see Father. I must hear for myself why he left us. And if there's a way to break the curse, or to free the castle of this overwhelming shadow, I must learn of it. I cannot do that from here. Were that possible, we'd have done it already, wouldn't we?

Please take care of the others while I'm gone. I won't be long.

Love,

Lulu

xx

Afterword

Find out what lies on the Other Side

in

Stormy Nights at Seventh House

Coming soon!

For the first news on this and all other books from Charlotte E. English, sign up to the reader circle at:

https://www.charlotteenglish.com/newsletter

You'll also receive a free copy of *Motley Tales*, an exclusive collection of short stories from the House of Werth series, Modern Magick, the Malykant Mysteries, and more!

www.ingramcontent.com/pod-product-compliance
Lightning Source LLC
Chambersburg PA
CBHW020903160726
47993CB00005B/1794